CRUEL KING

CRUEL KING

K.A. LINDE

CRUEL WORLD

Cruel Trilogy

Cruel Money (FREE!)

Cruel Fortune

Cruel Legacy

Cruel Spin Offs

Cruel Promise (FREE!)

Cruel Truth

Cruel Desire

Cruel Marriage

Cruel Kiss (FREE!)

Cruel King

PART I

THE GIRL WITH THE LAVENDER HAIR

WHITLEY

I negotiated lavender hair into my contract.

Well, not just lavender. All the colors of the rainbow. I'd gotten used to wearing my hair however I wanted in California. I intended to continue to do so now that I was coming back to New York City.

If I was honest, I might have been looking for a way to get out of the contract. Something that would make my boss roll his eyes and tell me I'd gone too far. This hadn't been the reason. Even if he hated agreeing to it. I was one of the best practicing plastic surgeons in the country. He was paying me a small fortune to move back to the city after I made an even bigger name for myself in LA.

But I'd left New York for a damn good reason.

And I had to face that reason tonight.

I was swabbing more mascara onto my already-long lashes when my phone rang on the bathroom counter. I pressed the video button, and my best friend, Anna English, appeared on the screen.

"Where the hell are you?" English asked.

She looked frantic, and my friend never looked frantic.

She was a celebrity publicist and could handle drugged-out rockstars like it was her job, which admittedly it was. It was another thing to have to manage her future mother-in-law.

"Leaving now."

"Oh my god, are you still at the hotel?"

I grabbed my overflowing Chanel bag and headed toward the exit. "I'm like three blocks away from The Plaza."

"You're still living on California time," English grumbled. "In New York, three blocks will make you *late*."

"You're actually from California, girlfriend." I snatched up a fuzzy white fur coat and exited my suite to the elevator. "Take a Xanax or something. I can handle monster-in-law when I get there."

"Wait, what the fuck is that in your hand?"

"A coat?" I deadpanned.

English huffed, but I saw a smile creep out. "I told you to wear something sensible."

"Oh, I heard you. Loud and clear."

"You're going to show up in something outrageous, aren't you?"

"No one will be worried about you when I walk in looking like a train wreck, now will they?"

English laughed this time. It was a beautiful sound. "Fuck, I missed you. You're going to be the best worst maid of honor there ever was."

"At your service," I said, stepping onto the elevator. I blew her a kiss. "See you in ten."

"Fine. Hurry. I love you."

I hung up and dropped the phone into my bag. Then, I slid the over-the-top fur coat on top of the slinky silver dress that I'd worn clubbing with my ex-girlfriend back in LA. She'd said it was the sluttiest thing in my closet, but I really thought that was underselling it. I'd paired it with strappy silver high heels that one of my clients had gifted to me as a thank-you for a nose job well done.

As I exited the elevator, I slipped on a pair of shiny aviators and sauntered through the overly bright lobby of Percy Tower.

A group of businessmen was laughing outside of the restaurant off to my left. Every single one of them turned to gape at me. A smile hit my lips. I still had it. Three years in California had made my pale skin a perfect sun-kissed tan. I'd had a personal trainer since I abjectly refused to work out unless someone forced me, and my body was toned in all the best ways. I liked a little appreciation from the peanut gallery to prove it had all been worth it.

Then, my smile slipped as I *recognized* one of the men.

In fact, the very *man* I'd been hoping to avoid for as long as possible.

Gavin King.

His look of interest turned to shock when he realized that the girl in the fur coat and lavender hair was *me*.

It had been three years since I'd laid eyes on Gavin King. Memory did not do him justice. His suit was black as night and tailored to his powerful build. He was somewhere in the six-and-a-half-feet range with burnished red-brown hair, styled with gel to stay out of those emerald-green eyes. He held himself like the wealthy Upper East Sider he was. Old oil money, mixed with a Harvard education, made him practically drip with arrogance.

But when our eyes met, I saw, underneath the charismatic playboy, he was haunted at the sight of me. I'd cracked the veneer of his mask, and he wasn't fast enough to get it together.

I wanted to scurry away. To pack up my shit and leave, like I had three years ago when things got too complicated.

But I was back. I was *back*, which meant I was going to have to face Gavin one way or another. I'd just wanted to do it on my terms.

Oh well.

When life gave you lemons, add a little vodka and soda.

I wasn't ready for this confrontation. Not by a long shot. If he hadn't seen me, I would have found a way to avoid this, but he had seen me. We had an audience, and it wasn't like we could get into it in front of all of his friends. I didn't want to get into it at all. Three years hadn't been long enough for me to be ready for this conversation. Maybe I'd never be ready to talk about it. And certainly not in this moment.

Which meant that I needed to let the outrageous, wild Whitley Bowen that he was all too familiar with off her leash.

My hips swayed seductively as I made for the group of businessmen. My eyes were only for Gavin King. One of his friends nudged him and laughed. Gavin didn't look back at him as I approached. He couldn't look away from me, as if I'd put a spell on him in my too-short skirt and too-high heels and too-purple hair.

I ripped my sunglasses off when I reached him, standing way too close for total strangers. Which his colleagues clearly thought we were—and we were very much *not*.

"Hey, you," I said with a grin.

"Hey," he said on a breath.

I took his tie in my hand and threaded it between my fingers. His eyes were impossibly green this close. They stared at me with three years of distrust and confusion. I needed to end this or my knees were going to go weak, and we just couldn't have that.

"You know this isn't your color," I said, flipping the blue tie over his shoulder.

A knowing smirk crossed his sullen little mouth. "That so?"

"Green," I said with a wink. "To match your eyes."

"I'll take that into consideration."

One of his friends elbowed him. "You going to introduce us to your friend, King?"

Gavin and I snapped back to reality at the same moment. And reality was not a plane that I enjoyed existing on.

Gavin looked flummoxed for a whole second as if he had no earthly idea how to introduce us.

"Love to, gentlemen," I said, stepping back with a flourish. "But I have business to attend to. You understand."

Gavin's mouth turned into an O of confusion. I could see every single thing he wanted to ask on those perfect, pouty lips. The *what was I doing here* and *what business could occupy my time* and *how had he not known that I was in New York*. A million things that I didn't want to discuss and couldn't bring down my mask enough to acknowledge.

So, I didn't let him get the questions out.

I wagged my fingers in farewell and shot him a wink. "See you later, King."

I swallowed back my apprehension and sauntered away from the group. A whistle followed my exit. I kept the smirk on my lips the whole way, tossing the sunglasses back into position before exiting Percy Tower onto the Manhattan streets.

It wasn't until I cleared the front doors that my shoulders slumped and a frown replaced the ridiculous smirk. My hand dropped to the stone exterior of the building, and I took a steadying breath. Gavin King knew I was back in New York City. I'd survived that interaction. Barely.

It'd get easier the next time and the time after that. Like

exposure therapy. The more I saw his beautiful face and that muscular physique and the skilled fingers, the more I'd replace the memory of him using all of that for my pleasure. The more I'd replace the look of betrayal on his face when I'd gotten back together with his best friend. The more I'd replace the horror he must have felt when I'd left New York without so much as a good-bye.

I'd agreed to come back.

I knew what that meant.

I just hadn't wanted to face the fact that I still had feelings for him on my first day.

2

———

GAVIN

"Holy shit, King. I know you pull hot girls, but *that* girl?" Blake Holliday asked to my left.

Yeah.

That girl.

I watched Whitley Bowen traipse out of Percy Tower in that ridiculous fur coat with lavender hair swishing at the same tempo as her ass. Seeing her had momentarily paralyzed me. I couldn't even get words out.

Blake wasn't wrong. I could get with plenty of hot girls. Even by my own standards, I was a notorious playboy. I'd dated celebrities and models and socialites alike. I had a different girl on my arm at every event. None of them made much of an impression on me. In fact, I'd been so bored the last couple months that I showed up stag to events. My friends joked that I'd gone through every eligible woman in Manhattan. But that wasn't it. I was just over the monotony.

None of them were Whitley Bowen.

A certified wrecking ball, who tumbled through relationships about as destructively as I did. We had been close friends for a few short years before we crossed a line we could never come back from.

"Who was that?" Merritt Locke asked next to me.

I glanced over at the guy who was soon-to-be family. In a month, Locke would be marrying my cousin back home in Midland, Texas. New York royalty officially merging with the King oil dynasty.

A wedding that I still didn't have a date for.

"*That* was Whitley Bowen."

Blake and Locke exchanged a look. They'd been best friends since their Stanford days, when they both were college swimmers. Now, Locke was Olympics bound, the fan favorite. I thought he had a real shot at gold. And Blake was returning to New Mexico were his family ran a ski resort.

"Can't believe you let a girl like that walk away," Blake said.

Again.

I didn't say that out loud, but it was an echo through my mind. I'd let that girl walk away once before and regretted it. I damn well wasn't doing that again.

I winked at them. "Gentlemen."

Then, I dashed out of Percy Tower, my lunch plans forgotten as I chased after Whitley. She had a head start. If she wanted to escape me, she could thoroughly disappear into the New York City traffic.

But when I rounded the corner, looking right and left, hoping to catch a glimpse of her lavender hair, I found her with her hand against the building, taking a deep breath. She hadn't run away at all.

"Whit," I called, catching up to her.

She jolted. For a split second, we were back in time. Three years ago, when I'd chased after her after the Fashion Week debacle. I wanted to make things right after what happened with Robert. But when I'd slipped outside, looking for the rush of tulle, she'd already sunk into a cab and disappeared from my life forever.

I didn't regret much in my life, but I regretted everything about that day.

"Hey," she said, a wide smile hiding any trace of fear from her face. "What are you doing out here?"

"What am *I* doing out here? Whit, you're in New York."

"I am." She shrugged. Her petite shoulders barely noticeable under the mound of fur. "But weren't you in a business meeting or luncheon or something?"

"Oh, that? No, Locke is marrying my cousin."

She arched an eyebrow. Right. She hadn't been here when Locke moved back to New York. She hadn't been here for any of it.

"It doesn't matter," I said in a rush. "What are you doing here? And dressed like this?"

"What? Can't a girl get dressed up?"

I chuckled. "Sure. Where exactly are you going?"

"I'm meeting English at The Plaza."

"Dressed like that?"

"What do you have against my outfit, King?"

Not a damn thing. In fact, my first thought was, *How long would it take me to get it off?* But I couldn't exactly say that.

"It's great."

She gestured up the street. "Can we walk and talk?"

"Yeah. Sure," I said, falling into step beside her. "I have to get back to work but—"

"Aren't you the boss?" she teased.

I was heir to the Texas fortune, Dorset & King. My cousins ran the main branch of the oil corporation back home in Midland, where they could handle the day-to-day operations in the field. But I ran the New York division, which meant meeting with investors and business executives and handling the northeast refineries. Since I'd graduated from Harvard and I was friends with Upper East Side business types, I had volunteered. Anything to keep me out of Texas.

"I'm the boss," I agreed with a grin. This teasing behavior was way easier to handle than anything serious that was threatening to come out of my mouth. We'd always worked like this. Flirting was ninety percent of our personalities. "Now talk, Bowen."

She pushed her shoulders back. "I'm back."

"Back?"

"*Back*, back," she confirmed. "My old boss, Kevin Varma, poached me from my LA position. He put me up in Percy Tower until I can find a place in the city."

"You're moving back."

She laughed at my flabbergasted expression. "Yeah. I didn't think I'd ever do it. My clients were pissed when I told them that I'd be leaving, but the money was too good to turn down. Not to mention, Kevin is bringing me on as a partner."

"Really?" I asked after schooling my features. "You're going to run the place?"

"Well, Kevin's in his late seventies. He has three daughters. None of them followed in his footsteps, and he wants to see his practice, which he brought up from literally nothing, continue. For some reason, he sees me as surrogate family. You'd think I just annoyed him."

"That's probably why he thinks you're family."

She snorted. "Classic, King. Thanks."

When she smiled up at me, it felt all strangely normal. Like she hadn't left for three years and put thousands of miles between us.

Then, her smile dimmed, and she faced forward again. We passed Bergdorf on our left and stepped into the square, where The Plaza resided just off of Central Park. It was a trademark location with an enormous fountain at the center of the square, tourists galore, and even a few horse-drawn carriages.

Our close friends, English and Court, would be married here this fall. It was going to be the wedding of the year. Court's mother, Leslie Kensington, was the current mayor of New York and determined to have the blowout wedding she had been denied by her younger son. I wouldn't have blamed English and Court if they'd also eloped in Paris, like Penn and Natalie.

Whitley's outfit suddenly made sense if she was here to deal with wedding plans. She didn't care about anyone's approval and could take the heat off of English.

"Are you here for the wedding?"

Whitley nodded as we crossed the street, narrowly avoiding a gaggle of tourists. "English is frustrated with the wedding planner."

"And her soon-to-be mother-in-law, I assume."

She wrinkled her nose. "You have no idea."

"I think I do. I went to the engagement party."

Whitley's cheeks colored. She'd still been in California when that little catastrophe took place.

"Was it that horrible?"

"Worse than horrible," I confirmed. "I thought for sure that someone was going to come to blows. I ended up leaving early with my date because it was such a fucking mess."

Whitley's eyes widened a fraction, and then she dipped her head to dig into her purse.

Why the fuck had I said that? Of course I'd dated while

she was gone, but I hadn't had to bring it up. That was just how we'd always worked.

She had been the best wingman I'd ever had. Who could have known that all of that time we'd been trying to find people for the other to hook up with, the person standing right next to me had been the answer?

"Fuck," Whitley said. "English is SOS-ing me. I have to get in there before she does more damage."

I nodded easily. "Sure. I'm sure I'll see you around."

"Definitely," she said, but she still wasn't meeting my eyes.

I'd fucked up. Maybe I'd said it because I was mad that she'd left before we could figure this out. Now that she could barely look at me, I realized that I didn't want her to go like this.

"Hey," I said, reaching for the sleeve of her fur coat.

She blinked back at me, her hazel eyes a honey color in the afternoon sunlight. There was something in those eyes, like panic. She looked ... terrified. As if she thought that I might say something horrible to her.

I withdrew suddenly. I didn't like that look in her eyes. I didn't like it one bit. And I wasn't going to get rid of it by asking her out right here on the street when she had somewhere else to be. I'd need to play a longer game for her to see that I was serious.

"Good luck."

Her smile brightened, as if she'd dodged a bullet. "I don't need luck."

She winked at me and then disappeared inside.

Fuck. I was fucking *fucked* up about this woman.

I jerked my phone out as soon as she was gone, dialing Court Kensington without missing a beat.

Court's baritone filtered through the phone. "King."

"You fucking asshole."

Court laughed, low and resonant. "So, I'm guessing you heard Whit is back?"

"Heard? I just saw her in Percy Tower in a silver minidress. I walked her to English's meeting."

"She was wearing a minidress to the meeting with my *mother*? God preserve her."

"Yeah. I think she's trying to take the heat off of English, but that's not the point, asshole."

"What? Should I have told you that she was back? Still got a thing for her?"

I gritted my teeth. Court Kensington, Camden Percy, and I had met at Harvard. We'd become fast friends despite the fact that they had known each other their whole lives and didn't like outsiders. Court had known exactly what he was doing by not telling me that Whitley was back.

"That was three years ago."

"And?"

"And ... I didn't want to be blindsided."

Court snickered. "Sure. Keep telling yourself that. Anyway, that's why we're all going out tonight. We were going to surprise everyone."

Fuck. So, *that* was what that was about.

"I'll see you tonight," Court said.

"Yeah, whatever, fucker."

Court laughed and then hung up.

I shouldn't have been this worked up about it, but Court wasn't wrong. I'd never really gotten over what could have been with Whitley. She'd made herself perfectly clear that she didn't want to try this by moving across the country. And I didn't think that I could change her mind now ... but I was willing to try.

3

WHITLEY

English crashed into me. "There you are!"

I wrapped my arms around my best friend with relief. "Sorry I'm late."

"It's fine. I'm just glad that you're here."

She looked as sensible as she'd wanted me to dress. Her blonde hair pin straight with soft makeup and a neutral lip. She was in a Chanel suit with classic nude pumps. The friend I'd made at UCLA—who blew rockstars backstage at concerts because she had a thing for trauma to escape her Valley roots—was really and truly gone. Now, she handled rockstars with aplomb and was only flustered by the mayor of New York City, who was also about to be her mother-in-law.

"Are you sure about that?"

English laughed as she got a good look at me. "You're going to give Leslie a heart attack."

"Let's hope not. She's not a bad mayor."

"Fuck, I missed you. Promise you'll never leave the city again."

"I'll give it my best."

English looped her arm with mine. "What took you so long anyway?"

"Well ... I ran into Gavin King."

English choked. "You're kidding?" Her smile was predatory. "How was that?"

"It was ... I don't know."

I never could judge Gavin exactly. I'd been his wingman for so long. I watched him go home with more women than I could count on both hands. I'd never been jealous until we slept together. And even then, I'd had no right to be jealous.

But still ... I didn't know if his flirting was him being his normal self around me or if it meant more. The look in his eyes right before I left had made me reconsider moving back. I couldn't do this if he wanted to talk about what had happened. I'd moved on. I was well past that moment in my life. I might have feelings for him still, but that didn't mean I needed to act on them.

"Oh, you're going to hook up again."

I scoffed. "Bad idea. We all know what happened last time."

"Yeah. Yeah. Bad girlfriend. I know the drill, Whit. You're the one who gets revenge and who leaves behind glitter bombs on ceiling fans and watches the world burn before admitting that someone hurt you."

I bristled under that assessment, but somehow, from English, it was almost affectionate.

"But Gavin isn't dating anyone."

"He never is."

"No," she said, pulling me to a halt before we reached the tearoom. "Like, he hasn't even been bringing anyone to events."

I snorted. "Okay. Sure. He just told me he took home the girl he brought to your engagement party."

She arched an eyebrow. "One, we should consider why he told you that. And two, I haven't seen him with anyone since then."

I did the math. The engagement party was in July. That was almost nine months ago. There was *no way* he hadn't been with anyone in that long. That was ... unheard of for the Playboy Prince of Manhattan.

"I know his reputation precedes him, as does yours," she said pointedly. "But maybe he's growing up."

"I doubt it."

English laughed. "Fine. Have it your way. Just come save my life, would you?"

"My pleasure."

We strode into the tearoom. I recognized Leslie Kensington from the campaign advertisements and the news. She was currently campaigning for her third term, which would be voted on this November. Some part of me wondered how much of the fancy wedding was related to her campaign and how much was a mother wanting what was best for her son. A large part of me thought it was the former more than the latter.

Leslie was too composed to make a face at my appearance, but the wedding planner blanched as I was escorted over.

Leslie rose to her feet and shook my hand. "You must be Whitley. We've heard so much about you," she said.

"Mayor Kensington," I said with a grin. "I've only ever seen you on the news."

"Leslie, please, why don't you take a seat?"

"Whit, this is Fanny McEwan," English said, gesturing to the wedding planner, who was making *no secret* of her distaste for me.

"Hello," Fanny said without extending a hand. "Perhaps

next time, we can arrive on time." She looked around the place. People were definitely looking at me, but she was the only one who cared. Well, maybe the mayor cared, but she was too good at her job to show it. "And maybe in more appropriate attire."

I gestured to myself. "What? This old thing? Don't you recognize Elizabeth Taylor's old furs?"

I was lying through my teeth but betting a lot of money that she wouldn't know that.

Fanny looked way out of her depth. "I'm certain you know precisely what I'm talking about."

"Let's get back to the menu," English said, deftly changing the subject.

The wedding planner looked ready to skewer me, but I smiled brightly, as if I had no idea. The next hour continued in much the same fashion. Despite my extreme attire, I was a good maid of honor. I'd attended a ton of weddings for clients back in LA and had opinions about the sort of grand-scale wedding that the Kensingtons wanted.

English looked relieved by my input. She was a publicist. Handling events was her thing, but she hated weddings. I was one of the only people who knew that fact. Her last wedding to a cheating douchebag movie star had been a huge Hollywood affair with all the pomp that LA could throw at it. She would have happily married Court barefoot in the sand with just her friends and family in attendance. But she loved him enough to endure this whole thing a second time.

And I loved her enough to endure the likes of Leslie Kensington.

By the time we finished the meeting, I was on edge from all the parrying back and forth. English pulled me close, and we exited The Plaza together.

"Thanks for enduring that."

"Anything for you, bestie."

"You're still coming out with us tonight, right? I have that work thing for Fallon, and then I want to get a drink with my girl."

"Yes, yes, I'll be there."

"It probably ruined the surprise now that you saw Gavin though."

"Surprise?"

"We were going to invite everyone for your return to the Big Apple."

I groaned. "Seriously?"

"Well, it won't be much of a surprise."

"Thank god."

English elbowed me. "So, what happened with Gavin anyway?"

"Nothing. It was normal, I guess."

"You guess? You haven't dated a man in three years, and the first time you see the one who still holds a piece of your heart, you say, 'It was normal, I guess.' "

I wanted to growl at her. She wasn't wrong. I'd given up men entirely after leaving New York. There was too much drama. I'd only casually dated girls before and decided that maybe I'd dive in head first in LA. I'd even had a girlfriend for almost a whole year. Well, on and off.

Actually, maybe I was back to me being the problem.

"He doesn't hold a piece of my heart," was what I decided to focus on instead.

English nearly choked on her laughter. "Okay, Whit. I'll see you tonight at Club 360?"

"Sure. Sure. I'll be there." Then, I thought of something else. "Are you planning to surprise Katherine?"

English shot me a devious look. "Yep."

"Do you want to get stabbed? She hates surprises."

"I figure since it's you, I will be forgiven."

"Unlikely. I'll go see her before we go out. I do some excellent sutures, but I don't want to do them in public."

English kissed my cheek. "I love you. See you later."

I headed back the way I'd come, veering toward Percy Tower. Three years ago, when I'd left, Katherine and Camden had just worked out their differences. Of a sort. Now, she'd moved into his penthouse on the top of his hotel with their two kids.

Two kids.

It still amazed me that Katherine was a mother at all. Let alone to two little ones.

I took the private elevator up to the penthouse. It opened to the top floor, and I found Camden Percy striding toward me in a suit that probably cost a few grand. He looked ... fucking gorgeous and generally terrifying. He was all thunderclouds and venom and balls of steel. He always made me falter a step, and Katherine Van Pelt was the only one who could come close to matching him.

"Oh, good," he said, his voice a low rumble. "I don't have to tell her then."

"Wait, you already knew I was back?"

He arched an eyebrow. "There's nothing I don't know about in my city."

"Court told you then, huh?"

He didn't acknowledge that, just smirked dangerously. "She's in the nursery with Beckett. Up the stairs, first door on the right."

"And Helena? Do I get to see my niece today too?"

"Helena is with the nanny and her godsister, Gem," he said of his two-year-old daughter and their all but adopted daughter. "They went to run errands. She should be back within the hour. I'm off to a meeting."

"Will I see you tonight?"

"Where she goes, so do I."

Then, he disappeared into the elevator.

Who would have guessed? A few years ago, they hated each other so much that they couldn't even enter the room together without clawing each other's eyes out. Now, they were sickeningly in love. In their own way, of course.

I took off my shoes and then climbed the stairs to the nursery. I knocked softly once, and Katherine hissed, "Shh, I just got him down."

I hesitated a minute before peeking my head into the room. Her eyes rounded in surprise. That was as much of a shock Katherine Van Pelt wanted from her friends. She held up one finger as she rocked her six-month-old against her chest. Finally, she set the big boy down into his crib, fiddled with a white noise machine, and then tiptoed out of the room. Her eyes were all for Beckett fast asleep in the crib. I'd never seen Katherine look at anyone like she did her children.

She slowly pushed the door closed. "You," she said with a twinkle in her eye. Then, she pulled me into a hug. "What are you doing in my city?"

"Surprise!"

"You know I hate surprises."

"To be fair, English was going to surprise you tonight when we went out."

Katherine wrinkled her little nose. She was the most gorgeous person I'd ever known. If I hadn't known that I was bi before I met her, then she surely would have made me realize it. Long, dark hair and endlessly dark eyes with pale skin and forever red lips. Despite her features, she was more Evil Queen than Snow White.

"I would have let you hold Beck, but he takes forever to go down. He'll sleep for ages once he's there though."

"It's okay. I'm moving back, so lots of little baby snuggles from now on."

Her eyebrows rose. "Moving back? Since when?"

"Officially a few weeks ago. But today is my first day in the city."

Katherine went straight to the wine fridge and popped a bottle of champagne. She poured each of us a glass and passed one to me. "To my Whitley returning home."

I laughed and took a sip of the bubbly. "Thanks."

"Who else have you seen? Just English? Lark?"

"English and ... Gavin."

Katherine shot me a mischievous look. "Indeed. Gavin King. This sounds familiar."

"We ran into each other downstairs. I'm staying in the hotel, and he was here for a meeting."

"Coincidental then," she said with a conspiratorial smile on her red-painted lips.

"Don't give me that look."

"Why not? Should I not hope for my friends to be happy?"

"I don't know. It's complicated. Robert and I dated before and after Gavin and I got together. I tore their friendship apart."

Katherine waved a hand. "That was years ago. Robert is happily dating Harmony."

I jolted. I hadn't heard that. "Harmony? Really? I thought they were just friends."

"They were, but I gave them the push they needed, and now ... voilà."

"You're such a little matchmaker," I said with a laugh.

I had no feelings for Robert anymore. We'd been doomed long before I called it off at Christmas and hooked up with Gavin. Our fate was sealed when he found out at Fashion Week. But I'd never thought he'd end up with Harmony.

"So, let me give you a little push too," Katherine said. She put her hand on mine. "Don't make the mistake that I did with Camden."

"What? Moon over someone else for so long that he thinks I hate him?"

Katherine rolled her eyes. "Let's keep Penn Kensington out of this, why don't we?"

I laughed. "Can we leave matchmaking to later then too? Until I've been in the city for more than a few hours? I don't know what I want here, Katherine."

"Fine. I'll allow you to figure it out on your own, but I'm always here to give you good advice. As you did for me once. And look, I have two beautiful babies because of that advice."

"Yes, thank god I told you to fuck your husband."

"I need no such advice now." Katherine's eyes roamed down my front. "Now, may I dispense some fashion advice?"

I shook my head. "Oh god, let's not. This was a joke. Wait, can I raid your closet?"

Katherine's eyes glittered with delight. "It would be *my* pleasure to get you out of that ridiculous dress." Her fingers went to my hair. "And please ... let me get you in with my stylist."

"I like the purple."

Katherine sighed, as if I were such an inconvenience. "If you say so."

"You're such a snob."

"Yes. That's why you like me."

"It is."

We went back upstairs with the champagne as Katherine dressed me like I was her rag doll for tonight. It kept my mind off of what was coming next. I'd have to figure out what to do about Gavin, but not yet. Not quite yet.

4
———

GAVIN

Work dragged the rest of the day. It was impossible not to anticipate going out that evening and watch the clock tick slowly by. By the time five o'clock rolled around, I practically vaulted out of my top-floor office.

The building was located across the street from Kensington Corporation. I crossed the street in a hurry and was about to enter the building when Court Kensington stepped outside with Sam Rutherford. Sam was an attorney for Court's company and had turned our trio into a quartet after hustling us in our weekly poker match a few years back.

We'd taken to getting a beer after work before we left for our respective homes. Court back to English. Sam to his wife, Larkin St. Vincent. And me ... to my empty apartment. A fact that had only started bothering me in the last year. Well, before that, I'd always been sure to keep a steady flow of women in it.

Sam clapped me on the back. "So, you heard."

I glared at Court. "Does everyone know but me?"

Court shrugged. "Pretty much."

"You're all assholes."

Sam laughed. "Why? Should we have told you?"

"I don't even know why I put up with your shit."

"Because we're your only friends," Court said. "Now, tell us what happened."

"Nothing happened," I said as we entered our usual pub.

Court ordered a round, and we sank into seats at the bar.

Sam gave me a disbelieving look. "I remember when I saw Lark for the first time."

"You were engaged to someone else, dick."

Sam held his hands up. "Yeah, but I still knew something was there."

I shrugged. I didn't want to talk about this. I didn't even know how to begin to discuss my feelings on the matter. Whitley had left. She'd left and made *her* feelings perfectly clear. I didn't know if she had been lying all along when she said that we could try this out or if she'd just panicked.

"Let's forget about it. We're all going out tonight. I don't want her to run back to California because of you idiots."

"Fine. Fine," Court said. "We'll see how it goes tonight."

You and me both.

Whitley was there before I arrived. I heard her laugh across the room before I caught a glimpse of her lavender hair, which stood out like a stoplight in the hip New York City rooftop bar. Club 360 was on the top floor of Percy Tower and the place to see and be seen. Since Camden owned the building, we'd been going here for years. I hadn't realized how much I'd missed Whit's vivacious personality infecting the premises until now.

Katherine sat next to her, looking as prim and perfect as ever. Except she was laughing with Whitley, which was *not* normal. Katherine was one of those buttoned-up types. Few could bring out effusive laughter like that from her. Whitley was like that with everyone.

Camden leaned against the wall, watching his wife with predatory delight. He was slightly apart from what was happening, as was his norm, but he missed nothing as I walked inside. His eyes met mine, and he lifted two fingers in a hello.

I waved back. But the girls still hadn't seen me, and I could hear the beginning of one of Whitley's stories. She was known for them. *The Crazy Adventures of Whitley Bowen*™, as I lovingly referred to them.

"So, we had been dating for about a year ..."

"A year?" Katherine gasped out. "Since when have you ever dated someone that long?"

"It was on and off ..."

"What was his name?"

"Her name was Safia," Whitley said, breezing over the question easily. "And unimportant. Can I finish my story?"

"Well, when you leave out all the good parts ..."

"Anyway," Whitley said. She waved her hands and continued forward. "When I walked into the room, the girl that she'd dated before me was in my bed."

"No!" Katherine said.

"Yeah. I mean, she had clothes on and was sobbing about how she wanted to get back together, but she was there."

"And Safia?"

"Gone. I didn't know where, but the girl told me Saf let her in so ... I mean, I assumed the worst. In my opinion that's what happens. So, I did the only sensible thing ..."

Katherine sighed heavily. "You walked out?"

"Oh, no. I made the fucking crying girl on my bed

leave. Kicked her out and told her to cry somewhere else. Then, I took all of Safia's shit, put it in a few boxes, and left it on the front step, had the locks changed before she got home."

"Whitley! What if nothing had happened?"

"Then, I wouldn't have walked in on this girl *in my bed*. I was paying for the apartment. Saf hadn't paid a dime in six months. She was a struggling actress."

"Well, serves her right for living off of you. I would have left if someone poor tried to take advantage of me."

Whitley winced, and I winced with her. Such a Katherine thing to say. The point of the story wasn't that Safia was broke. It was that she'd broken Whit's trust, and in true Whitley fashion, she'd burned the entire relationship to the ground.

"Hey," I said when I realized that Whitley was done.

Katherine and Whitley whipped around at the sound of my voice. It was then that I grasped they weren't just laughing, they were *drunk*.

"Gavin King," Katherine said, coming unsteadily to her towering high heels. "Come over here and say hello to my guest."

Whitley's cheeks turned a light pink. "Yeah, King, come say hi to me."

"Whit," I said, taking her hand like a gentleman and kissing it. Her gaze was locked on mine, and she shivered slightly as my lips grazed her skin. "Welcome home."

"This isn't home," she said easily.

"Home is Texas for you both," Katherine said with a wrinkle to her button nose.

"That's not home," we said in unison.

I laughed. Texas was where I had grown up and where my family was, but I didn't miss it. That desolate hunk of land felt like work now. New York was home. It had been for me for a long time.

"Where's home then?" I challenged.

"LA," Whitley said.

I shook my head. "No way. You never would have taken this job if LA were home. No amount of money could have made you leave."

She drew her hand out of my grasp. "You just don't like California."

No, I liked New York. There was something about the city. The atmosphere. The food and the park and the shows. You could be anyone or no one in New York City. I'd always been in the shadow of my cousins back home in Texas. Midland wasn't exactly a small town, but the circle that I had grown up in, everyone knew everyone. In Manhattan, I could be as important or as invisible as I wanted.

"He's right," Katherine said, surprising me by actually agreeing with me. "New York is home."

"You've never lived anywhere else," Whitley said.

"So? I don't have to live anywhere else to know."

I laughed. "Who knew Katherine and I could agree on anything?"

"You and me, Gavin," Katherine said with a drunk grin. "We agree on two things."

"Oh yeah?"

"New York and Whitley."

Whitley glared. "Don't gang up on me."

"But we love you, dear Whit," Katherine said with a look that said she was joking even though I was sure she wasn't.

That was the moment that English appeared with her work in tow. Her work being the biggest rock band in the country—Cosmere. I'd been listening to their music for years, but their new single was next level. Campbell Abbey was a fucking incredible musician and lyricist.

I went to introduce myself. Lark and Sam were at the back of the group. Lark broke off to rush into Whitley's arms. Sam gave me a fist bump. English was in deep conversation with one of the bandmate's girlfriends when I overheard her discussing, of all the things to be discussing, my cousin's wedding.

I looked the small woman, Nora, up and down. "You're planning my cousin Margaret's wedding?"

"I am. It should be beautiful."

"Oh, I know Merritt Locke. I bet the wedding will be glamorous," English said. She gave the girl a shrewd look. "Have you ever done anything in LA or New York?"

Nora gulped. "I haven't."

"English," Court warned.

"I *hate* my wedding planner." English gave Court a *shut the fuck up* look. "My future mother-in-law picked her out, and she doesn't listen to anything I want. It's only a few months away, and I'm pulling my hair out."

"That's a tough place to be in. She should always listen to you first. It's your wedding, not your mother-in-law's."

English arched an eyebrow at Court. "See!" Then, she turned back to Nora. "Do you have a card?"

I tuned out the rest of the conversation. English wanted out of the big wedding, but maybe a change in wedding planner would make the whole thing better. Since she couldn't change her mother-in-law. I chatted with another woman for a while about the wedding, ignoring Sam's jabs at taking *Whitley* to my cousin's wedding. Yeah, because that would be a good idea.

I shook my head.

That would be a disaster.

My family was ... a lot. Under good circumstances, they were a lot. At a wedding, they would be oppressive. The easiest way to get a girl to run for the hills was to meet my family. I was an only child, but I had six cousins on my dad's side and another fifteen on my mom's side. When we were all together, it was fucking crazy. Someone either ended up drunk, injured, or drunk and injured. Everything was bigger in Texas, including my family and the hurt feelings.

But that didn't stop me from considering it for one moment as I watched Whitley stumble onto the dance floor with her friends. She was shaking her ass and laughing and being as effervescent as ever. She'd be the life of the party, and all the stupid fucking questions that people asked every time I was home about why I hadn't settled down would finally cease.

I'd put down a plus-one for the wedding.

I was sure that I'd have someone that I wanted to take between when I'd told Margaret that I was coming and when I actually showed up. So far, the only person I wanted was entirely off-limits. Even if I wanted to bring her, I wasn't risking our relationship on the chance she said no.

Fuck it. I was tired of thinking about this shit. I was just going to have a good time. Whitley was back in town. Which meant that I wasn't going to sit here with strangers and sulk.

Sam must have seen the glint in my eyes because he started laughing. "Good luck."

"You don't know shit."

"I know you're about to make a fool of yourself. I commend you on doing it so thoroughly time and time again."

I gestured to the redhead on the dance floor with Whitley. "Why don't you get out there with your wife?"

"Because my wife knows that to get me on the dance

floor would be a feat in and of itself and a short-lived victory. She takes her wins where she can get them."

I snorted. "Basically, you don't like to dance?"

"Nope. But go get 'em." He pushed me toward the dance floor, and I didn't look back.

I barged right in on the group of girls, dancing like a maniac on the floor until even Katherine Van Pelt had a smile on her face. Court appeared a minute later with a literal tray of shots. English giggled as she snagged one. I grabbed two shots and met Whitley's eyes with a raised eyebrow. She took two as well and winked.

Good. Good. That was way better. Just how it had always been. Real flirty and a current of desire under every interaction. I'd liked her the first time I met her, but she and I were the same in that neither of us ever seemed to want to settle down. I'd thought our endless flirting was standard order until I realized that maybe that flirting was going somewhere.

Sure, it'd gone somewhere—up in flames.

Court made some ridiculous toast, and then we downed the shots. Whitley wobbled on her heels. She was pixie short. Even in her heels, I towered over her. I liked that. Her makeup was light, highlighting her big honey eyes and her pouty, full lips. They were certified DSLs—dick-sucking lips —and looked like she'd injected several vials of filler into them, but they were just her lips. They were currently a soft pink color, and man, I was trying not to think about exactly what she'd done with them when we hooked up on vacation.

We danced the night away, as if she hadn't been gone at all. I was even on the drunk side by the end of the night. Whitley grabbed my arm as I stumbled toward the bar.

"Hey," she said, stopping me. "Can we talk?"

My eyes widened in surprise. "Yeah, sure."

We moved away out of earshot.

"I just ... I wanted to say thanks for not making this awkward."

"Why would it be awkward?" I asked, grinning down at her, waiting for her to admit why she'd left.

"Shut up. You know why."

"Oh, but I want to hear it." I leaned toward her.

She rolled her eyes and slapped my arm. "You're obnoxious."

"Am I?"

"I'm trying to thank you, and you're flirting with me."

"Have we ever done anything else?"

She paused, as if giving it real thought. "I think we have."

She was right. We had. We'd spent two weeks in paradise, doing a lot more than flirting.

"I want things to be like before. *Before*, before. You know?"

"Before what?" I asked, really pressing the issue.

She giggled. "Stop. Stop. I don't want to talk about that."

She was drunk and her shoulder was pressed tight against mine. I could smell the perfume she wore. Lavender to match the color of her hair. I could have devoured her whole in that moment, but my brain was catching up to what she was really saying.

"Tell me what you want, Whit."

She bit her bottom lip. Fuck, I wanted that in *my* mouth right now.

"You know, just be friends, like before."

Friends.

A cold bucket of water was thrown over my head. She wanted to be *friends*.

Fuck, I could do that. But I didn't *want* that.

I didn't want to lose her either.

"You want to be friends."

"Yeah. I mean, like how it's been tonight. It's been great. I was worried that you'd want to talk about …"

"What exactly?" I asked, pressing again.

She gulped. "You know."

"You've said that. Maybe you should enlighten me."

Because I remembered her watching me masturbate in the shower and the feel of her lips on my cock and how it had felt to sink into her cunt. And for a second, as our eyes met drunkenly, she thought about it too. Then, her eyes shuttered.

"That's what I mean, King," she said, swatting at me and pulling away at the same time. "I don't want things to change with us. You don't either, do you?"

"What if I said I did?"

She froze at those words. Her lips opening to a silent O. Her eyes going wide. She didn't know what to do with that. And Whitley Bowen was terrified of relationships. She thought she was the stereotypical "bad girlfriend," and if she felt the slightest pressure, she'd ditch. I'd seen her move across the country because of it. I could see her brain, even her alcohol-addled brain, considering it now.

"I'm kidding," I lied.

She broke out into laughter. "Jesus, you're the worst. Such a goddamn flirt."

"That's me."

"I'm still the best wingman you've ever had, right, King?"

"Something like that."

"Glad we had this talk. I need another drink. Come dance with me."

"I'll be right there."

She bit her lip and winked at me as she scampered back

to the dance floor. I kept my smile on my face until she disappeared. Then, I let it fall. I wanted to punch something or someone. Whoever had hurt my little pixie enough to make her run away from the first sight of something real.

Fuck.

Just ... fuck.

5

WHITLEY

M y brain was mush when I woke up the next morning, naked in my hotel room, alone. I reached haphazardly for my phone and saw the three missed calls from Lark.

"Fuck," I croaked.

I clicked the voicemail button. "Are we still on for today? I can meet you at the building in ten."

Beep.

"I'm here. Where are you? Whitley, are you still drunk and in bed?"

Beep.

"Well, the apartment was lovely. Are you going to be able to come to the next one, or should I reschedule with my real estate agent?"

"Fuck," I repeated and scrambled into the shower.

Twenty minutes later, I was uptown in a sort of presentable outfit. My hair was still wet, but it was a rainy morning. So, I sort of got away with it. Lark barely held back laughter as I scrambled out of the cab and to her side.

"Sorry, sorry!"

"You look drowned."

I brushed my hair off my shoulders. It looked much darker when it was wet. The lavender deepening to a gray-purple. But I hadn't had time to blow-dry it. Not when I had enough hair that even with a fancy blow-dryer, it took a half hour to dry on a good day.

"Yeah. But I'm here, and I haven't had coffee."

Lark shook her head. "Come on. Let's get you some coffee before we meet Cassie. She's the best real estate agent in the business. She works for my dad in commercial real estate but helps out friends and family for personal residences."

Larkin St. Vincent was heir to the St. Vincent's Resorts conglomerate. They had resorts and villas all over the world for their upper echelon clientele. We'd gone to one in Puerto Rico for two weeks over Christmas three years ago. That was where Gavin and I had fallen into bed.

But Lark had no interest in the family fortune. She was Upper East Side through and through, but now, she worked for Leslie Kensington on her mayoral campaign as the head campaign manager. She'd helped get her elected to her second term despite Court acting like the train wreck he'd been before he met English, and she'd been with the mayor ever since.

"Thanks for doing this," I told Lark after I had coffee securely in my hands and could function as a human being again.

"You know me, I love to help."

"Well, I appreciate it. I know you're busy with the election in November."

"Things are picking up," she agreed. "But it'll really get busy in the fall. English's wedding couldn't have come at a worse time."

"And here I thought that was the point."

Lark rolled her eyes. "I told Leslie to plan it for after or to have it in the summer when she wouldn't be quite so busy."

"But she saw English and Court's wedding as a chip in the campaign game."

"Don't tell English."

"Oh, she knows exactly what family she's marrying into."

"She wants to elope," Lark said. "I'd be for it if Leslie wouldn't have a fit."

"Plus, you want to be there."

Lark grinned. "Well, yes. I love English, but I didn't get to see Penn and Natalie get married."

Once upon a time, there had been a group of Upper East Side teenagers who were so obsessed with each other that they had their own name—Crew. Cruel Crew, if the rumors could be believed. Penn Kensington, Katherine Van Pelt, Larkin St. Vincent, Lewis Warren, and Archibald Rowe ruled the Upper East Side. They were inseparable. Then, Natalie had appeared, and the fissures in the group had turned into chasms. They still met every Labor Day weekend at the Kensingtons' Hamptons home, but it wasn't the same. And maybe that was for the better.

Natalie and Penn had eloped. Katherine and Camden had gotten married in the city. Everyone went on with their lives.

We stopped in front of a building just off of Central Park. My heart skipped as I looked up at the towering thing. I couldn't believe that I could afford an apartment here. It had been my goal the last time I was here, but it had felt unattainable. Just a dream. Like I'd never really fit in with all these fancy Upper East Siders.

Not a girl from Dallas, Texas, who had shunned everything her parents stood for. Mom and Dad were wealthy in a Texas way. Land and ranching and horses. They were Junior Leaguers and country clubbers and the sort. They'd wanted to turn their daughter into the beautiful, brainless blonde that matched the rest of the town.

My brother was home, married to the version of me that I would have become if I'd stayed, with the requisite two and a half children. They went to the right schools and participated in the right activities and belonged to the right clubs. They were everything that I wasn't.

My first dream had been to sing. They'd laughed at me when I brought it up. It was one thing to sing in the church choir. It was another thing to sing at weddings on the weekends for extra money. Another thing *entirely* to want to go to LA to pursue a singing career.

They wanted a daughter to fit a mold and find a good husband, not to be a starving artist in LA, pursuing a once-in-a-lifetime dream. A dream they made clear that I wasn't good enough for and they wouldn't support.

I was supposed to go to college to find a husband. When that didn't happen, I went on to medical school because it looked good to level up my MRS degree, not to actually become a doctor. Certainly not a plastic surgeon.

Not that I could do anything right in their eyes. Plastic surgery had worked out. They'd been right about my voice. The dream was too far-fetched. I didn't sing in front of anyone anymore. But I hadn't gotten that MRS degree either.

I was better for it now that I was looking at a Central Park–facing apartment.

Lark introduced me to Cassie, and we toured the home. Lark shot me a look and shook her head. The one that I'd missed earlier that morning was nicer. We skipped to the next one and the next and the next.

They were all wonderful in their own way. Much nicer than where I'd lived last time I was in the city. I'd been making good money. But good money didn't buy you much in the city. Only legacy money or stupid money did that. And now, I—who was far, far from the trust funds of my peers—was making *stupid* money. So, I would hold out for *the* apartment.

"Oh," I whispered as we stepped into the last one on our list.

"Now, this one is a little higher than your initial price point. The building fees are double, which I understand is a sticking point," Cassie said, walking me through the apartment. "But it has a doorman and bell service. There's a whole list of amenities, including twenty-four-hour-a-day security, a courtyard, a gym, and a rooftop pool."

I tuned out the rest of the sales pitch as I walked through the apartment in a daze. It was perfect. Modern and sleek. Everything was updated and fresh. It smelled like a new home.

Lark came to my side in the master bedroom, which had a view overlooking the park, and arched an eyebrow. "You like this one?"

"Yeah."

"Me too."

I glanced at her. She was hiding something. "What?"

"Nothing. Nothing at all."

"Lark, I can read you. It's been three years, but I'm not stupid."

Lark laughed. "Most people can't see my tells."

"I'm not most people."

"I suppose not." She ran a hand back through her red hair and smirked at me. "Gavin lives in this building."

I froze at those words. They hadn't been what I was expecting at all. "What? I thought he lived by Court."

"He did. He moved last year."

"Oh."

Lark grinned. "Is that a problem?"

"Why would it be?"

"Well, you were all over each other last night."

I blinked. "Uh ... we were?"

"God, how drunk were you?"

"I don't know. Katherine and I started drinking in the afternoon. I was pretty gone when everyone showed up."

"Did you hook up?"

I shook my head. "I would have remembered *that*."

Lark snorted. "God, let's hope so."

"Well?" Cassie said with a kind smile. "This is my favorite. What about you?"

I nodded. "Mine too."

"When you said it was more, how much more?" Lark asked.

"Let me pull up the information for you."

Lark followed her into the kitchen. I took my phone out and snapped a picture of the bedroom with the view. I bit my lip and then sent the picture to Gavin.

What do you think?

I didn't expect a response right away, but my phone dinged almost immediately.

Is that an invitation?

I snorted. Typical Gavin.

It's an apartment I'm looking at.

That's quite a view, Bowen.

I grinned.

I thought so too.

Moving up in the world.

Lark tells me this is your building.

The ellipses that said he was typing was visible for a minute before disappearing. I frowned. What had he been planning to say?

It's a great building. The people are nice, and the rooms are soundproof, so you can't hear your neighbors. You'd like it.

I reread the text. He was pitching the building to me. As if everything was totally normal and being in each other's orbit like this wouldn't be difficult for him. Maybe I'd read everything wrong about him.

That's good to know. Anything else?

Well … as your friend, I have to tell you … the coffee downstairs sucks. I go out of my way every morning to get the good stuff.

Friend. As his *friend.*

Words I'd never heard Gavin utter. We were friends. Of course we were. I'd been his wingman long before things changed. But there had always been some kind of undercurrent between us. He would only say we were friends if there was no chance that this was going to happen.

"Whit?" Lark called from the kitchen.

I shook myself out of that train of thought and headed toward her. "Hey, sorry."

"What do you think?"

I glanced down at the text again. Well, there was no reason to be worried about seeing Gavin King on the regular if we were just friends. Wasn't that what I wanted anyway?

Just because I had feelings for him didn't mean that I had to act on them. It would be better if I didn't. Things had been terrible after Robert found out and I bailed. I didn't want to ruin anything. I didn't want to run again.

"This is the one," I told them both.

"Excellent," Cassie said, beaming. "We'll get started on the paperwork. I have a friend at the bank who can expedite the purchasing process."

Lark threw her arms around me. "I'm so glad you're buying a place. It feels so permanent."

"Don't try to scare a girl away."

She laughed. "I know you don't like anything permanent, but you're here to stay. None of us want you to leave ever again."

And neither did I.

6

———

WHITLEY

Three weeks later, I moved into my new apartment. Katherine insisted on throwing a welcome party. Having all of my friends in my new place was magic. Katherine certainly knew how to throw a party, and there was enough charcuterie and finger food for me to munch on for the rest of the week after everyone left.

That night, Gavin had been as friendly as he'd been in text. Nothing out of place. Not any more or less flirtatious than normal. He was doing an incredible job of pretending like nothing had ever happened between us.

I was confused by it all, but I couldn't deny that it made me relax. There had been this undercurrent of fear in every interaction before this. That every moment was being watched and judged and filed away for later about what Gavin and I were going to do. Even my friends had been waiting.

Once they saw that nothing was different, they'd all backed off. They still wanted us to get together. But the excitement of *will they, won't they* was gone.

We were friends. Just friends.

The Monday after I had my housewarming party, a knock sounded at my door. I'd just finished blowing out my hair and thrown on something for work.

I yanked open the door to find Gavin King standing there with two cups of coffee. "Hey, neighbor."

I blinked. "Hey."

"Got you coffee before heading to the office."

"Oh, thank you." I took the cup in my hand and blew on the top. I took a sip and glanced up at him in surprise. "This is delicious."

"Yeah, I told you, you have to go around the block to get the good stuff."

"Well, you were right."

"As per usual," he said with a smile. "You headed out?"

"I have to finish my makeup, and then yeah. You have to go?"

He nodded thoughtfully. "I have to be in at seven thirty. Try to leave a half hour ahead of time with the car service." He trailed off as he saw me eyeing him. "What?"

"Car service? In this city? What a pain. Just take the subway."

He looked at me for a minute, as if he'd never considered the possibility.

I laughed at him. "Go to work, King. Thanks for the coffee."

I closed the door on him and finished my makeup. Work was grueling. Dr. Varma was already trying to lay on more responsibilities. I'd only been there a few weeks, and I could see that he was itching to take the entire summer off to visit family in Pakistan.

I didn't have any plans until English's wedding. I'd left all my wedding invites and party plans and the rest of my life back in LA. As long as I kept my weekends for my sanity, I'd be fine.

The next four days, Gavin appeared with coffee at my door promptly at seven in the morning. On the fifth day, when it didn't appear, I peeked through my door in confusion. Maybe I'd gotten used to him bringing me my morning fix.

I worked on my makeup and grabbed a light jacket and my purse before heading down the elevator. I left earlier than normal so that I could find this coffee shop that he'd proven was the best.

But when I stepped off the elevator, Gavin was standing there with two cups of coffee in his hands.

He laughed when he saw me. "Sorry, running late."

"You don't have to do this every morning." Even if I liked it. "I can get my own coffee, you know?"

"Sure," he said, handing me my coffee. "But if I'm going anyway ..."

"Then, you can take your car service straight to your office instead of walking all the way back up to my apartment."

He grinned. "What do you have against my car service? I could drive you?"

"Or you could take the subway with me."

"I'll stick with being above ground, thank you."

I snorted as we passed through the front doors. A sleek black car waited out front.

"Well, that's me," he said with a grin. "Until Monday."

"You really don't have to get me coffee," I said, holding the cup in my hand protectively.

"Ah, but then I wouldn't get to see you in the morning."

I rolled my eyes. "Such a flirt, King."

"You're the one who moved into my building, Bowen. These are the consequences."

Then, he hopped into his car and disappeared into the New York City traffic.

What an infuriating man. Yet I couldn't stop smiling.

Coffee continued for another week. I'd make sure I was finished getting dressed by the time that he brought it, so we could take the elevator downstairs together. He'd hop into his little black car and drive away while I traipsed to the subway to get to work. Showing up a half hour early wasn't a problem. In fact, it was almost necessary with paperwork stacking up in my office. I had client meetings all day and surgeries the rest of the week. Though it was a tremendous amount of work, I never regretted a minute of it. I loved it. I loved it more than my work in LA.

As Dr. Varma made his plans for the summer, he encouraged me to take time off when I needed it. My time off was in my hands. He didn't want me to burn out.

Maybe there was something in the coffee that was placed in my hands every morning because I felt more invigorated than ever. The doctor laughed at me and called me young.

In time, I'd need more time off.

But plan for it?

I shrugged it off.

After another week, I started meeting Gavin downstairs to go to the coffee shop with him. The place was magic. My regular black coffee was phenomenal, but I tried all the varieties that he recommended. An iced Americano was probably my favorite, but unsurprisingly, I was really into lavender lattes.

We were walking back to the apartment so that he could catch his car for work when he touched my arm and pulled me in the wrong direction.

"Uh, where are we going?" I asked.

"I told my car service to come back tomorrow."

I blinked at him in surprise. "You did what? How are you getting to work? Oh my god, are you playing hooky?"

He laughed. "When I take off at my own company, it's not playing hooky, Whit. I'm the boss. I can take off when I want. So can you."

"Right. Still not used to that. So, what are you doing?"

"I was going to take the subway. With you."

"What?" I asked in disbelief. "You hate the subway."

"I don't *hate* it," he said with a laugh. "I'm a New Yorker after all. It's a way of life. I just prefer the morning to myself in the car."

"Then, why are you taking the subway with me?"

"I thought I might spend the morning with you instead."

I eyed him skeptically. "Why?"

"Because we're friends. That's what friends do."

I didn't believe him, but I scanned my MetroCard and saw that he had one already as well. We passed into the busy underground, taking seats on a train heading north. My office was in a fancy, stuffy part of the Upper East Side. He worked somewhere nearby. Maybe a subway stop or two away from me.

Still, he got out at my stop and laughed when I gave him another curious look.

"I can walk a few blocks, Whit. I promise, my shoes are comfortable, and it's a beautiful day."

It was. May was when New York finally left the dreary,

wet spring behind, and the world began to bloom with clear skies and bright colors everywhere. It was hard to believe a city of steel would blossom along with the park at its heart, but it did. The world came alive.

I decided not to argue with him. Just headed inside to my building, to the mountain of work on my schedule, and left Gavin King at the door. He'd told me that he had drinks with Court and Sam after work every afternoon, which was why I never saw him around the building when I got home.

Still, he took the subway with me every morning. I was surprised he hadn't tried to convince me to take the car service instead. He must have still taken it home every afternoon because we never saw each other, except for coffee in the mornings and when we had stuff with our friends.

But the spring was busy for everyone with Lark working on the campaign, Court and English preparing for the wedding, Camden brokering a new international deal for Percy Tower, and Katherine spending more and more time with her children. Summer was usually when things slowed down and we could all get together more. Weekends in the Hamptons and evenings on the rooftops. I was looking forward to it all again.

A knock came on my door.

I checked my phone and saw that it was midnight. I should have been asleep already, but I'd started a new true crime novel. I hadn't been able to put it down. I wanted to know who had done it before I started the Netflix series based on the book. I had my suspicions, but it was keeping me on the edge of my seat.

Still, none of that explained why someone was knocking on my door.

I peered out the peephole and found Gavin King with his hands in the pockets of his suit pants and his tie undone and loose around his neck.

"What the hell?"

Despite us meeting every morning during the workweek, Gavin had never shown up at my place in the evening. I certainly hadn't been expecting him.

I yanked the door open. "Hey. What's up?"

He leaned forward against the doorframe. "Hey, Whit."

"Everything all right?"

"Can I come in? I need to talk to you."

Adrenaline coursed through my body. I nodded, pulling the door open wide. "Sure. What's going on?"

He stumbled forward, catching himself on the kitchen island. He laughed hoarsely and then shot me a winning smile. My heart skipped at that look. Then, he headed into the living room, collapsing onto the couch and lying there.

I slammed the door closed. "How drunk *are* you?"

"Drunk? Me?" He shot me that same smile. "Just a little bit."

"You're falling all over yourself."

"Yeah. True." He lay back and stared up at the ceiling. "I blame Locke, Blake, and Mal."

"Who?"

"Fuck. I forgot you weren't here when they moved here. Mal is my cousin. Malcolm King. Well, he doesn't live here. He lives in Midland, but he was here for the bachelor party."

"Bachelor party?" I asked, my voice rising.

"Yeah. Locke—Merritt Locke—is marrying my cousin Margaret next weekend. Blake Holliday is his best friend and his best man. Mal and Blake have known each other since childhood. Mal's a groomsman. I showed them a good time."

"Lord, I can only imagine what that means." I headed to the kitchen and poured him a tall glass of water. "Here. Drink this."

He sat up and downed it in one long drag. "Crisp."

"Okay. So, you were out for the bachelor party tonight. Why are you here exactly?"

"I need your help."

I stared at him in confusion. My help. That ... that wasn't what I'd been expecting. I'd been—I didn't know— expecting some kind of drunk confession. We'd been hanging out every morning. It was what *friends* did. That was what he'd said. Our flirting meant nothing. I needed to get over myself.

"How can I help you?" I sank into a seat across from him.

I was in nothing but a tiny tank top and shorts. Gavin's eyes roamed my body. I could see the snide comment he'd throw out flirtatiously at the way I'd phrased that.

"Keep it together, King."

He laughed. "Right. Okay. So, I have a dilemma."

"What sort of dilemma?"

"I kind of told everyone that I had a girlfriend."

"Why would you tell anyone that?" I asked with a chuckle. "You are as likely to settle down as I am. I mean, have you ever had a girlfriend?"

"I had a girlfriend," he growled. "Once."

I snorted. "Okay."

"Anyway, the problem is that I said that I was bringing said girlfriend to the wedding."

"That is a problem. Just tell them you don't have a girlfriend."

"No, no, no," he said, standing and walking aimlessly around my living room. "You don't understand my family. They're ... a lot. Like *a lot*, a lot."

"I can understand that," I said softly, thinking about how over the top my own family was.

"No way. I have a million cousins and aunts and uncles. It's so much, and I've never brought a girl home to meet them all. I couldn't even imagine doing something like that. I should have never told them I had a girlfriend, but once I did, it spread like wildfire. Everyone is so excited to meet her. Especially because I'm so secretive about her. Do you see my dilemma?"

"Your lie turned into a wildfire."

"Yes," he said, pointing at me as if I understood.

"Just tell them the truth."

He laughed. "Or you could go with me."

I stared at him, waiting for the punch line. But he was just standing there, staring at me, judging my reaction. "I'm not your girlfriend."

"No, I know. Of course not. But you could *pretend* to be my girlfriend for the wedding."

"What?" I gasped. "I couldn't do that. Everyone would know we weren't dating."

"No, no. See, we could act like we always do. We're already flirty and ridiculous together. You would act like that and tell everyone you were my girlfriend."

I cringed at that word. "I'm a terrible girlfriend, King."

"That's not true."

"It is," I told him vehemently. "I'd never pull it off. Plus, I have appointments all week. I can't take the time off."

"You're the boss," he reminded me in the way that I always reminded *him*.

"Not fair."

"Come on. Please, do this for me. I'll do something for you. Whatever you want," he urged with that heart-melting smile again. "It's a few days in Midland, where you smile and laugh and pretend we're a happy couple. We can plan a huge breakup afterward, if you want, so everyone will know it didn't work out. Please. Come on. This is what friends do."

What friends do.

Because he didn't want me there as his real girlfriend. Something I'd honestly be terrible at. But a *fake* girlfriend.

No, fuck, I hated the idea of being a girlfriend. I didn't like that at all. I was the sort of girl who ruined relationships as soon as they touched me. I was never quite what anyone needed. And I didn't know how to stop it or how to escape the spiral of it all.

"I'm a bad girlfriend," I repeated. "Even if I could get away, I'd ruin it."

"Explain this *bad girlfriend* thing to me again, Bowen. All I remember is that people treated you like shit, and so you left them. I've heard all the stories of you being cheated on and all that."

I blushed. Yeah, I had been cheated on a lot, but it was more than that. It had always been more than that. It had started in high school. My parents were worried after I was asked to my first dance. I was the rebel, the heartbreaker, even before I'd broken my first heart. I went to that dance and danced on tables and not given a single fuck. Apparently, not caring about your date meant that date was probably going to abandon you halfway through the night. Whatever. I'd ended up having a good time without him.

I'd long ago discovered that not wanting to settle for anything less than perfection meant that I spent a lot of time alone.

"I don't get the whole dating thing. I've done it. I've done it over and over, and it all ends the same way. With the other person saying I'm too wild or too indifferent or too *something* that doesn't quite fit their definition of a girlfriend. Then, when I see the first sign of it going bad, I don't just end it. I sunder it to the fucking cinders. I can't let it go. I have to ruin it beyond measure. So, believe me," I said in a desperate attempt for him to understand what a terrible idea this was, "I'm *bad* at it, King. I don't think I can even *pretend* to be good at it."

Gavin opened his mouth, as if he were going to disagree, but then stopped, as if a thought had struck him. "Wait, you wouldn't have to be my girlfriend."

"What? That's what you told everyone."

"What if you were my fiancée? My fake fiancée."

I narrowed my eyes. That didn't make it better. If I was a bad girlfriend, then, I'd be a bad fiancée, too.

But he kept speaking. "You've never been a fiancée. You ... you don't know if you're bad at it. It'd just be for fun, Whit. Come on. Give me a few days. I'd owe you big."

I bit my lip as I turned the idea in my mind. I imagined myself on Gavin's arm at his cousin's wedding. I'd meet his family and pretend like I was besotted with him. It wouldn't even be hard. We already acted like that around each other. We always had, even before things went down. It was just our personalities. We clicked. And we could click this way too.

Varma *had been* trying to tell me to take some time off. Surely, he hadn't meant to a wedding in Midland, Texas. But with Gavin's pouting face staring at me with such hope, I found my walls coming down.

Would it be so bad to pretend to be his for a few days? Maybe I'd get the entire thing out of my system, and I could finally move on from what had happened. Maybe I'd prove that I was as bad of a fiancée as I was a girlfriend. It had been the thrill of being with him on vacation. I'd convince myself that it wasn't going to work, and things could finally go back to normal.

"All right," I said on a sigh. "When do we leave?"

PART II

BLONDES HAVE MORE FUN

7

———

GAVIN

She said yes.

I still couldn't fucking believe it.

I'd wanted to invite Whitley every day for the last two months leading up to my cousin's wedding. I wanted her to go as my date. But every time we got even remotely close, she backed off. Her eyes shuttered. Her body stiffened. She'd really meant it that night she told me that she wanted us to be friends.

Then, I was down to the wire about getting a date, and I was an idiot. I asked her to be my fake date. Even though I wanted her to be my *real* date. But she wouldn't decline when it was a game. She never would have said yes if I'd been serious. As serious as I wanted to be.

Regardless, she'd said yes.

Now, I was fishing around in my apartment for the one thing I needed to give her to make this fiction a reality.

I was minutes away from heading upstairs to help her with her bags. We were flying out that afternoon, and I still couldn't believe that we were doing this. She'd gotten her clients rescheduled for the week. She'd gone shopping and gotten a dress that she refused to show me. And now, we just had to get on a plane and head back to the town where I was raised.

God, my family was going to be a pain in the ass about this.

I continued to rummage through my drawers. I could have *sworn* I'd stuffed that thing back here somewhere. Admittedly, it had been a few years since my mother had given it to me, and I'd rolled my eyes, tossing it unconcerned into the back of a deep dresser drawer. When the hell was I going to need that anyway?

But now, I fucking needed it.

I reached my arm farther back into the drawer and felt the edge of a velvet box.

"Aha!" I said triumphantly, retrieving the little black box.

I popped it open and glanced inside to make sure it wasn't empty. That would have been one hell of a surprise. Satisfied, I pocketed the thing with relief.

All set.

I slung my suit bag over one shoulder and pushed my suitcase toward the door. I took the elevator to Whitley's floor and knocked twice. I couldn't deny that I'd liked having her only an elevator ride away for the last couple of weeks. Getting coffee for her had been a pretense to see her.

What had happened in the following weeks still surprised me. We'd started to get coffee *together*. I gave up my car in the mornings and took the *subway*. Me. Who the fuck would have guessed? And it hadn't even been terrible. Not when I had her at my side to make jokes with all morning on our way uptown.

The door creaked open, and I looked into Whit's apartment at a gorgeous blonde.

My eyes rounded in shock. "Your hair!"

She laughed, almost self-conscious. "Thanks, King. That makes a girl feel good."

"But the purple," I said regretfully. "I liked it."

Her smile was genuine then. "Me too. But I know what Texas weddings are like. Bleach is a safer choice than color."

Before I could stop myself, I reached forward, threading my fingers through the now–Marilyn Monroe–blonde color. She stilled under my touch.

"You could have just been yourself. You didn't have to change it."

She gulped and pulled back with another laugh. "Oh, don't worry. I'm dyeing it again as soon as I get back."

"Good," I said, stuffing my hand into my pocket to keep from touching her again. "Are you ready to go?"

She looked half-ready to run. I could see that all over her.

"I still can't believe I'm doing this. It's crazy, right?"

"It's going to be fun," I told her with ease. I didn't want her to back out now. "You already have the time off and a new dress and new hair."

"I do, and I did. Yeah. But this is wild, even for me."

I laughed. "Is it? I've heard some of your stories."

She rolled a suitcase to me. "A fake fiancée at your cousin's wedding for the weekend. This one is going down in the books."

"Then, let's get this started."

She nodded, as if she were determined. "I'm ready as I'll ever be."

I wheeled her suitcase into the elevator, and she slung an oversize boho bag and a purse on before locking up. We headed downstairs to the limo that waited to whisk us to the airport.

Her eyes rounded. "Fancy as fuck, King."

The driver put our bags in the trunk, and I offered for her to get inside first. I slid into the seat next to her. The limo pulled away from the curb, and we were off.

"We should probably plot our backstory," Whitley said.

"Our backstory?"

"You know, the things that parents are likely to ask. How we met and how you proposed and all that."

"Probably should stick to the truth as much as we can."

"Yeah, sure, but the proposal."

"About that," I said, clearing my throat.

Suddenly, I was sweating. I'd never considered what this moment would feel like. I'd never wondered who the woman would be or how it would look like or that I'd be sweating. Jesus, it wasn't even real, and I was so fucking nervous. She could still say no, right? Fuck.

Whitley's head whipped to me. "What about that?"

I withdrew the black box I'd spent this morning trying to locate. "Whitley Bowen, would you do me the honor of being my fake fiancée?"

Her jaw dropped when I opened the box and revealed my grandmother's enormous five carat engagement ring. My mother had given it to me when Grandma died a few years back. She told me that she wanted me to hang on to it and give it to someone who deserved it when I was ready. I laughed and told her that day would never come. But she'd closed my hand around the ring and said there was someone right out there for me. Now, I was offering it to Whitley.

"What ... what is that?" she whispered.

"This is my grandmother's engagement ring. My mom passed it to me."

"I can't wear that!" She looked up at me with big, frightened eyes. "That's your grandma's ring."

"I know. But no one will believe that you're my fiancée without it."

"What if it doesn't fit?"

I plucked the ring out of the box. It was heftier than I remembered. Well, I'd never even touched the thing. It felt terrifying to even consider giving this to someone. Even though this was fake, I couldn't deny that I wanted to slip the ring onto Whit's finger.

I took her left hand in my own and slowly slid the ring onto her ring finger. It slipped into place, as if the ring had been designed for her. As if it hadn't been on my grand-mother's hand for fifty years and passed down to me for some unknowable future bride.

Whitley's eyes were wide. "Oh," she whispered, breathy and uncertain.

She held her hand out in front of her, looking at the huge ring on her dainty finger. Her nails had been done, and the whole thing looked like a picture-perfect moment. Her hand shook slightly.

"It's beautiful."

I'd never seen this expression on her face before. It was almost uncertainty, as if she had confronted a fear she'd had her whole life and realized that maybe she wasn't that different from other girls.

"It is," I said before adding softly, "And so are you."

She met my gaze. All of her bravado fell away. "Thank you, Gavin. I'll take care of it."

"It looks good on you," I admitted. "Now, you can say I proposed in a limo."

She laughed, and her gaze went back to the ring on her finger. "That will be so romantic to tell the kids one day," she joked.

"Very romantic. That's me."

She rolled her eyes. "Surprisingly so."

I didn't have anything to say to that. I'd just sort of proposed to my fake fiancée. Maybe it *was* romantic. Maybe it was because it was Whitley.

Either way, we let the subject drop as we neared the airport. We were flying private. Normally, I took the company jet home when I had business, but this was the first time in a while that I'd used it for pleasure.

Whitley was still staring at her ring as we walked out toward the Dorset & King plane. She pulled her phone out and snapped a picture of it on her finger with the plane in the background.

"What are you doing?"

"Sending a picture to the girls."

I arched an eyebrow. "Is that wise?"

She shot me a calculated Cheshire cat smile. "They're going to freak."

"Again, is that wise?"

"Guess we'll find out."

I read the text over her shoulder. Sunlight bounced off my grandmother's ring, and the plane was blurry in the background, but it was very clear what was happening.

> Don't freak out but …

I snorted. "Oh, you're courting trouble. Katherine is going to kill you."

"English," Whitley said, putting her phone purposely on airplane mode and following me onto the plane. "She'll hunt me down and murder me for not telling her what I'm doing."

"You've been friends a long time. I'm sure she'd expect you to tell her you got engaged in person."

"Oh no, she absolutely would be offended if I got engaged and she wasn't there to witness it happening."

I tucked that tidbit away. "But you weren't there when Court proposed."

"Nope, but it's English. That's kind of her job. She'd feel like she failed in her friend duties."

We climbed onto my private plane. Whitley's eyes roamed the interior before settling on the champagne that I'd been sure to have on ice before we got there.

"For the future Mr. and Mrs. King," the flight attendant said, handing us each a glass of bubbly.

Whitley's cheeks heated, and she looked over at me accusingly. "You told the staff?"

"We're about to tell everyone, darling," I joked, pulling her into me.

Her eyes widened in surprise at how forward I was. But this was what we were going to have to pull off for the next few days. With my family, who knew me better than anyone. It was easier with Whit because none of it really felt like pretending.

Having her pressed against my chest with my hand at the small of her back brought back a riot of memories. And no matter how fake this was, I couldn't stop the desire that shot through me at her nearness.

"Well, to us then," she said, lifting her glass.

I clinked mine against hers, and we tipped them back. She stayed in my embrace with her eyes on mine, assessing me for the trick in all of this, but she didn't know that the trick had already happened. I'd wanted her here. I had gotten her here. Everything else that happened along the way would just be icing on the cake.

8
———

WHITLEY

idland, Texas, was a desolate, dusty mess of a place
with oil rigs as far as the eye could see. Despite the
sight from the airfield being less than ideal, I took a deep
breath of relief. Texas. I'd refused to say it was home, but it
had a different smell than the rest of the country. Like blue-
bonnets and longhorns and BBQ and Friday night lights
and big oil. It smelled like home.

I hated admitting it. When I went back to Dallas, which
was rare to start with, I focused on getting in and getting out.
But here in West Texas—where the land was flat as a
pancake that stretched across the entire world, the cerulean
skies had not a cloud in the sky, and the air was dry and
clean—it was hard to remember why I hated it so much.
Why I'd stayed away for so long.

"Not much to look at," Gavin said quickly. "It's nicer in
town." Then, he paused and reluctantly added, "Sort of."

"You don't have to convince me. I'm from Texas,
remember?"

"Yeah, but Dallas isn't Midland."

"No."

Dallas was … chock-full of bad memories. Midland was a blank slate.

"But I like it."

He gave me a disbelieving look. "If you say so."

We stepped off of the plane directly to an awaiting car service. Once I was safely out of the dry heat, I turned my phone back on. Immediately, the thing lit up like a Christmas tree. Gavin laughed, watching over my shoulder as the messages flooded in a cascade and the missed calls and voicemails racked up.

"I told you," he said.

"Yeah, yeah," I said with a laugh.

I clicked through the wave of texts in the group chat first. Katherine, Lark, and English were going insane because of the ring. And how could I blame them?

I'd gone out of my mind at the sight of it. Of Gavin fucking King proposing to me. Fake proposing. Whatever. My brain clearly could not tell the difference.

My breath had gone short. My mind all fuzzy. And tears had nearly come to my eyes. Not only was it utterly massive, but it was also *stunning*. Maybe the prettiest ring I'd ever seen in my entire existence. It fit perfectly, like it was *mine*. Except it wasn't mine.

Gavin had made a joke out of it, like we both always did, but it wasn't a joke. In that moment, it had felt so very real. I couldn't stop staring at it. Even as we flew across the country. I continued reading the crime novel Gavin had interrupted the night before. But I'd kept getting distracted by the weight of the ring on my finger and the way the diamond cast rainbows across the room when it caught the light.

"They are really freaking out. Should I put them out of their misery?"

"It's the right thing to do," Gavin said with that sly grin. He was tapping away at his phone.

I pulled up the group again and selected video chat. A few seconds later, all three of my friends were on the screen, shrieking at me.

I held my hand up. "Oh my god, hold on. My eardrums, Christ. Not all at once."

"What in the fuck was that picture, Whitley?" English asked first.

"Yeah. What is going on?" Lark asked.

Katherine tugged little Beckett closer and shot me an imperious look. "Explain yourself."

"Well, I might have done something rash."

English snorted. "That's your MO."

"When he asked, I said yes."

"Who?" they all asked as one.

Gavin leaned into the camera and waved. "Hi, ladies."

The phone went deathly quiet. All three girls had wide eyes and shocked expressions.

I couldn't keep my face neutral. "You can all breathe. It's a joke."

"What the fuck, Whit?" English snapped.

"I don't get it," Lark said.

"You're at the wedding," Katherine guessed intuitively.

I pointed at her. "Bingo. I flew with Gavin to Texas for his cousin's wedding. He needed a plus-one." I grinned at them. "I just wanted to raise your hackles."

"You're a bitch," English grumbled. "I actually went to your apartment to try to yell at you."

"Sorry, airplane mode. I missed all your calls."

Gavin leaned over again. "Don't worry. I'll take good care of her."

Katherine smirked. "I bet you will."

I snorted at Katherine's quip. Typical Katherine.

"Okay, I'm going to let you all go now. We're almost to the hotel."

English shot me a look. "Call me later, okay?"

"Love you."

Then, I hung up.

Gavin chuckled. "They were having a fit."

"I knew they would. Especially when I sent them a picture of the ring."

"I thought you were going to tell them our grand scheme."

"It might have been too much, even for them."

English had still looked pissed. I was probably going to get an earful when I finally called her back. She wouldn't want to rage in front of Gavin. That was more Katherine, but she'd just smirked, as if she had known this was all going to happen.

"I'll tell them how it all turns out when I get back."

"You and your stories."

"Hey, I have good stories," I argued.

"Ah, yes, *The Crazy Adventures of Whitley Bowen*™."

I arched an eyebrow. "You're the one who brought me here to be another crazy story, King."

His smile was genuine. "I never said otherwise. And I like the stories anyway."

That look told me he was telling the truth, but I still felt wary. The girls always thought my stories from my ill-conceived relationships were a riot. But the people I dated thought they were a time bomb, waiting to blow up in their face. Not that Gavin and I were dating ...

"Here we are," Gavin said as the car rolled up to the front of a fancy hotel downtown. "Everyone from out of town is staying here."

I followed him up the stairs as a bellman dealt with our luggage. The hotel looked like something straight out of New York. Maybe not as nice as Percy Tower, but still swanky.

I had to remind myself that this was a Texas oil dynasty. Of course they'd put everyone up at the nicest hotel in town. And they had done it because they wanted to, not to keep up with the Joneses, like my parents.

Gavin checked us in and then passed me a key. We took the elevator to one of the top floors, and he opened the door to a massive suite. There was a balcony overlooking the city and oil fields beyond. A king-size bed was set back into its own bedroom with a bathroom that made me want to crawl into the enormous tub and live there permanently.

"Wow," I muttered. "Nice digs."

Gavin peeked into the bedroom, and a slow smile came over his features. "It'll do."

I shivered at that look. One bed.

I'd be lying if I said that I hadn't considered that I'd be in a hotel room with Gavin King, all alone for a couple of days. I wasn't sure that I'd considered the fact that there would be only one bed.

But of course, there was.

I sauntered past him, brushing his shoulder. "I call the right side. I always sleep on the right side."

He laughed. "You'll have to fight me for it, Bowen."

"I'm scrappy. I'll win."

"Maybe," he said with that unrelenting smirk. "I look forward to you trying."

I rolled my eyes at him to keep back how good that inviting quality sounded in his voice. "What's next?"

"My aunt and uncle are throwing a party tonight at their place."

"Time to meet everyone."

"Are you ready?" he asked sincerely.

I popped open my suitcase and withdrew a pink sundress. "Going to be fine. I'm great with parents."

He chuckled. "I have no doubt."

Sometimes, I thought I was better with parents than I was with my dates. Maybe because I'd been raised to say *yes, ma'am* and *no, sir* until it was ingrained in my very being. When I saw an authority figure, my entire body snapped right to attention. This was a hundred percent nurture, and I'd never found a way to get around it.

It was probably the reason that Dr. Varma had decided I should take over his business when he wanted to retire. All those *yes, sir*s had really stuck with him. Even though I might or might not have broken the heart of one of his daughters.

As we drove up the winding drive toward Gavin's aunt and uncle's house, that same thing started to happen to me again. I sat up a little straighter. I checked my hair and makeup in the mirror of the Wrangler one of his cousins had dropped off for him to drive around while I was getting ready.

"I never thought I'd see you in a Jeep," I told him as I snapped the visor back into place.

"I used to drive a truck."

I leaned my chin on my fist on the center console. "Was it lifted?"

He winked at me. "Not a true West Texas boy without a lifted truck, Bowen."

"Do you have pictures? I must see this."

"I hope they burned them all."

"Aww, I bet you were adorable. Did you have boots and a hat and belt buckles and shit?"

He huffed. "Of course. Who do you think I am?"

"Do you *still* have them?"

"We don't talk about that."

I laughed. "Oh my god, you do. Please tell me you'll wear boots and a hat for me."

"Why? So you can make fun of me?"

"Hey, I was raised in Texas. I can appreciate a man in his Sunday best jeans and a hat."

Gavin shot me a conspiratorial grin. "Are you saying you're hot for cowboys?"

"As if you aren't," I said with a wave of my hand.

"It might shock you to learn that I've never hooked up with a cowboy."

I shot him a filthy look. "Oh, I have."

"I bet you ate them alive."

"Good ole boys make for tasty treats. As long as you don't stick around long enough for the misogyny."

Gavin choked. "You're something else." Then, he nodded his head toward the drive. "We're here."

I faced forward again, and my jaw dropped. I'd known that Gavin was of the King oil dynasty. I'd *known*. Obviously if he fit in with his other richie rich friends in New York. *My* richie rich friends. But Upper East Side was different than Texas. This was acres of land without an oil rig in sight and a three-story *mansion* on flat property with its own river and horses grazing freely. This was *Texas* rich. Exactly the kind of family my parents had wanted me to associate with all those years ago.

"Whoa." I popped open the door and jumped out of the Jeep.

"Yeah," Gavin said, coming to stand at my side. "Last chance to back out."

I glanced up at him in surprise. "You're the one who begged me."

"I know. But I'm still a gentleman."

"A gentleman?" I asked with a laugh.

Gavin King was a rogue and a rake and a playboy. Gentleman was the last thing that anyone would ever call him.

"That's adorable, King. Let's do this."

He tucked my arm into his, and we headed up the drive together.

As we got closer, I noticed the white roses blooming from verdant bushes all around the house. The scent was so sweet, almost cloying. Someone had an incredible gardener to get roses that stunning to grow.

"What's with the roses?"

Gavin grinned. "It's my family flower. White roses. The Dorsets, who my family runs the oil business with, they're red roses. Sort of a long-standing rivalry."

"Well, they're beautiful. Whoever they hired to do them has a great touch."

"That would be my aunt Susannah," he said. "She has a green thumb."

We climbed the stairs, and Gavin knocked once. A second later, the door swung open, and a woman of undetermined age appeared.

"Gavin!" she said, pulling him into a hug. "Honey, we're so glad you're home."

"Hi, Aunt Susannah. This is Whitley. She was admiring your roses."

"They're beautiful, ma'am."

"Ma'am," Susannah said, winking at Gavin. "I see you

got a good one here. I'm so excited to meet you, Whitley. We've all been *dying* to meet Gavin's girlfriend. He never brings anyone home, and he's too wonderful not to have someone good for him."

"I couldn't agree more," I said easily at Susannah's gushing.

"Come. Come inside," Susannah said quickly. "Your parents are already here. I know they can't wait to see you and meet Whitley."

We let Susannah pull us through her enormous house and out onto an outdoor patio that should have been on some TV show.

There was a fireplace and several mounted televisions with elaborate patio seating. All of it looked over an oasis in the middle of the otherwise dry land. Her gardening skills were on display, surrounding a massive pool with an actual lazy river and diving board. It looked like something out of a resort. And sounded like it with a few dozen people floating in the water, sitting under covered cabanas, and laughing over drinks.

The patio had an outdoor kitchen bigger than most indoor kitchens with two built-in grills and a grilling egg. A man was manning one of the grills, and the smell of hamburgers wafted toward me. I tried to keep my face neutral, but, fuck, it was hard.

He stepped away and drew Gavin into a hug. "You're home."

"Whitley, this is my uncle Richard."

"The lady of honor," Richard said genially. "A pleasure."

"My baby," a woman said, jumping out of her seat and sloshing her margarita as she rushed toward Gavin.

"Hi, Mom," he said with a laugh.

They hugged, and then his father was there, giving him

a hug as well. Without waiting, his mom scooped me up into a hug too.

"You must be Whitley. Oh, we've heard such good things about you."

"So nice to meet you, ma'am."

What exactly had Gavin said about me? I glanced at him, but he was just beaming at his family.

"Oh, please call me Julianne," his mom said. "And this is my husband, Edmond."

"We're so happy to have you here."

I laughed and drew back with surprise. They were all so *nice*. So fucking nice. Wow. My parents' friends were all that fake nice. That sugary-sweet, backstabbing nice that put you on edge. These people weren't like that at all.

"Sit. Sit," Susannah said. "Whitley, can I get you a margarita?"

"Actually," Gavin said, clearing his throat, "before we get to drinks, we have news."

He wore a wide smile as he turned to face me, taking my hand in his. A shiver of anticipation ran down my spine.

He held my hand up so that everyone could see the ring on my finger.

"We're engaged."

9

GAVIN

The next several hours went by in a sort of blur of delight. My family was ecstatic. To put it mildly. My mom cried at the sight of my grandma's ring.

Suddenly, Whitley and I were whisked around the backyard, and I was introducing Whitley to all my King cousins, plus dates and friends and children. It was an overwhelming number of people on a first visit. Whitley handled it like a champ, laughing and greeting everyone like this was a common occurrence.

"Okay, remind me of names again," she said with another secret grin.

"There's a lot of them. I don't expect you to remember everyone."

"I'm going to get it right," she said determinedly.

"All right. Malcolm, Margaret, Trent, Nathaniel, Cora, and Lawrence. We call them Mal, Maggie, Trey, Nate, Cor, and Law." Which I realized was probably even more confusing.

"Do they call you Gav?" she asked.

"Actually, yes."

"And I'm Whit. I fit right in."

I snagged a glance at her. She did fit right in.

We moved away deeper into the crowd, me pointing out each of my cousins again. When we reached Margaret, she grasped Whitley's hand in hers and stared down at the diamond.

"I am *so* jealous. Who said you got to have this one?" Margaret said. She winked at Whitley.

"I *am* the oldest," I reminded her. "Grandma wanted me to have it."

Margaret still pouted. "You are one lucky girl."

"You're marrying a Locke tomorrow," Malcolm said dryly.

He arched an eyebrow at me. There was a question in it. Malcolm and I were the closest in age, and he was the kind of person who could read someone with a glance. He'd always been an intuitive person, and under his scrutiny, it felt almost as if the whole house of cards was going to come tumbling down.

"I suppose I am." Margaret made a face seemingly before she thought better of it. Then, a big fake smile came onto her lips, and she shoved her ring into Whitley's face.

"Gorgeous," Whitley confirmed.

"Say, what are your plans tonight?"

Whitley looked over at me in question, and when I shook my head, she shrugged. "No plans."

"Well, we're having a little girls' night. I had a bachelorette party already, but this is for family and my bridesmaids. You're going to be family soon. So, you should come."

"I *love* girls' nights," Whitley said with a grin at me, which I knew all too well meant she was going to do something devious.

"Oh lord," I groaned.

"What?" Margaret asked. "Are you worried we're going to corrupt her?"

"No. I'm worried she's going to corrupt *you*."

Malcolm chuckled. "As if someone who intends to marry Gavin can't already keep up with him."

"Fair," Margaret agreed.

"If only he could set a better example for Nate."

"Hey," Nate said, overhearing. He was chatting with a blonde who must have been his date. "I take offense to that."

"No, you don't," Mal said.

"Good one," Trent said, pointing at Malcolm as he leaned back lazily on a lounger.

Nate snorted. "Fine. Gavin is practically a role model."

"Says the thirst trap," Margaret said with a pointed eye roll.

"What can I say? TikTok loves me."

Whitley glanced between the whole group of siblings. "If Gavin is your role model, I fear for the women who cross your path."

Margaret burst into laughter. "Oh, I like her, cos."

My eyes wandered to Whitley's pleased face. I liked her too. I liked her a lot. Especially how she could hold her own with my enormous family. Maybe I shouldn't have played this game. With her wide smile and easy demeanor, I found that I didn't want this to be fake at all.

"So, yes on the party tonight?"

"Yes," Whitley acquiesced. "As long as we're not doing anything?"

"Nope."

"We have the poker night tonight anyway," Malcolm reminded me.

"Shit, right. Yeah, I already have plans. So, by all means,

and lord help you ladies with Whitley in your midst. What exactly is the plan?"

"Karaoke," Margaret said.

My grin went feral. "Oh, that's good. Whitley can *sing*."

Whitley smacked me on the arm. "I regret *every day* that I told you about my singing roots, King. Every day."

"Oh yeah? I remember you serenading me on the beach all night with that voice, Bowen," I crooned. "Can't get out of it now."

"That was a secret," she teased. "No singing for me!"

"Oh my god, stop!" Margaret groaned. "Y'all are so *cute* that it's almost disgusting."

Whitley's cheeks colored. "Thanks for the invite. I'll be there so long as singing is optional."

"Totally optional. We'll have ... other entertainment anyway."

"Is tonight actually karaoke, Maggie?" Malcolm teased his younger sister. "Or are y'all just going to get strippers?"

"Big bro, you know that I am always truthful," Margaret teased. "Us girls are going to have a great time."

"Strippers?" Whitley asked with an expression I'd read on her before.

I placed my hand on the small of her back and brushed my lips against her ear. I didn't miss the shiver that shot straight through her at my touch.

"I know what that look means," I teased. "Maybe don't hook up with any of the bridesmaids."

Whitley leaned into my touch with a husky breath. "No promises, King."

I circled my fingers against her back. "Can we at least share if you intend to bring them back with you?"

"In your dreams."

I released her with another laugh. "Oh, you know me so well."

She rolled her eyes at our usual banter and then moved toward Margaret to discuss the night out. I tracked her as she moved away. Because she was wrong. My dreams were nothing of the sort at present. They all revolved around this one little pixie.

Whitley switched out sundresses and disappeared with my cousin Margaret later that evening. They had been thick as thieves before the day even wore off. They were probably going to burn some buildings down by the end of the night. Whitley was the sort of person to do that with, and Margaret had her own rules about the world.

I'd have been shocked she was marrying at all if I hadn't known the circumstances.

I frowned when I remembered it, but there was nothing to be done about it.

So, I snatched up my wallet and headed downstairs. Malcolm was hosting the poker night at his home on the outskirts of town. It was nearly the size of my aunt and uncle's place with the same white roses that thrived for our family. Malcolm had risen in the ranks of Dorset & King spectacularly. He was what I could have been if I'd stayed. Not that I'd wanted to stay. Not even for a shot at running the whole damn company.

I parked alongside Malcolm's lifted pickup and headed inside without knocking. I could already hear the raucous behavior within. I bypassed the living room and stepped into the game room. The space was already cloudy with cigar smoke. Whiskey sat in crystal glasses around a green felt poker table. A pool table was unused across the room.

"Hey, you made it," Locke said, coming to his feet to shake my hand. He was the man of the hour and already intoxicated.

Blake stood up next, elbowing me in the side. "You sly motherfucker."

I laughed. "So, you heard?"

"That you're fucking marrying *that* girl?" Blake said with a hint of admiration in his voice. "How did that happen?"

Malcolm shuffled the card deck while my youngest cousin, Lawrence, looked on in awe. Malcolm was seated between his two other brothers, Nate and Trent. Both toasted me when I stepped into the room.

"Got lucky, I guess," I finally said.

"No way. We saw that girl in New York," Blake said. He punched Locke. "Back me up."

"She's hot," Locke agreed. "But I feel ripped off that we weren't introduced now that I know you're getting married."

"What's all this about?" Malcolm asked.

I took a seat and crossed my foot over my knee at the ankle. "I was having lunch with Blake and Locke when Whitley came downstairs from Percy Tower. I hadn't expected to see her. We flirted, and she left."

"She was wearing a minidress and fur coat," Blake said. "She acted like she was going to eat you alive."

So, I hadn't been the only one who thought that. Whitley had nearly given me a heart attack that day. Course, they didn't have to know the real reason behind it.

"She does. Pretty regularly," I joked.

Blake slapped my arm and guffawed. The rest of the guys chuckled too. It sounded sexual, but they didn't know Whit. The phrase was literal.

"Were you already engaged then?" Locke asked.

"I don't remember a ring," Blake said.

Locke rolled his eyes. "As if you've ever looked for one."

Malcolm snorted.

"Ouch," Trey said.

Nate called out, "Shots fired."

Blake didn't even seem miffed. He shrugged good-naturedly.

"I proposed after that. Before we came here."

Which was the truth.

Unlike Margaret and my mother, who had grilled us about the proposal and future wedding plans, the guys were content with bare-bones information. Soon, we got into the game.

The poker match I played in New York with Camden, Court, and Sam was regularly high stakes. More money was played at every match. Sam was ruthless and cleared the table more often than not, but I'd honed my skills off of his playing.

When I sat down for this match, everyone expected the old Gavin King, who relentlessly lost every penny he put down. They were in for a surprise as I slowly began to sweep the table.

"The fuck, Gav?" Nate asked when I took him for every chip in one spectacular hand. "When did you get good?"

"Me?" I asked with a gleam in my eye.

When Blake, Nate, and Law were out of money, they moved over to the pool table. Locke's money was running low, too, and he looked at the pool game with regret.

I put my hand down. "Go on. Play with them. I need another drink anyway."

Locke didn't argue. He got up to play the game. At least he knew when to cut his losses. I headed to the wet bar, and

Malcolm followed me with Trent on his heels. As it always was.

"The man of the hour," Trey said, shaking my hand.

"That would be Locke."

"He's marrying our sister, but he's not family yet. Your occasion feels more momentous."

"Don't let Margaret hear you say that," Malcolm grumbled under his breath.

Trent shrugged. "I mean, we always knew Maggie was going to settle down. She *dreamed* of weddings. But Gavin?"

I clapped him on the shoulder. "I'm just full of surprises."

Malcolm quirked an eyebrow. "That's putting it mildly."

Trent grabbed a beer and tapped my glass with it. "Happy for you."

Then, he headed over to the pool table, leaving me and Mal alone.

"He's right, you know," Malcolm finally said. He was smiling, but it didn't quite reach his eyes. "We didn't expect this with you and Whitley. That seemed to happen fast."

I shrugged, lifting the glass to my lips. "When you know, you know, right?"

Malcolm pursed his lips, as if he'd never considered that before.

"What about you, Mal? I'm the infamous bachelor," I said with an eye roll. "But you haven't even been dating."

This time, Malcolm smirked. "I've gotten better at keeping it hidden from our nosy family."

I arched an eyebrow. "Yeah? You're seeing someone?"

"You could say that," he said with a shrug.

"Is she coming to the wedding?"

He shook his head. "I'm not ready for that. I don't know how you are."

"You don't know Whit."

Malcolm shot me a thoughtful look. Almost as if he was going to say something more. He was the intuitive one. The only one I hadn't been sure would swallow the pill I was feeding them. But he finally smiled.

"I'm happy for you. Let's hope it happens to me one day."

"I'll drink to that."

We clinked glasses together to an unknown future. One where we both swore ourselves to another, like Locke was doing this weekend. In my fantasy, I imagined a girl who knew all of my tricks and wanted me for who I was anyway.

10

———

WHITLEY

Margaret was a riot, and she seemed to have no interest in getting married in a matter of days.

I'd met *a lot* of brides-to-be. I had sung at weddings in high school, had been a bridesmaid at any number of weddings for my sorority sisters and then as a guest for a lot of my LA clients. I knew a bride who was ready to tie her life to another. This girl seemed more like she was selling her soul to the devil for ten years of good fortune.

"Come on, Whit. One more dance," Margaret said. She reached for my hand to try to steer me into the chair.

Margaret actually *had* hired strippers for the party. Or someone had. All the bridesmaids were laughing and dancing on the poles or getting lap dances. I'd been worried about karaoke for nothing. The machine had been discarded for shots and strippers within the hour.

"You take it." I pushed Margaret into the chair, and a male stripper started gyrating on her.

I took a step back from the fun and gestured to the bartender for waters. Margaret's younger sister, Cora, had been sitting by the bar with rolled eyes since about the time karaoke had ended.

"Are you trying to take care of my sister?" Cora asked. "It's a waste of time."

"Is this normal behavior?"

Cora shrugged. "It's Margaret. She believes anything that can be done should be done over the top."

"Well, I don't disagree with that."

"She probably shouldn't be smacking that guy's ass days before she marries someone else."

I patted her shoulder. "Maybe. Maybe not. Probably depends on the boundaries already set in the relationship."

"Would you be okay with Gavin going to a strip club?"

I laughed despite myself. I still wasn't used to thinking of Gavin as mine, but this question was easy. "Honey, I'd go to the strip club with him and buy the lap dances."

Cora laughed. "Oh. Well, never mind. Maybe it doesn't matter about Margaret and Locke, and I'm the only one who is upset."

"What do you mean?"

Cora came to her feet and waved her hand. "Nothing. I'm a downer. I'm going to head home. Make sure she drinks all of this water. She has the worst hangovers."

I was too drunk for this conversation. So, I let her go, brought Margaret some much-needed water, and closed down the bar.

It was three in the morning when I finally stumbled back into the downtown hotel. I took the elevator up to our suite, fumbling with the key in my purse. I dropped it and nearly collapsed on the floor in a heap of laughter before getting the card to tap correctly against the door. It swung inward, and I tiptoed into the room with my heels dangling in one hand.

I made it halfway across the room before hitting something in the dark. "Oof!"

My body pitched forward. I tipped over and went sprawling, landing hard on my hands and knees. I laughed maniacally as I realized there wasn't anything at all in the middle of the room.

I needed to stand up and figure out where the hell the bed was in all of this, but I was still too tipsy for that. I was reaching for my phone to try to figure out the flashlight when a light flicked on, silhouetting a figure in the doorway.

"Hi," I said with a Harley Quinn–esque grin.

Gavin King stepped out of the bedroom in nothing but fitted boxer briefs. My mouth went dry. He was ... a god. Literally. His physique was cut from stone with so many abs that I couldn't even count them. Or maybe I was seeing double. But I could tell that his chest was broad, his waist was tapered, and he was as fit as I'd ever seen him.

"Hi," I repeated, a little huskier.

He smirked. "Have a good time?"

"The best."

"Do you need help?"

I held my arms out. "Please."

Instead of taking my hands and helping me to my feet, he stooped down and lifted me into his arms in a bridal carry. Aptly named.

"What?" I gasped before he straightened and raised me clear into the air.

"You're wasted."

"I ... am."

"Were there actual strippers?"

"Maybe."

"I'm surprised you came back at all," he teased.

"Cora put me in charge of watching Margaret. I am shockingly soberer than I was."

"Why do I doubt that?" he asked.

"Oh, I was. I almost considered singing."

Gavin snorted. "I bet. Why would Cora leave?"

"Cora said something about being a downer because she was the only one who cared about Margaret and Locke."

"Ah," he said. "Cor has always been the most sensitive."

He reached the bed and gently set me onto my feet. When he pulled the covers back, I was on the right side. He'd been lying on the left side even though we'd fought over the right earlier. Something contracted in my chest at the gesture. Something that I definitely did not want to look at.

"There," he said.

"Thanks." I flopped back on the bed even though I was still in the dress I'd worn to the party. The hem that had crept up nearly to my hips along the way.

Gavin's eyes went to my legs. He stiffened slightly as his gaze ran over my body. I bent one knee and turned toward him invitingly. I was drunk, but I wasn't stupid. Gavin King wanted me in that moment, and I wanted him. Maybe I was drunk enough for *that*.

Then, he cleared his throat and turned away. "I'll find you something to sleep in."

I blinked at his back in surprise. Wow. I hadn't thought it was possible for Gavin to walk away like that.

He came back a minute later with one of his T-shirts and a pair of shorts. "I couldn't find anything in your stuff. Just wear this."

I took it from him, starting to lift the hem of my dress. He coughed and hastily turned around. I smirked. Well, this was unexpected.

The dress came off in one swift movement. I threw it past Gavin and into my pile of clothes. I drew Gavin's oversize shirt onto my figure. I was so short that it nearly hit my knees. The shorts were useless with a T-shirt this large.

"Done?" Gavin asked.

"Yep."

He turned around to find me still clutching the shorts. A Cheshire cat smile crossed his face. "You look good in my shirt, pixie."

I laughed and threw the shorts at him. "Don't make fun of my height."

"I'd never," he said solemnly before hoisting me back up into his arms.

I yelped again at the manhandling. But damn, I couldn't deny that I liked it.

Our lips were inches apart as he gently deposited me down onto the bed. I arched into him, my body going supple and wanton. My head might be spinning and limbs all fuzzy, but my core knew exactly what it wanted. All I had to do was lean forward and claim those lips for my own.

With one arm under my bare legs and the other under my back, Gavin hesitated over top of me. As if the same thoughts were flitting through his mind. The same desire coursing through his body.

Everything hinged on that second in time. The whole world slowed on its axis as our breaths mingled for the first time in years and our hearts beat as one again. A hitched sigh escaped my lips as I waited with bated breath for the instant when everything changed and we tipped over the edge.

The moment I saw him again, I'd known that this hadn't gone away. That moving to California hadn't changed the desire that clung to him like a wet coat. I'd thought we'd evaded it all these weeks. That maybe this friendship thing was actually viable.

Pour a little alcohol in me, and I was as hot as a firework and just as likely to explode if he set me off.

But Gavin removed his arms and stepped around me.

I made a noise of protest.

I heard his chuckling as he walked around the bed and slipped under the sheets. "Go to sleep, pixie."

"But ..."

"You're drunk."

"So?"

"You'll feel differently about this in the morning."

I rolled over and met his green eyes. "Will I? How do you know?"

"Because you told me."

I tilted my head in confusion. "Maybe you could kiss me and find out?"

"You're trouble."

"But the good kind?" I asked, moving into the middle of the bed.

"If I kiss you, I'm not going to want to stop."

"Who said you had to?"

He sighed, as if caught in the middle of his own angst. "Whit ..."

"Gav ..." I trailed a hand down his muscular shoulder and over his bicep. "I'm right here."

He trapped my hand against his and fingered the ring on my left hand. "We don't have to make it more complicated."

I huffed. "You don't want to play?"

His eyes raked over my body. How eager I was. I couldn't guess what he was thinking, but the seriousness of his expression was making me second-guess whether I should have come on to him. Maybe he was right. Maybe I should have stayed far, far away.

He tugged me forward until I was nearly pressed against him. He clutched my wrist in his grasp and didn't let go as he held me in place. Then, his lips landed on mine, hard and unyielding. I gasped at the force of the kiss. The need etched into every line of him.

His tongue darted out and traced my bottom lip. I shivered at the taste of him, the feel of him, the want that radiated off of him.

Suddenly, it was over. Far too soon.

He pulled away, leaving me caught in the space between with my mouth slightly parted and eyes closed.

"There."

"Oh," I whispered.

"Now, go to sleep. If you want more in the morning, I will ravish you."

He tucked a strand of hair behind my ear as my eyes fluttered open to look at him.

"Promise?" I purred.

He held a pinkie out, and I linked mine with his. "Pinkie promise."

11

———

WHITLEY

My head pounded the next morning. I rolled over with a groan as sunlight streamed into the room and flung my arm over my eyes to shield them from the stabbing pain.

"Morning, sunshine," Gavin said, stepping out of the bathroom.

I was rewarded with the sight of him in nothing but a towel. His hair was still wet and floppy. There was an impressive amount of abs on display.

"Morning."

"I thought you might sleep all day."

"What happened last night? I remember getting Margaret into a car, and it sort of all goes fuzzy after that."

His smile faltered for a second. "I had to carry you to bed."

My cheeks heated. "Sorry." It was starting to come back to me. Seeing Gavin in nothing but boxer briefs and coming on to him. Fuck. "And ... you kissed me."

"You weren't going to let me sleep otherwise."

"Right. Yeah. That ..." I trailed off. I didn't normally feel bad about this sort of thing, but Gavin and I had set bound-aries, and I'd crossed them. That was okay. "I probably shouldn't have done that."

"I'm guessing that means you don't want me to ravish you."

That memory flared too. The pinkie promise before I'd promptly passed out. He had offered more when I was sober. And now, I was sober.

He laughed softly at my expression. "I'm kidding, Whit. You look like you could use a hangover cure. But if dick is what fixes you, by all means, I'm game."

I snorted, rolling my eyes, hopping out of bed, and bypassing him for the bathroom. He'd made it a joke again, and that was good enough for me. I could roll with that.

"I haven't had dick in three years. I've survived thus far."

His jaw dropped, and I smirked as I slammed the door in his face. I pressed my back against the wall and took a deep breath. Well, this was not going as expected. We'd been fine together all those mornings that we went for coffee. I hadn't considered the tension that would bloom when we shared a bed.

"Fuck," I whispered.

I should have taken him up on his offer. Maybe we needed to get it out of our systems. Except that was the exact thought process that had gotten us into this mess in the first place.

Showering made me feel better. I blew out my bright blonde hair and applied some makeup. Today was the rehearsal dinner, but otherwise, we were free to do what we wanted during the day. Gavin showed me around his hometown and then drove us to his parents' house. Julianne and Susannah regaled me with stories of Gavin growing up, and his mom pulled out an old photo album.

Gavin groaned, trying to object, but I sat in the living room and looked at tiny pictures of him throughout the years. So many cowboy hats and boots. A picture of him roping. Something I never would have guessed my suit could do. High school football pictures and old prom shots.

"You're so cute," I said, pinching his cheek.

"Yeah. Yeah," he grumbled.

The whole thing was shockingly ... normal.

In fact, there was next to no acting at all. I'd known Gavin for years. It took no effort to talk to his family like he was someone important to me. He always had been until the rug was pulled. And his parents liked me, as I'd suspected they would. They wanted to like me because they loved their son.

We finished at Gavin's house and toasted the bride and groom at the rehearsal dinner with the packed crowd that had to be nearly as large as the wedding itself. Who was I kidding? I knew small-town Texas weddings were an entire event. If this was only a fraction of the wedding, it was going to be enormous tomorrow.

Gavin and I stayed late into the evening at the dinner. Only returning long enough to collapse into bed from the desperate need for sleep. I only had moments to wonder if we were going to move on to that ravishing when I could hear his deep breathing on the other side of the bed.

The wedding morning dawned bright and beautiful. Clear blue skies that traced their way across the horizon. Not a single cloud in the sky to mar the upcoming outdoor wedding.

"Perfect weather," I mused, sipping on the coffee Gavin had run downstairs to get for me.

"Couldn't have asked for better."

"Can't wait to see Maggie's dress. Maybe I can sneak into the bridal suite for a peek."

He snorted. "I'm sure it'll be outrageous and worth a small fortune."

"As it should be. You only get married once, right?"

"In theory."

"Yeah, I suppose in theory. The romantic in me says it's one and done. I'd kill you before letting you leave me."

Gavin shot me an exasperated look. "That's sufficiently terrifying."

"I'm all bite."

"And since when are you a romantic? I didn't think you ever wanted to get married."

"Who says they never want to get married? Even you had a wedding ring handy like in your sock drawer or whatever. You clearly had planned on it or at least thought about it."

"Yeah, well, my mom gave it to me after my grandma died. It's been chilling in my drawer for a while."

I shrugged and lounged back. I was still in the shorts and tank I'd fallen asleep in. I'd already fixed my hair and makeup, but I wasn't quite ready to get into my dress. Gavin slipped his suit jacket on with the pink tie hanging loose around his neck.

"Romantic, King."

I set the coffee down and crossed to him, threading the tie through my fingers. My dad had taught me how to knot a tie at a young age so that I could help him get ready for church services. He had a thousand different ties, and I'd loved being the one who got to pick it out. I'd practically learned tie knotting before I could tie my shoes.

That was a long time ago. Dad and I weren't on great terms. But old habits die hard.

"What are you doing?"

"Tying a *perfect* full Windsor."

"Is that what we're calling it nowadays?"

"Stop moving," I ordered. "I've got this."

I felt Gavin's eyes on the top of my head, but I didn't lift my gaze to meet his until I pulled the tie knot through.

"My masterpiece," I said when I finished.

There was no amusement in his expression when I met his gaze. My breath hitched at the look in his bright emerald eyes. Not desire—or not *simply* desire. It was tinged with something deeper—admiration and trust. Something much more dangerous than pure desire. Desire could be thwarted and cast off. This look could cleave mountains.

I stepped back hastily. "Go look in the mirror."

Gavin moved to the full length and admired my handiwork. "You're good at this. Where'd you learn?"

I shrugged. "My dad."

Then, I snagged my dress and went into the bathroom to change. The dress was a marvel. I'd found it at a boutique on Fifth Avenue. Katherine would be upset that I hadn't taken her along for the ride, but I'd been on a deadline. And frankly couldn't explain what I was doing to my friends yet. Even though they'd been messaging me all week and asking questions. English had even tried to call me, but I'd been too busy to answer.

The miracle of the dress was that it was a light layer of ice blue that fell to my feet in my four-inch heels. It was nearly impossible to find long formalwear that didn't have to be hemmed six inches at bare minimum. I had been looking for *anything* that didn't require a hem, and this had been the best fit. It was almost Roman in style with a deep V at the front and a cinched waist. It was easy to move in, modest—well, for me—and, most importantly, the right length. Not to mention, it made my hazel eyes look almost blue in the right light.

I stepped out of the bathroom and said, "Well?"

When Gavin faced me, he froze. "Jesus Christ," he whispered, barely audible.

"Good?" I twirled for him, the skirts fluttering around my ankles.

"You look stunning." He caught my hand and pulled me into him. "I'll be honored to have you on my arm."

My cheeks heated at the unexpected words. "Thank you."

"I'm going to be the envy of every guy in the room."

"You don't look so bad yourself."

That was an understatement. I'd been trying not to ogle him as I fixed his tie, but the suit fit him as if it had been made for him, which, of course, it had. The angles intensified his height and the breadth of his shoulders. It came in sharply at his waist with a single button done. The pants were trim, just hiding the powerful thighs underneath.

A well-made suit was to women what lingerie was to men.

He winked at me and then offered me his arm. "Shall we?"

I nodded. It was safer for me to get out of this room right now or I might have second thoughts about stripping him out of that suit. But we hardly had time.

Even though it was an afternoon wedding, Gavin's family had asked him to be there for pictures. He was an usher and dressed to match the groomsmen. I didn't mind arriving with him and ingratiating myself with Margaret.

Gavin parked in the gravel lot before the gorgeous barn that would house the reception. The wedding itself was being set up outside in a meadow surrounded by large oaks. Already, the caterers, florists, and other event planning specialists were getting ready. A tent was being pitched next to the barn for overflow seating, a dance floor, and drinks.

The wedding planner rushed by in mile-high heels as she spoke to the men carrying a circular wooden arch. I recognized her as the woman that Gavin and English had been speaking to that first night I was back in town. Nora.

She saw us, and her smile brightened. "Hi, y'all," she said with a wave in our direction.

Gavin waved back, and then Nora was gone, off to pull off a five-hundred-person wedding for two American royal families.

The groomsmen were already standing under a gazebo. I could see Blake passing a flask to Malcolm. Locke waved Gavin over.

"You sure you'll be okay?" Gavin asked me.

"Sure. You know me."

He tossed me the keys. "If you get bored, you can head out and come back later."

I stuffed them in my purse. "I'll be fine. You don't have to worry about me. Maybe I'll get coffee or lunch for the bridesmaids. Maggie would appreciate that."

Gavin opened his mouth to agree, but then his aunt Susannah appeared from inside the barn in a panic. She had a cell phone pressed to her ear. "What do you mean there's no replacement?"

"Oh no," Gavin muttered.

Susannah's eyes widened at the sight of us. She put a

finger to her mouth and then continued her conversation. She looked ready to yell at the person on the other line and then just ended up hanging up. "Fuck."

Gavin laughed. "Aunt Susannah, you never cuss."

"I know. I know. It's just ... Maggie is going to be so disappointed."

"What happened?" I asked. "Someone had to cancel?"

"Yes. I need to get with the wedding planner."

"She went that way," Gavin said.

Susannah sighed. "She's from Lubbock. I don't know if she'll have a replacement singer for today. We'll see if she knows someone in town."

"Singer?" Gavin inquired.

"The only thing Mags said she wanted was someone to sing that song that Grandma always sang to you kids growing up. You remember the one—'Love Me Tender'?"

Gavin nodded. "Of course. She was always singing that."

"We hired someone to perform it, and she's sick. Laryngitis. Can't sing for two weeks," Susannah said in dismay. "I'll have to find a replacement."

Slowly, Gavin turned to face me, and I realized exactly what he was going to say before it left his mouth. "Whitley can do it."

"Gavin," I groaned.

Susannah's eyes widened. "Oh my god, you sing? That would be a literal godsend."

I opened my mouth to object. Because of course, I didn't sing anymore. My parents had stamped that out of me. Years of chorus, singing in church, and filling in as a wedding singer weren't exactly the making of a real singer. LA had taught me that having a good set of pipes didn't mean anything. Now, they were only utilized when I was in the shower and on car rides.

"She used to be a wedding singer," Gavin said instead. "Have you ever sang 'Love Me Tender'?"

Only a thousand times.

Silently, I nodded.

Susannah grasped my hands tightly in hers. "Would you sing for us? I'd be eternally grateful. Margaret wouldn't even have to know that there was a change. I don't want to worry her. Please, Whitley."

As I stood there, holding the hands of Gavin's aunt, knowing this was *the* thing she needed to fix everything, I found it impossible to get the words out. To say no to this woman would be like kicking a puppy.

"Okay," I agreed slowly. "Yeah. I'm a bit out of practice, but I can do it."

It was Gavin's look of admiration and intense relief that put me over the edge. A smile finally came to my lips as Susannah pulled me aside to walk me through the ceremony and everything I needed to know.

I glanced back once to see Gavin still looking at me. His hands in his pockets. A broad smile on his face. I quickly looked away. That man would be the death of me.

12

———

GAVIN

I never thought Whitley would agree.

Even as I'd suggested that she sing at my cousin's wedding, I had been sure she'd throw it back in my face. She would have. If Aunt Susannah hadn't plowed forward with the guilt trip, Whitley would have flown away like the lost, broken bird she was. I wasn't going to regret that we got her to say yes because that meant, in a few short hours, I would finally get to hear those incredible vocal cords work.

Not to mention, I had a feeling she actually *wanted* to sing. She had just convinced herself that part of her life was over. As if there were a before and after singing. And I was here to show her that wasn't true.

After Whitley was whisked away, I was pulled into the groomsmen troop. Locke's other friends from New York had arrived. As well as his brother and sister—Micah and Margot.

Micah acted sullen, as if he'd been bullied into attending the event. Which ... was possible. From my limited interactions with him, he thought the world shone out of his sorry ass. Margot, however, was Micah's polar opposite. She was sneaky and cunning and hilarious. The youngest of the three and probably the cleverest. I rarely expected the youngest to be the peacemaker, but she wrangled both her older brothers and managed to make them both laugh.

Luckily, there was Blake Holliday filling up all the space and doling out shots. The day should have been merrier than it was. I was glad that Whitley had a task and couldn't tell the false at all the edges.

Finally, pictures were taken, I walked little old ladies down the aisle to their seats, and there was nothing left to do but for the ceremony to begin.

Whitley met me at the back of the church. When I'd left her, she'd looked nervous, and now, she seemed more than ready.

"Know all the words?" I teased.

She wrinkled her nose at me. "I will get you back for this."

"Hey, you agreed."

"Like I had a choice."

I laughed. "Is it going to be that bad to perform again?"

She paused, as if actually contemplating the answer to that question. Then, she turned her face away from me and shrugged. She released a soft, "No."

My finger caressed her cheek, and I drew her face back to me. Her eyes were wide with something like desire and concern, all trapped together and rattling around inside her.

"You're going to be magnificent."

She smiled. "I know."

It was my turn to laugh. I released her and then offered her my arm. "Walk with me?"

She slid her hand into the crook of my elbow by way of answer, and we walked down the center of the long stretch of outdoor seating toward the large circular arch on display. People from New York and a full half of Midland were in attendance to watch the momentous occasion. This would seal the Lockes and the Kings together in a way that nothing else could. An old-fashioned sort of bond.

Whitley and I had reserved seats near the front by my parents. I took the inside seat so that she could get up when it was her turn to sing. My mom squeezed my hand excitedly. My dad gave me a reassuring smile. Locke stood at the front of the room in a suit with a similar pink tie with his troop of groomsmen behind him. The band struck up a tune. Everyone turned around in their seats. It was finally time.

The bridesmaids came forward first in their blush gowns that almost grazed the grass at their feet. One by one until Cora was the last. A smile was plastered on her face. Only I could tell that it was false. Cora never smiled like that.

Then, Canon D was played, we all rose to our feet, and Margaret appeared at the end of the meadow in a dress as pure as snow in a full princess motif, complete with a tiara and my aunt's glittering diamond necklace on her throat. Uncle Richard was at her side, keeping his head held high as he walked his oldest daughter down the aisle.

Words were exchanged at the altar before all assembled. Then, the pastor announced a special performance. Whitley rose to her feet on wobbly legs. They strengthened as she strode toward the band and stood before the microphone.

Her hazel eyes were wide as she surveyed the enormous crowd. For a second, I thought my brave, valiant girl would faint from the pressure. But as soon as the first note came from the band, she entered a trance.

Her body was taut as a bow, and it began to melt as she surrendered to the music. Her eyes fell closed, and her body swayed ever so slightly. As if her very being had been capti-vated before she even released.

And release she did.

The tune was low and almost haunting. A séance in the middle of a wedding. A call to worship. Her voice was so deliriously good that it felt like swallowing honey.

As the song picked up and the chorus took over, Whitley opened her eyes and met her audience. Her voice rose with her. I was entranced by that voice, unable to look away, and I wasn't the only one. I could feel the rest of the wedding guests paralyzed by her. My mom's grip on my hand tight-ened, and I heard a sniffle. Tears tracked down her face, and Aunt Susannah blew into a tissue in the seat in front of us. Margaret had tears in her eyes at the front of the aisle.

She sounded nothing like my grandmother. And some-how, it was as if she had been reincarnated into Whitley's voice. Her soul singing through her voice. There was pres-ence in each syllable. A force that I could no more walk away from than the gorgeous woman singing.

I'd thought that I felt something for her before.

I knew I did now.

At the end of the song, the word suspended in silence.

Then, a roar of approval came as everyone applauded her rendition. Margaret rushed forward and hugged Whit-ley. Whitley looked baffled by the reaction, hurrying back to the seat next to me and sitting down.

She was shaking.

"Whitley," I got out hoarsely.

She shook her head. "It was awful. I know. Not my best performance. I was so pitchy at the start. But I thought the end was okay."

I looked at her as if she had sprung a second head.

She reared back at the look. "What? I know everyone clapped. Was it that bad?"

"Believe me when I say, that was the best performance I have ever seen in my entire life."

She rolled her eyes. "Yeah. Sure."

I took her hand, threading our fingers together. She looked at me in surprise, but I didn't release her. "I know that I joke about almost everything, but you were phenomenal. I have no idea who told you that you weren't good enough or why you would hide your gift because what you have is a gift, Whit. It was incredible."

She flushed then, bright pink, and ducked her chin to her chest. A tear ran down her cheek, and she brushed it away hastily. "Thank you."

We could get to the bottom of this. Because, holy shit, that woman should sing. Even if it was only for me, she should sing as often as possible. No one should ever have told her otherwise. No one.

13

WHITLEY

Susannah was currently crying as she thanked me at the reception. Margaret and Cora had already come over. Malcolm, Trent, Nate, and Lawrence had followed. Aunts and uncles I didn't know were whispering about the performance. Everyone was talking about it, offering their praises, and generally making me incredibly embarrassed.

I'd thought it was mediocre at best.

I'd certainly sung it better in high school than at present.

But that didn't seem to matter to anyone.

Let alone Gavin. Who had been looking at me with no less than abject admiration from the moment I sat next to him. That same expression still graced his face as his mother stared at the engagement ring and wiped her eyes.

"My mother would be so happy right now. The perfect woman is wearing this ring," Gavin's mom said.

Susannah nodded. "I couldn't agree more."

A knot of worry formed in my stomach. This was all supposed to be a cover story for the week. Gavin had needed help, and I'd thought, *Why not?* And now, I was realizing why not. Because, now, they thought we were getting married, and they'd be genuinely upset when we called it off next week.

My gaze must have shown something like that because Gavin intervened. "Give her some room to breathe, Mom."

"It was just a song."

"It was more to us," Susannah said.

Gavin took my hand. "Let's get you a drink."

"Yes, please." I smiled wanly as we retreated. "I really didn't think it was anything crazy."

"They're sentimental, and you're wrong."

I laughed softly as we got in line for drinks. "I'm glad everyone enjoyed it. It was worth the hours I spent working on it with the band. My voice felt like popcorn when I started."

"So, why don't you sing anymore?"

I shrugged. "Went to UCLA. Didn't get famous. Same old story."

"They don't know what they're missing."

"Nah, it worked out in the end. I became a doctor instead."

"Which you're also brilliant at."

Gavin ordered our drinks and then passed me a whiskey sour.

"That I can agree with." I took a big swig of my drink. "But, yeah ... I have so many bad memories attached to singing from when I was growing up. My parents didn't approve. They thought I sang just fine, but I was smart, so it was a waste of time."

"How can it be a waste of time when you have such talent?"

"Well, they wanted me to get married to a rich man. That's how. Medical school was my *in* to marry a doctor, not become one. So few people become famous singers. They didn't approve."

"That's horribly outdated, even for Texas," Gavin said with an arched eyebrow.

"Tell me about it. That's my parents."

"I never hear you talk about them."

I snorted. "For good reason. There's nothing to say that would be worth repeating." He looked like he wanted to ask more, so I quickly changed the subject. "But why don't you talk about your family? They're amazing. You made it seem like it would all be overwhelming and terrible."

"Oh, no, they're great. It's just that there's so many of them, and we all have giant personalities. Bringing us together usually results in some sort of enormous fight."

"There's been no fighting."

Gavin shrugged with a grin. "I am going to let you take all the credit for that."

"Me? Why?"

"You know, they don't want to upset my fiancée."

I rolled my eyes. "You're ridiculous. That is not the reason. They're happy for Locke and Maggie."

"Could be."

When we finished our drinks, Gavin took my hand again and led me out onto the dance floor. A slow song was play-ing, and I molded into his embrace. We'd never danced like this before. Most of our dancing had involved sweaty night-clubs, where I was grinding my ass against him.

Here, he held me tight and secure, as if he'd had ball-room lessons. We moved easily across the floor because I'd also had many, *many* lessons. Thanks, Junior League.

Gavin looked down at me with that same wicked smile I'd fallen for three years ago before I screwed it all up. I could easily fall again. I was hardly acting with any of it.

Gavin and I fit into each other's world. We always had. First as friends and then as more, and now, even pretending, we seemed to fit just fine.

I exhaled with relief when the dance turned to more common dance songs, and all of Margaret's friends ran out to the Wobble and then the Electric Slide. I moved right into the middle of the group, following along with the steps I'd done a hundred times. Then, Gavin barreled into the middle of us and did an exaggerated dance. We all laughed. Life of the party, and he ate up all the attention.

The rest of the night went through much of the same motions. We danced until I was exhausted, until my feet were numb, and then we danced some more. Margaret and Locke's exit was an insane affair with a horse-drawn carriage and sparklers for the night sky.

Gavin set a sparkler in my hand, and we each held one aloft as they dashed down the makeshift aisle we'd made. They stopped in the middle and kissed for the camera while we all cheered. Then, they were off into the carriage. Maggie waved good-bye to the crowd until they disappeared.

Gavin took my sparkler to dispose of it safely. While he was gone, a man I'd thought looked familiar all night sidled up to me.

"Hey, you're Whitley Bowen, right?"

"That's me," I said.

"I'm Curt Smith, out of Dallas."

I nodded once, wondering where he was going with this. Dallas was a big place. Like New York, you could get lost in the people there.

"Nice to meet you."

"Is your brother Wyatt Bowen?"

Now, I froze. "Oh. Uh, yes."

"Cool. Cool. I wasn't sure you were *that* Bowen."

That Bowen. Shit.

"You ... know my brother?"

"We golf at the same club. His wife is friends with mine. Here, you can meet Anna Kate."

"Oh, I think we were leaving," I said, hastily retreating. "Nice to meet you."

Then, I turned and fled toward Gavin. *Shit, shit, shit.* I hadn't considered that someone from Dallas would both know the Kings and my family. There wasn't a lot of cross-over between the cities, even with the two big family names.

When I glanced back up at Curt, he was already heading back inside with some other guys. I blew out a breath. It was fine. He was probably drunk enough that he wouldn't even remember that we'd had that brief conversation. No reason to freak out.

Gavin's hand landed on my shoulder, and I jumped. "Hey, you okay?"

"Yeah. Just ready to get back."

"Me too. There's some cleanup left, but it's late. We should get you to bed."

I looked up at him, expecting that to be an innuendo but it wasn't. He looked serious. Like he was taking care of me after a long day.

After that kiss the first night, there hadn't been anything else between us. Just hand holding and temple kisses in public. There had been tension in bed, but Gavin hadn't made another move. Maybe I'd been misreading him.

We said our good-byes to his family and then drove back into town. Gavin had stopped drinking hours ago so that he could get us home. I was only a little tipsy. Neither of us needed alcohol to have a good time. Though it was nicer in New York, where we didn't need a designated driver.

By the time we got back to the hotel, it was after

midnight, and I was actually tired. I fought back a yawn as he pushed his way into the hotel room. We'd been up since dawn to get there in time for Gavin to be in pictures. I could crash face-first into the mattress and not wake until the next morning when we needed to catch our flight.

Then, I caught Gavin watching me, and I was suddenly *wide* awake.

"What?" I whispered.

He shook his head and stepped into the bedroom. "Nothing."

"That didn't look like nothing."

He plucked the perfect knot I'd created for him this morning and let the ends of the tie hang loose around his neck. He faced me again, his expression a mask of indecision.

Then, he crooked his finger at me.

I swallowed hard and moved toward him. I didn't stop until I was directly in front of him. His hands moved up into my hair, tilting my face up to meet his. I was frozen in place, my stomach roiling with anticipation of his practiced touch.

"What are you doing?" I managed to get out.

"Kissing my fiancée," he growled.

Then, his lips landed on mine, and everything within me went pliant. His perfectly pouty lips were heavenly against mine. We'd had that one hot kiss a few nights ago, but I'd been drunk at the time. This was ... so much better than that had ever been. He tasted of pure sin, and I wanted to dive headfirst into the heady lust that sprang like a well.

When he pulled back, my eyes fluttered open to look into the emerald orbs. "I'm not your fiancée."

He laughed deep in his throat. "You are until I take that ring back." He fingered the ring on my left hand.

"That so?"

"Mmhmm."

"Well, in that case, I remember a certain pinkie promise."

His eyes widened in surprise. As if he'd thought that I had completely forgotten about that. "Really?"

"Yes." I glanced down and then back up at him through my long lashes. "Something about ravishing me."

"I said, if you wanted that when you were sober." He cleared his throat, looking hopeful. "Are you sober?"

"Ish," I teased.

He drew me in closer. "And here I thought, you were offering."

"Maybe I was," I said in a breathy whisper. Then, I stood on my tiptoes again and kissed him.

All restraint left Gavin in that moment. As if he'd barely been containing himself, waiting for me to give him the okay. By the way he was kissing me, like a drowned man, that had cost him.

He'd said we should be friends. Now, I was wondering if that had all been a front, because he was not currently kissing me or biting my lip or grinding against me like any friend I'd ever had.

"How hard was sleeping in the same bed with me?" I gasped against his lips.

"Torture."

"And you were so good."

"So good," he said, backing me toward the bed. "I deserve a reward."

I snickered. "Am I the reward?"

"No," he said as his hands slid down to my thighs. He lifted me into the air and then dropped me backward on the bed. "Your pussy is."

I gasped as he buried his head between my legs, hiking

up my skirt and kissing his way toward my awaiting pussy. All thoughts of stopping completely fled my mind. I'd wanted Gavin for far too long. I didn't know what tomorrow held. But until I gave this ring back, I was going to enjoy every luxury Gavin King offered.

The first brush of his lips against my clit nearly sent me over the edge. I had been anticipating having him like this too. Lying in bed next to his body and imagining all the ways he would make me come and forcing myself not to have the thing that I wanted. I had never been good at self-restraint, which explained why I'd broken the instant he kissed me.

"If I remember correctly," he said, sliding his tongue all the way from my lips to my clit, "you come hard when I eat you out."

I nearly blacked out just from the words. Gavin King was filthy. Something I'd forgotten in the intervening years.

"Isn't that right?" he demanded.

"Yes," I cried as he flicked harder against my clit.

"Tell me how you like it."

"Faster."

He did as I requested until I was panting and breathless under his ministrations. Then, as I neared the edge, he slipped two fingers into my wet, aching pussy.

I whimpered as he started a rhythm in and out.

"Imagine me fucking you," he said in between strokes.

"Yes."

"Deep inside of you." He thrust hard back in, and my walls contracted around his fingers.

"Are you remembering?"

And I was. My body shuddered as the memory of our vacation washed over me. The feel of his huge cock inside of me. The way he had certainly known how to use it to bring me to orgasm. Like he was using his fingers and tongue right now.

I came apart in a mewling mess, shaking from exertion. I saw stars as he moved in and out twice more before slowly removing his fingers.

"Fuck."

He smirked as he came to his feet. He worked his belt loose. The button and zipper went next. Then, he was freeing himself from his boxers.

If it was possible, he was bigger than memory served. The first time I'd seen his cock, I'd stumbled into him jacking off in an outdoor shower. He was leaning one hand heavily against the wall, pumping his fist tight against his cock and demanding an orgasm from himself. Then, he'd confessed he'd been thinking of me, and I'd been a goner. Just thinking about it now made me even wetter.

He produced a condom, sheathing himself with practiced ease, then settled between my thighs.

"Fuck, Whit."

"Yes?" I panted.

"I've wanted this."

"Me?"

"To own you," he growled.

I raised my chin, defiance on my face. "No one owns me."

"Then, I hope you enjoy watching me try."

To punctuate his words, he slid inside me, and everything tightened.

I'd forgotten. Vibrators and toys and fingers were all well and good. It wasn't like I was missing sex with a guy. If I'd wanted it at any time in the last three years, I could have had it. But ... shit. His cock worked miracles.

He smirked down at me, stroking my hair out of my face. "Having second thoughts about my ownership?"

"Yes," I admitted.

His hand circled my throat, and my eyes dilated with need.

"Good girl."

My body melted at those words. From anyone else, I would have laughed in their face and bucked from the depravity. But coming from Gavin, it felt like a compliment. Like I should be pleased that he had called me a good girl.

I was more than pleased. I was willing to do whatever it took to hear those words again.

Then, Gavin started moving. A long draw out that had me trembling with need before a hard, quick thrust deep inside me again. I cried out every time he pushed back in. He increased the pressure on my throat, which only increased the pressure I squeezed on his cock. And everything went fuzzy at the edges. Everything contracting and tightening and begging for another release.

He leaned forward to brush his lips against my ear. "You're going to come for me again."

It wasn't a question.

"Please."

He smiled too that time. That lovely Gavin smile. "You asked nicely." As if he couldn't believe it.

He withdrew and pushed in harder and faster. His tempo turning almost brutal. He grunted, and I could tell he was close too. Then, he threw back his head and cried out in satisfaction as he emptied himself in me. I came at the same time, shuddering with relief.

His hand gently released from my neck, and he bent down to trace kisses across the spots he'd been holding.

"You were perfect," he breathed.

"Fuck."

He laughed. "Yes."

He moved out of me, discarded the condom, and then returned to the bed. After I cleaned up, I crawled into bed, and he tugged me tight against his chest.

The silence was peaceful. As if I'd been sleepwalking for so long and I was suddenly in a daydream.

"Whit."

"Hmm?"

"We're going to have to talk about this," he said into my shoulder.

I stiffened, but he stroked my back until I relaxed again. "Not tonight. But sometime."

I bit my lip. And didn't answer.

The last thing I wanted was to talk about the past and figure out a future. Those things sounded terrifying. I just wanted to live in this moment right now. No past or future. Just the present.

"Whit?"

"Okay," I whispered softly.

"Good girl," he repeated again against my shoulder. His breathing already evening out as he fell into a heavy sleep.

14

GAVIN

I woke up with a head between my legs.

I'd fallen asleep naked, and already, I could feel my cock swelling. A hand was stroking it up and down. And it certainly wasn't mine.

After a moment, that hand was replaced by a mouth, and I came suddenly, forcefully awake.

Whitley.

We'd had sex last night.

That was *her* mouth on the head of my cock.

"Fuck, Whit," I groaned, slumping back in the bed and trying to make it seem as if I wasn't going to immediately nut in her mouth.

Whitley responded by taking me deeper. I groaned, low and feral.

A beautiful woman hidden under the sheets with her mouth working me like a popsicle. Her head bobbed up and down, shaking the sheets. I flung them off of her to watch her work and was given the sight of her DSLs wrapped tight around me. She was still naked. Her breasts dangling between my thighs and her ass in the air. The exact way I was planning to fuck her after she finished.

"That's it," I encouraged.

Her hand slipped between my legs and cupped my balls. I jerked against her hand, and I swore she smirked like a cat. After only a few more strokes, my hands were in her hair. My breath came out in pants, and I forced her to take more and more of me.

"Close," I warned.

I expected her to back off and let me finish in my hand or on my stomach, but she did nothing of the sort. She took more of me, and at the sight of her deep-throating me, I came in long, hot spurts into her welcoming mouth.

"Fuck, fuck, fuck," I said incoherently as she sat back on her heels and swallowed.

"Morning."

"Good fucking morning to you, pixie."

I grabbed her round the middle and threw her down on the bed. She giggled and let me nuzzle kisses against her neck. My stubble scratched against her skin and left a row of red marks that I deeply enjoyed, and by the way she squirmed, she did too.

"I could get used to this," I muttered into her neck.

She laughed and shoved me backward. "I bet you could."

I sat back on my heels and looked down at her, sprawled on the bed. We had a flight to catch later, but I wasn't sure I'd ever be ready to leave. I couldn't even think past this moment. Past her naked body with her arms over her head, unabashedly beautiful, and a smirk on her lips.

"What? You couldn't get used to this?"

I pressed my hands into her wrists, applying pressure to

hold her in place as I ran my cock against the slit between her legs. She groaned, and her eyes fluttered closed.

"Look at me, pixie."

Her eyes snapped open. The hazel nearly as green as mine in the morning sunlight. They said eyes were the window to the soul, but Whitley's were usually so hidden that even I couldn't figure out what she was thinking. But not this morning.

This morning there was a challenge in her eyes. A look that said, *I dare you.*

My cock lengthened at that look. I released her just long enough to slide a condom on before returning to the position we'd been holding. Then, I slipped inside of her. She kept her eyes focused on me, even as we both panted and groaned. It wasn't until I brought her fully to climax that her eyes snapped shut and she trembled from head to toe.

We both released our breaths at the same time. She gave me a satisfied smile as I slid out of her.

"You're right," she finally said. "I could get used to that."

I laughed in a self-satisfied way and then hoisted her over my shoulder.

"What are you doing?" she cried.

Without explanation, I carried her into the bathroom. I set her on her feet in the shower and turned the water to steaming. After discarding the condom, I joined her.

"I could have walked. It was a handful of feet." She grumbled something under her breath that sounded like *barbarian.*

"Barbarian, huh?" I asked with a laugh. "That's a new one."

"I'm not used to being manhandled."

"Pretty sure that's not true." I reached for the soap.

"Fine. I'm out of practice then. Women have much better manners."

I snorted. "I have manners."

"You just carried me into the bathroom like a Neanderthal."

"And then? I wanted to get you clean. That sounds like manners."

She made a noise of dissent, but it was half-hearted. I didn't think that she actually cared. She was just making a fuss.

Once she was all lathered up, I gave her the spray of water and went to soap up myself. I was almost done when she took the soap from me and worked on my back. I wanted to fall to my knees for her right there. I didn't know what it was about that simple gesture, but it did me in. Intimate, but not sexual, and I was a goner.

I cleared my throat when she stepped back, trying to cover the fact that my cock was lengthening again. Which was nearly impossible since we were both naked in the shower.

She snickered at me, shaking her head. "*Again*? You just came twice!"

"You're naked in the shower with me. What did you expect?"

I reached for her, and she stepped into the spray. She was so short that I had to bend down to press my lips to hers. I could have taken her right there, slippery wet and somehow still horny. But I enjoyed the thrill of her tongue darting into my mouth and her soft, pouty lips against mine.

Whitley reached behind me and turned the water off with a smirk. She stepped out of the shower, handing me a towel. We both dried off, and she'd already thrown on panties and an oversize T-shirt by the time I was calm enough to come out of the bathroom again. If she thought that was going to help, she was sorely mistaken.

"Jesus, you're sexy," I said, crashing into her and knocking her back on the bed. Our mouths moved together again, and I pulled her on top of me. She leaned against my chest and ran her fingers along my collarbone.

"You're insatiable."

"Would you rather we talk about this?"

She froze. Her gaze flickered to mine. Whitley never wanted to *talk* about anything. Everything was easier if it was a joke or a game or sex. Those things she could handle, but real conversation made her run in the opposite direction. That was why I'd hatched this elaborate plan to get her here rather than just ask her to be my actual date.

"Talk about what?" she asked hesitantly.

"This. Us."

She pulled back, rolling off of me. "I don't know what there is to talk about."

I came to my elbows. "Well, we could start with why you ran away three years ago and end with you being here as the perfect date, who my entire family loves."

She swallowed hard. "Do we have to complicate things, Gavin?"

"Is it complicating things when you're wearing my grandmother's engagement ring?"

"As a cover up for you with your family."

"Sure. It worked. I'm grateful. But three years ago, we had something. You know we did. Then, you went back to Robert. I didn't begrudge you dating him again. Robert was ... serious. He loved you desperately. I never would have come between you two, but then, after Fashion Week ..."

She held her hand up. "Please, I don't want to think

about it. We had a great week. Can't we just ... figure it out after?"

I sighed. Of course she didn't want to talk about it. Of course she was going to hole up at the first talk of something more than this. It was all fun and games until there was talk of more.

"We don't have to talk about it today, but can we talk about it when we get home?"

Her big hazel eyes finally met mine, and I saw something I hadn't expected there—fear. Normally, she was so reticent about all of this, but it was just her normal avoidance behavior. This was something else. This was actual terror in her expression, and I had no idea why she would ever look at me like that.

"What? What's wrong?"

"Nothing," she said at once. The expression cleared, and my Whitley was back. "Okay, fine, will you kiss me again and be the playful Gavin if I agree to have a real talk when we get home?"

I grinned devilishly, grabbing her hand and dragging her toward the bed again. "I'll do whatever you want me to do to you for that."

Her eyes twinkled. "*Whatever* I want? Are you sure you can promise that?"

"I'm not afraid of your desires, Whit."

Her cheeks heated at those words. I held up a pinkie, and she slipped hers into mine.

"Pinkie promise," I told her.

She nodded once, and then I yanked her back onto the bed, kissing my way down her navel. If she wanted to forget what had happened in the past with sex, I could do that. But I was going to have to tell her the truth when we actually had that conversation. She needed to know that I was serious and that it wasn't *just* sex with me either.

But not today.

Things would work themselves out when we got home.

In the meantime, I needed to keep my promise.

PART III

THINK PINK

15

WHITLEY

The first thing I did when I got home was squeeze in an appointment at the hair salon. I left Sunday afternoon with a fresh cotton-candy pink do that I adored. The blonde had been fun for the week, but I hadn't negotiated hair color into my contract for nothing. I wanted to be fresh for Monday when I finally had that conversation with Gavin.

I was adding curls to the left side of my head and wondering how this conversation was going to go. Gavin's grandmother's ring was on a ring tray beside the sink. I'd slipped it off this morning. I couldn't explain why I'd kept it on all day yesterday ... even when I went to my hair appointment. My stylist had nearly had a fit.

I stared at it as I finished my hair. I bit my lip and reached for it. The thing literally fit like it had been made for me. I hadn't known that wearing it for less than a week would make it mold to my finger. Now with it missing, the finger felt blank. I slid the ring back on my finger.

A knock sounded on my door.

I jumped. Fuck. Was Gavin already here with coffee? I wasn't ready.

I threw off my night dress and hastily pulled on my work clothes. I was still jumping into my pants to get the damn button to close as I called out, "Coming!"

Straightening with a gasp, I wrenched the door open with a wide smile for Gavin. Only to freeze in place at the sight of my *parents*.

"Whitley! What did you do to your hair?" she asked with a look like she'd just sucked on a lemon.

"Mom?" I said in disbelief. I touched the pink strands of my hair.

My mom didn't throw her arms around me or start crying happy tears. She just bustled inside my apartment, as if she'd been there a hundred times. When, in fact, she'd never visited me while I lived in New York. She'd only come to California once, lamented the sin of my relationship with Safia, and then left in a hurry. My brother, Wyatt, had come with his family and apologized a hundred times for Mom. His wife, Carrie, was slightly more progressive than our dinosaur parents. Their two kids—Wesley and Wynona— had both thought Safia was cooler than me, which was why they'd stayed, even as my mom had flown straight home.

"Dad?" I said next as he shot me a bemused look and shuffled in after his wife.

"Hi, sweetheart," he said cheerfully.

"What are you doing here?"

"Oh really!" my mom cried. She whirled on me and grasped my left hand. "Our baby girl is getting married!"

And I was still wearing the goddamn engagement ring. Fuck.

"Oh, Mom, that's ... that's not ..."

"To a King no less!" she cried.

My dad patted me on the back twice. "We're real proud of you, honey."

Mom gazed down at the massive rock on my finger. "All those years, we thought you were a lost cause. Living with that woman in California." She made a face. "And now, you've clearly come to your senses. Marrying a real Texan man. And this ring! I heard it was his grandmother's."

I tugged my hand out of her grasp. "Heard from who?"

"Rumor mill," Dad coughed under his breath.

My mom shot him a dirty look. "The ladies at church came by to congratulate me yesterday. You must have seen all my calls."

I frowned. I had seen them. I'd seen them for weeks. But I hadn't really been talking to my parents since the Safia incident. I'd answer my brother, but never my mother and only rarely my dad. Since he'd stood by as Mom made a fool of my girlfriend and said not a word before giving me a look filled with so many unsaid apologies and then left.

"But how did the ladies at church find out?"

"Oh, what does it matter?" Mom gushed. "Surely, getting engaged would have been reason to call your parents. You knew we'd be excited for you."

I didn't know how to tell them I'd hoped that they never heard. Was it because I had run into that guy at the wedding who knew Wyatt? Was that how it had all gotten out? Jesus.

I hadn't planned for *my* parents finding out. The Kings were one thing. They didn't have expectations of me. My parents were another story. This was their dream come true, and I'd never wanted to make their dreams a reality less than in this instance.

I opened my mouth to tell them the whole thing was a sham and they'd flown all the way out here for no reason when another knock came from the door. I cursed under my breath. I'd forgotten about Gavin and coffee due to my parents' surprising appearance.

"Hold on," I muttered.

I pulled the door open just enough to catch a glimpse of Gavin in a charcoal-gray suit, holding two coffees. His smile was bright when he saw me.

"Your hair!" he exclaimed. The opposite sentiment that my mother had used when she said something similar. His smile broke into a full-on beam. "I love it."

"Uh ... Gavin, it's not really a good time."

"Gavin?" my mom gasped. "He's here. Oh, come in, come in. I want to meet my future son-in-law."

The door swung the rest of the way open, and my parents got a good look at Gavin King. The exact sort of man they'd always wanted me to marry.

"Uh, hello," Gavin said.

He passed me my coffee, and I took a long gulp for fortification.

"Gavin, these are my parents," I told him. "They flew out ... when they heard about the engagement."

His eyes flicked to my left hand, which still had the ring securely in place. He arched an eyebrow in confusion. We'd agreed to talk about what had happened and where this was going, but I was sure he hadn't imagined I'd still be wearing this ring. I hadn't exactly planned to either.

"Oh, you're so handsome," my mom cooed. "Perfect for our Whitley."

My dad put his hand out. "Nice to meet you, son. I'm Walter, and this is my wife, Cynthia. Sorry for barging in on y'all. We're just so happy to meet you."

Gavin shook my dad's hand solemnly. "The pleasure is all mine."

"Well, have you set a date yet?" my mom asked.

"Mom," I groaned.

"I know. I know. You're a modern woman. You don't care about all this stuff." She shot Gavin a conspiratorial look. "I'm sure you know that about our Whitley."

"That I do," he agreed easily.

I glared at him, and he smirked. My dad just guffawed at the interaction.

"But you can be excited about your wedding. I sure am. Are you having it here? Or back in Texas? In Dallas, or do you want it in Midland?" My mom spat her questions so fast that there was not a space to answer any of them.

I didn't know how to even tell her about it all right then and there. If she kept throwing questions like that at me, then I was going to blow a gasket and toss them out of my apartment.

Gavin slid an arm around my shoulders and interrupted my mother's tirade. "I'm sure you had a long flight, getting here. Why don't we do dinner tonight to discuss all the finer details?" he suggested smoothly. "Whitley and I both have to get to work. I'll make a reservation, if that suits you?"

My mom nearly swooned. A man taking charge. I almost rolled my eyes. I would have if I wasn't so grateful that he'd shut her up. Had he seen that I was *this close* to strangling her?

He glanced down at me, and I mouthed a thank-you.

"That sounds good to me. Where are you staying?" I asked my parents.

They rattled off the hotel, just south of Central Park. It was nice, but it wasn't Percy Tower. That sounded like my parents.

Gavin insisted they take his car downstairs. I thought my mom would kiss him, but in a matter of minutes, he had them out of my apartment without a fuss. He sent a text to his driver before glancing up at me.

"Wow," I muttered. "You *handled* them."

He blinked at me. "That's half of my job."

"Is it?"

"Pretty much. Lots of meetings and charisma and directing people to do the things I want."

"Well, you were excellent at it," I admitted. "I've never seen anyone get my mom to do anything she didn't want to do."

"So, you have that in common?" he teased.

"Hey!" I swatted at him. "I'm nothing like my mom."

He snatched my hand up and pressed a kiss to it. "You're still wearing the ring," he said softly.

I tugged my hand back self-consciously. "I'd taken it off. I was just ... trying it on again." My cheeks colored. I started to tug it off. "You can have it back."

He stilled me. "Keep wearing it. We'll have to figure your parents out before you take it off."

"What the hell am I going to tell them? We're going to have to stage some elaborate breakup at dinner."

"Hold on." He set his coffee down and then put his hands on my shoulders. "Let's figure this out."

"You don't understand."

"Then, help me understand."

I wrenched away from him. "You're exactly the kind of guy my parents want me to marry."

He gave me a quizzical look. "Thank you?"

"Gavin!"

He laughed. "What? Should I be insulted that your parents like me?"

"They don't like you. They don't know you," I insisted.

"They only care that you're a King from Texas oil money and that I'm finally letting a man take care of me."

"Is that so bad?"

I snorted. "Gavin, I'm telling you that all they have ever cared about is me marrying the right guy and giving up my life for him. That *is* bad. And worse," I said as I began to pace, "when they came to LA to see me, my mom was *furious* that I was dating Safia. She barged out of there after insulting my girlfriend and taking my dad with her. They've never accepted me for who I am. I don't want them to accept me for this." I glanced up at him. "For something that isn't even real."

Gavin's face hardened at those words. "I see. Well, that's terrible of them. I have to imagine that your relationship with your girlfriend was every bit as real as any of your other relationships." His voice was hard and unyielding when he added, "More real than this one."

"Exactly," I said, though some of my bravado evaporated at the way he'd said that.

"But couldn't we tell them after dinner or after they go home? We can pretend for a few more days. Then, just tell them we broke up."

I shook my head emphatically. "That would work with your family, but not mine. You met my parents. My mom would a hundred percent blame me for ruining my only chance at what she considers happiness. She'd go out of her way to make me try to work it out with you. Even if it was your fault, it would be my fault."

"How would it be different if we broke up in front of her?"

"Well, she would *see* that it's your fault."

Gavin's expression was flat. "Would that change her

mind? After everything you've told me about her, I don't see a good out for you in all of this."

I deflated at his words. I was being hysterical. I *knew* I was being hysterical. My mom always put me on edge like this. I'd done everything I could not to be her little princess and to defy all her expectations. I didn't want to be the little girl who married the right man for her praise. And still, the prospect of having her approval was so tantalizing.

But I wasn't marrying Gavin. I wasn't sure I wanted to get married at all.

I didn't see a way for this to work out in my favor. Again, the same old, same old with my family. I was going to be the disappointment once more. Well, what else was new?

"You're right. We can tell them after they go home. I'll … I'll give you the ring back then."

His face was perfectly blank at those words. "Are we still going to talk about all of this after that's done?"

I bit my lip and nodded. "I promise."

16

———

WHITLEY

"Ready for this?" Gavin asked.

We were seated in the back of his black car, heading toward our dinner reservations. I'd come home from an anxiety-ridden day of playing catch-up to throw on a midnight-blue dress and head out again. I'd considered wearing something outrageous to get a reaction from my mom. Show the rebel I'd always been, but I'd given up on that. I just wanted them to go home. Back to Texas, where they belonged, and not in my beloved New York.

I shrugged and chewed on my bottom lip. Gavin reached across the car and took my hand. I jerked my head back to him as he threaded our fingers together.

"What are you doing?"

"You're nervous."

"Well ... yeah. Pretending for your parents was easy. They wanted to see you happy. They didn't know who I was."

"Your parents want you to be happy," he said, drawing calming circles on the top of my hand.

I scoffed. "They want me to be happy in the way *they* want me to be happy."

"Do you really care what they think? We could walk in there and tell them the truth."

I trembled at that suggestion. It would be the easiest route, of course. Much easier than telling them later that it hadn't worked out. But it wasn't the right thing to do either. They wouldn't understand. It might actually be *worse* than breaking off a relationship they deemed fitting. This was making a mockery of the thing they wanted.

Slowly, I shook my head. "I can't do that either."

He nodded approvingly. "A few more days then? It shouldn't be too bad."

No. No, it wasn't bad at all. Being Gavin's fiancée was ... better than I'd imagined it would be. In the moments when I let myself consider it at all, I found the whole thing as easy as breathing. I didn't know what that meant.

I liked Gavin. I'd liked him for a long time. But I wasn't *girlfriend* material. Not really. And he'd see that too one day, if he hadn't already.

The car stopped in front of the restaurant, and Gavin stepped out first, offering me his hand. I took it and set my heels down on the wet sidewalk. It had been raining on and off since we'd gotten home. It felt like an ominous portent.

Gavin was greeted by the maître d' as soon as we entered the restaurant. My parents were already standing nearby. Their expressions of discomfort disappeared at Gavin's presence and his clear command. My mom looked overly pleased with herself as we bypassed a long line of people and were immediately seated.

"This way," the woman said with a wide smile.

"What service," my mother said, delighted.

"We're always pleased when Mr. King graces our restaurant. We've reserved you the best table," she said, gesturing to a seat at the window overlooking the city street beyond.

"Thank you," Gavin said with his winning smile. He pulled my seat out for me. "After you."

"Thank you. I didn't realize you were a regular here."

"A man has to have his secrets." He shot me a look with one arched eyebrow. There was jest in his eyes.

This must have been where he took dates. Classic Gavin.

I forced back a laugh as my parents took their seats. Dad groaned slightly as he settled into his chair. My mom fluttered about him, but he just pushed her off.

"Leave it, Cynthia."

"Walter," she whispered.

He glared at her once and then scooted his chair in. She dropped it with a gulp and then forced her cheery smile back into place.

We perused the menu. I saw my mom wince at the entrée prices. We were pretty well off, but still, a couple hundred dollars for a steak wasn't a regular meal. She probably hadn't considered where a King would take them for dinner. That was the Upper East Side for you.

Gavin ordered a bottle of wine for the table as we went around and ordered. I wasn't surprised that my mom got a salad or that she sneered at me for getting steak. If I was going to get a King dinner, I was going to get a King dinner.

Gavin just smiled when I ordered and looked up at the waiter and said, "I'll have what she's having. She has good taste."

My mom's face pinched at those words. Caught between wanting to tell me to eat less to please my future husband and the realization that Gavin didn't give a shit.

"So, tell me all the details," Mom said once the waiter was gone. "How did you meet? How did he propose?"

I glanced at Gavin. Well, at least we'd practiced this much. "We've known each other for a few years. We met before I moved to California."

My mother looked aghast at this news. As if we could have been married then.

Gavin reached across the table and took my hand. "I was glad that Whitley took the job in LA. It was perfect for her," he said as if we'd rehearsed this part. "She deserves every good thing in her life. We were a classic *right person, wrong time*. But when she moved back to New York, I didn't miss a beat."

"That's right," I said, catching on to the part of the conversation we'd actually said in Midland. "It was a whirlwind. I've only been back a few months." I glanced down at the ring. "The whole thing was unexpected."

"How romantic!" my mom gushed. "And the ring is beautiful. Where did you get it?"

"It was my grandmother's," Gavin said, confirming what the rumor train had already told my mother. "When she passed, my mom entrusted it to me. She said she always knew I'd find the right person to give it to." He was looking deep into my eyes now. I was ensnared. I couldn't have possibly looked away if I wanted to. "And I found her."

My mom dabbed at her eyes. "Oh, isn't that romantic, Walter?"

"I'm happy that our Whitley has finally found love."

I cleared my throat and removed my hand from Gavin's. I was supposed to be playing a part. Playing up our love and all that. But the more Gavin stared lovingly into my eyes and held my hand and treated me like I was the most precious thing on the planet, the more something happened in my stomach. Butterflies of excitement. A new pull to him, like a string connected us and he was tugging me ever closer.

The wine appeared, breaking the connection. Gavin tasted it first and approved it with that same dimpled grin. Wine was poured, and we all held up glasses to toast the wedding.

"So, will the wedding be here in New York?" Mom asked. "Or back home in Dallas? Or would you prefer to have it in Midland?"

Gavin turned the full weight of his attention on me. "Whatever you want, dear."

I nearly scowled at him. "Definitely New York."

My mom sighed, as if she'd known I would say that. "Are you sure you don't want to come back to Dallas for this? All of your family and all of Gavin's family are in Texas. It would be much harder—not to mention, more expensive—to get everyone up here."

"We can send the jet if it's a problem," Gavin said offhand.

I thought my mom might turn purple as she sputtered in shock. Yeah, we weren't *private jet* rich.

"Plus, Camden Percy is a close personal friend. I'm sure he could put in a room block at Percy Tower so that everyone could stay in the heart of the city," Gavin said as if he'd already thought this through.

"That would be ... incredibly generous," my mom said.

"Sounds like y'all have this all figured out," Dad said with a nod of approval toward me.

I shot Gavin a questioning look. "It sure does."

He took my hand again and brought it to his lips. "Our best friends are getting married right now. So, I've heard all the hoops they've jumped through. Their wedding will be much bigger than ours though since Court's mom is the mayor."

"The mayor of New York?" my mom asked in awe.

She was starting to get the sort of people that I hung out with here in the city.

"Yes, Court is the mayor's son, and he's marrying English. Remember her?"

My mom's eyes widened. She'd thought English was some lowly slut who worked with degenerate rockstars and probably did drugs. She hadn't even thought better of her after she married Josh, who was a legitimate movie star. But apparently, marrying the son of the mayor was something else entirely.

"Anna English?" she asked, just to be sure.

"Yep. We went to UCLA together."

"I do remember her now," Mom said.

"She's a nice girl," Dad said. "I'm glad she's happy."

"Me too."

My dad changed the subject to my brother as dinner was served. I dug into my steak, only half-paying attention to the life my brother was leading back in Dallas. The kids were going into kindergarten and second grade this year. Carrie was working at some MLM business that kept her busy on the weekends when she wasn't carting the oldest to baseball. Wyatt was helping dad run the business, of course.

I opted out of dessert, hoping that we could have this entire charade over sooner rather than later, but Gavin shook his head.

"I have never known you to skip dessert," he said. Which was true, but damn it.

He ordered us each the cheesecake, which I'd been eyeing. I had no idea how he'd known it was what I wanted. He just smirked, as if he already knew me that well. He ordered a port for himself and my father while Mom insisted that she couldn't spare the calories.

I nearly choked right then and there. Ever since Katherine's anorexia scare, I'd been firmly in the anti-diet culture stance. No calorie counting, no scales, none of that bullshit. Just intuitive eating and living a healthy lifestyle. Just hearing her mention calories was triggering.

Dad and Gavin were talking about the baseball season. I hadn't even known Gavin liked baseball, but he apparently could carry on an entire conversation about the Texas Rangers. We ate dessert as they chatted.

Unbeknownst to the rest of us, Gavin picked up the entire tab and wouldn't hear a word from my parents about covering it. "My treat."

I knew he had the money, but still. "You didn't have to do that," I said as we walked out of the restaurant.

"I absolutely did," he whispered against my ear. "Not every day I get to take out my fiancée's parents."

"You're a scoundrel."

He chuckled. "You like it."

I grinned up at him. The night was over. We'd both survived. Maybe we could go back to my place and have sex. That'd be the correct end to this night.

But my mom intercepted us. "Could we come over and talk some more?"

I blinked at her. "To ... my place?"

"Yes, we want to discuss the wedding more with you."

"Could we do it ... tomorrow?" I asked, seeing my plans of seducing Gavin going out the window. "How long are you staying?"

"We're leaving tomorrow evening. And, no ... I think we need to discuss it tonight." She glanced at Dad, and he nodded.

Gavin beamed. "Absolutely. Why don't you all come to my place instead? Whitley and I live in the same building."

"That would be lovely," my mom said gratefully.

Gavin bustled us all into the car and swept us back to our building on the Upper East Side. I couldn't even express my displeasure at this new arrangement. Dinner hadn't been as bad as my anxiety had expected it to be, which was normally the case, but you never knew with my parents.

Despite Gavin being in the same building, I'd never actually been to his place. We always met at mine or in the lobby or at the coffee shop. I marveled at how much *nicer* his apartment was than mine. It shouldn't have surprised me since, even though I was making stupid money now, I hadn't grown up with it. Gavin's place was probably twice the size of mine and had clearly been put together by an interior designer. It exuded bachelor and wealth. It was absolutely Gavin King in every way.

I tried to act like I'd been here many times before, sinking into the plush leather sofa and kicking my heels off. Gavin offered my parents a seat and then poured more wine for everyone. I would have killed for the whiskey on his wet bar, but I wasn't going to ask for harder liquor before anyone else did.

Gavin sank into the seat next to me, dropping his arm across my shoulders, as if it were perfectly natural. My parents glanced at each other. Neither touched their wine. They were being weird.

"You wanted to talk more about the wedding?" I prompted.

"Right," Mom said, glancing to Dad and then back. "There's been a new development. We tried to call, but you didn't answer. We knew we'd have to see you in person."

"Development?" I asked, sitting up.

"Your dad is sick," Mom blurted out.

I blinked. That ... wasn't what I'd been expecting at all. My gaze shifted to my dad, who looked uncomfortable.

"I have cancer, sweetheart."

The words registered, but they didn't seem real. My ears were ringing. I could barely hear the rest of the things they were saying. Cancer. Moved to spine, hips, and bladder. A few months to live.

Those words were incomprehensible. I had my problems with my parents. They'd never been the people I wanted them to be. But I didn't want them to *die* either. I didn't want my daddy to *die*.

"That's why we're here," he said. "I just … I want to walk you down the aisle."

I choked. "What?"

"I know that would move the timeline up for you two," Dad said hoarsely. "I understand it would have to happen before the end of the summer. But … it's my last wish."

17

———

GAVIN

Whitley wasn't breathing.

Her mouth was agape, eyes wide and tear-brimmed, and she just *stopped*. As if time had frozen.

I'd suggested we move to my apartment, thinking that we could have one glass of wine and then we could busy her parents out of the place. That it would be a lot easier to get rid of them if we were in my apartment. I hadn't considered that they were going to drop a bomb in the middle of my living room.

"Whitley?" her mom said softly.

She said nothing. She stared at her father in abject horror.

"Whitley, honey," her dad began.

"How ... how long have you known?" she forced out.

"About a week."

"We tried to call," her mom interjected. "We bought the tickets to come see you when you didn't answer. The engagement was just ... a happy coincidence." Her smile widened at the words, but Whitley's didn't.

They were asking her to process a lot right now. Even if

our engagement hadn't been fake, this would have been a whole lot to ask of anyone.

Finally, she got to her feet and stumbled toward her dad. "I'm so sorry, Daddy."

"It's okay, honey. It's okay."

"It's not," she said through her tears. "It's not okay."

"I know." He patted her back. "I've had a good life."

"But ... but treatment," she said, immediately going into doctor mode. "There's so much cancer treatment. A few months is ... that's absurd."

"He's still going to do immune treatments," her mom supplied. "But it's at such an advanced stage that they don't think chemo or radiation is going to help."

Whitley had this look in her eye, like she thought she could solve this. I would have smiled at that look under other circumstances. But right now, there wasn't a whole lot that she could do.

When that realization hit Whitley too, tears came to her eyes again. She closed her eyes and tried to fight them from falling down her cheeks. I hated this. I hated every minute of it. There was nothing I could do to make this easier for her ... for any of them. And watching her in this much pain was terrible.

"I know it's a lot to ask," her dad said, looking at me now. "Moving the wedding up would mean so much to me, but if you can't, we understand too." He came to his feet and offered me his hand. I shook it immediately. "I don't expect you to know if it's possible right now."

Whitley's eyes finally met mine, wide with fear. Our engagement was fake. Her dad wanted us to get married in a matter of months. What the fuck could we even say?

"Daddy," Whitley said with a hiccup in her voice, "I ... we ..."

She was about to tell them that it was fake. I saw it cross her expression, but she couldn't do that. Not right now. Not with everything else.

"We'll have to discuss it," I told them quickly. "Can we talk about it more tomorrow? It's been a long night."

Her mom sighed with relief, as if she had just been waiting for a reason to leave and escape all of this. "Tomorrow would be lovely. We could always talk more on the phone once we're home too. Nothing has to be decided yet."

"Of course," I said amicably as I bustled her parents out of the apartment.

It wasn't until the door closed behind them that silence finally settled over the place. Whitley had her arms crossed over her stomach, as if trying to hold her intestines in from spilling out of the split that had just opened in her gut.

"What am I going to do?" she whispered.

"First, you should take a seat," I told her. She did that promptly. I stalked to the liquor bar and poured her a hefty portion of whiskey. "Drink this." She took it gratefully and took a long sip.

"I can't believe this is happening. I can't believe ..." She trailed off as her eyes went glassy again.

I took the seat next to her, gently wrapping an arm across her shoulders again. She leaned her head onto my shoulder.

"We can figure this out."

"How? My dad is dying. He wants to walk me down the aisle. But Gavin, we were going to tell them we had broken up in two days. We're not really engaged."

"I know," I said slowly. I let the silence linger longer before adding, "But I'd still do it."

"Do what?"

"Marry you."

Her head tilted up to look into my emerald-green eyes. She blinked twice, as if she hadn't heard me right. "What?"

"I'd do it. I'd let your father walk you down the aisle."

"You would fake *marry* me?"

"Yes," I said, brushing a stray pink strand out of her face. "And ... it would be a real wedding, Whitley. You'd be my real wife."

"But it wouldn't be ... *real*. It would be wrong. We're not ... we're not together like that."

"No," I agreed easily. "It's not like I planned to get married, but that doesn't mean we have to say no to your father's request."

She squeezed her eyes shut. "I don't want to think about this."

"I know." I ran my fingers back through her cotton-candy hair. "I can't imagine you'd want to discuss this. I can't believe they dropped this in your lap. It's not fair, and it's awful, but, Whit ... it doesn't change the reality."

"I know," she croaked. Tears clustered in her long, dark lashes. She blinked them away, curling further into me. "What are we going to do?"

"I think ... we should go through with it. If you'll have me."

Her eyes opened again, and she shook her head. "You don't *want* this." She pulled away from me, dropping her glass on the table and running her hands back through her hair. "I could never ask you to do that."

"You didn't ask," I reminded her.

"No, but ..."

"In fact, I offered."

"Gavin ..."

"Hey," I said, tilting her chin back toward me, "look at

me." Her eyes lifted to mine, and she froze under my gaze. "I don't think it's a mystery that I like you, Whitley. I liked you three years ago when we were together and when you left for California. I respected your wishes, which was to leave, but we're in a different place than we were then. The wedding doesn't have to be real. None of this has to be real, if you don't want it to be. But ... it's real to me. What we're doing here is real to me."

She swallowed down terror. "It can't be real."

"Why not?" I demanded. "Why can't we at least try?"

She jerked to her feet and put her hands around her stomach. "Because I like you," she admitted with such force that I thought it might shake the windows.

"So?"

The fact that she'd admitted that much must have cost her. Whitley kept her own counsel. She always had her own rules. Rules that protected her from the sort of heartbreak that could really be possible here if she let herself be more than just the bad girlfriend she'd written herself as.

"I don't want to hurt you."

I was taken aback by that. Never in all of this had I considered that Whitley would fear hurting *me*. I had thought all of her fears resided over the fact that she didn't want to be hurt. That she ran to escape the possibility that she would give her heart to someone. She'd always held it so close, never quite making herself vulnerable enough.

I rose to my feet and took an easy step toward her. "And here I thought, you were worried about me hurting *you*."

She scoffed. "No. I'm the one who leaves, Gavin."

"In my relationships, Whitley, I'm the one who leaves."

We stared at each other in the space of those confessions. We were the same. We'd been the same for so long. It was why we'd been the perfect wingman for one another and effortless friends. It was why soaring over that line had felt as easy as breathing. And why this wedding would be equally as simple, if she gave in to it.

"Why did you really leave?" I asked.

"Because I liked you ... and I didn't want to hurt you."

"Did you ever think that *leaving* would hurt me?"

"No. I ... I didn't want to tear friends apart, and I ... didn't want to like you."

"Why not?" I asked, dragging a finger down her jaw.

"I told you, I'm going to hurt you."

"You don't have to be scared."

She laughed, slightly hysterical. "I'm not *scared*." But I could see that was a lie. She was terrified. She was petrified to let her guard down and find that she actually enjoyed what we were doing here. "All liking someone has ever gotten me is heartbreak. I'm the bad girlfriend, remember?"

"Why don't we put the labels aside? We're good together. You've seen that for the last week. It was *easy* with my family because *we're* easy, Whit."

"We ... we are."

The admission felt like a balm. "I'm not asking you to marry me." *Yet.* The word was left unsaid as I stared down into her wide, frightened eyes. "I'm asking you to see how this goes while we do the right thing by your dad."

"You really mean it?"

"It's your father's dying wish, Whitley. It seems cruel to deny him that."

She nodded once, folding herself against my chest. I wrapped her tight against me, and it was the most incredible feeling. I wanted to hold her like this for eternity. She sniffled against me, and I brushed a kiss on the top of her head.

"We'll figure this out together, pixie."

18

WHITLEY

The next morning, I woke in a big, comfy bed. Gavin's bed. I rolled over and found the other side of the California king empty. The shower was running in the next room. The man showered more than anyone else I knew.

I sank back down into the plush mattress and tugged the comforter up to my chin. I was in one of Gavin's oversize T-shirts. Nothing had happened. I'd fallen asleep in his bed, and nothing had happened. Well, I'd cried a lot, and he'd held me, stroking my hair, without complaint. I didn't know what to make of that.

Or the conversation we'd had last night.

Or my dad's diagnosis.

It was the first time that I'd ever been furious that I had chosen plastic surgery instead of something more helpful ... like oncology. I could have been curing cancer this entire time. Not that I'd ever *wanted* to, but that seemed irrational at this present moment.

I had no more expertise in this than an oncologist had in a face lift. And still, I was mad that I'd put myself in this position.

I wanted to avoid the reality of my father's cancer nearly as much as what had happened last night with Gavin.

Did this mean we were dating? A spike of fear shot through me. I'd told him the truth. I broke relationships, and if we had a real relationship, whether or not the marriage would be real, I was sure I'd hurt him. Of course, he thought the same thing. So, we were at an impasse there.

It was all too complicated to focus on. Last night felt like a fever dream. None of it could have possibly been real. Let alone all of it.

And yet here I was, in Gavin's apartment, with two missed calls from my mom and a text message from my dad about meeting. It was real. I wasn't going to wake up to a new world. This was my reality.

"Morning," Gavin said, jolting me from my spiraling.

"Hey."

I might have been depressed, but I wasn't blind. Gavin was wearing nothing but a towel slung low around his waist, and he looked fucking fantastic. Water still clung to his red-brown hair. It dripped into his eyes, and he brushed his hand back through it, slicking it backward.

"How are you feeling?" he asked.

I tilted my head to get a clearer view of the eight-pack abs. "Better now."

He laughed softly. "At least you haven't lost your sense of humor."

"Please, humor is all I have left."

Then, I snatched up his towel and ran across the room with it. Gavin's jaw dropped, and without warning, he chased after me. There was nowhere to go anyway, but he caught me with ease, slinging me over his shoulder and plopping us both on the bed.

"You're mischief incarnate."

"Why, thank you," I said with a teasing smile.

He shook his head and then dropped his lips onto mine. The moment they touched mine, the rest of the world fell away. It would have been nice to live here in this point of time. To not have to face what was coming after that. I could delude myself about a lot of things, but not that my dad was dying. No amount of freezing time was going to change that fact.

Gavin pulled away slowly, looking down at me with those mercurial eyes. "How are you really?"

"I don't know."

"Do you still want to go through with this?"

"Do *you*?"

"Yes," he said automatically.

I still couldn't believe that Gavin was suggesting what he'd suggested. A fake engagement for a week to deal with his family was one thing. A *real* marriage to satisfy my father was something else entirely. We could annul it or whatever … divorce. But he'd taken it a step further. He wanted to try this. *Actually* try this. Might as well see if it worked while we were going through with it anyway.

Yet, as I looked up at him, I saw a future in those eyes. I saw all those promises we hadn't quite made become reality. Would it be so terrible? It was certainly terrifying.

But there was something else there. Something … exciting too.

We were getting married one way or another.

Why not see if I could fall in love with him too?

"Then, let's do it."

His smile was brilliant as he bent down to kiss me again, sealing our promise.

It was nearly an hour before I got back to my apartment, took my own shower, and was ready for the day. We met my parents at H&H Bagels and broke the news to them. My mom cried. My dad pulled me into a tight hug. This was a big ask, and I had *no* idea how I was going to pull this off in two months, in New York City.

Back home, we could throw it together, but here?

I knew exactly who I needed to make this work. Now that the train was running down the track, there was no backing out. The engagement ring was on my finger. I was going to have to tell my boss, my friends, and the rest of the world too.

Which meant I needed *help*.

The SOS went out to my girlfriends that morning, and by the evening, we were all seated around a table at Katherine's favorite sushi restaurant with sake for the four of us.

"Finally," English grumbled. "I was wondering if you were going to avoid us forever."

Lark arched an eyebrow. "So, are we going to get the whole story?"

"You know we do love a Whitley Bowen original," Katherine purred. Her eyes were as clever as a cat. As if she'd already sussed out what this whole thing was about. Which felt impossible, but it was Katherine. I put nothing past her.

"I didn't mean to avoid you. It's been an interesting couple of days since I got home, which was why I wanted to get with you."

Katherine tapped the diamond still on my left hand. "And explain why you're still wearing this."

English's eyes widened. She must have missed it. "Oh my god, are you actually engaged?"

"No," I said quickly. Then stalled. "Well, sort of."

All three of my friends looked at me in various stages of astonishment. English had known me since college. I was the least likely of our friends to *ever* marry. Lark looked equally shocked. I was known for my daring breakups and petty revenges. Not for *this*. Katherine just arched an eyebrow and waited. She didn't like to be out of the know.

"Start from the beginning, Whitley Bowen," English demanded. "Don't leave anything out."

So, I did as she'd asked. I confessed about our clever fake engagement. How I'd sung at the wedding and made everyone fall in love with me. And how we'd planned a big breakup after we got back.

Then, my parents had blown up my entire world. By the time I explained that Gavin had not only agreed to go through with the wedding, but also been the one to suggest it, all three girls' mouths were open.

"Gavin actually wants to do it?" Lark asked with wide eyes. "That's ..."

"Incomprehensible," English finished for her.

"And *you* want to go through with it?" Katherine asked. "It's not as if you've been dying to get married."

"No, I'm not dying to get married. But my father *is* dying. So, I'm going to do it. I'm going to give him this thing that he wants."

"Then what?" English asked. "It's a great thing you're doing, but are you going to *stay* married to Gavin?" She glanced at Katherine hesitantly. "Just because we've seen arranged marriages work doesn't mean that they work."

"I don't know. No. I think we'll get it annulled or get divorced or whatever."

"Unless it works out," Katherine said.

I laughed, forcing the sound to be as ridiculous as her

suggestion. "Come on. Not everyone is you and Camden."

"No one else is me and Camden," she said resolutely. "But it's not as if you two don't fit. Maybe it could work."

"Katherine," English growled low, "don't push her."

"She's right," Lark said. "Whitley shouldn't be forced into anything she doesn't want, and they should end the relationship if it isn't real."

"We'll figure it out as we go."

I bit my lip, wondering if I should tell them the rest. How Gavin wanted to try this for real ... not just as a favor to my dad. Maybe not a real wedding, but something beyond what we were doing. It complicated thing, but I liked him. I'd been fighting it for so long, and I couldn't fight forever.

English shot me a quizzical look. As if she could read my mind. I shook my head slightly. I wasn't ready to admit that to everyone.

"Anyway," I said hastily, "that's not why I brought us together. Well, not exactly. I have to be married in two months. There's no way I can do that without you."

Katherine threw her long, dark hair off of her shoulder. "Assuredly."

Lark shook her head. "I can't believe I'm agreeing to this, but I'm in. I'll help however I can."

I looked to English. She still seemed skeptical. Like she wanted to change my mind about this whole thing. She was the only one who knew the full extent of my distaste for my parents. How they'd hurt me in the past. But just because we didn't get along didn't mean that I was going to refuse my own dad his dying wish. I would walk down that aisle with him as his little girl before he passed away. If I didn't, I'd regret it for the rest of my life.

"English?" I asked softly.

She sighed heavily and then pulled out her cell phone,

immediately switching into publicist mode. "Okay. First, we need an estimated head count, so I can get you a venue. Do you have a preference?"

"About any of it?" I asked, shaking my head. "Not a thing."

English was already typing. "I'll handle it. I'm going to guess two hundred."

I nearly choked. "That many?"

"You're marrying Gavin King," Lark reminded me. "No chance it'll be smaller than that."

I nodded. Margaret and Locke had had five hundred. It had seemed obscene to have that many people at the wedding.

"I can work on a photographer and caterer," Lark said. "I know a few who work with the campaign on occasion. They can let me know who to work with."

Katherine waved her hand. "And I've got the dress."

"Oh, right," I whispered. "The dress."

"I'll get with Harmony."

I winced slightly at that. Harmony and Robert were dating now. "Uh ... would it be weird for Harmony to make a dress for her boyfriend's ex?"

Katherine rolled her eyes. "Harmony and I are friends now. She probably doesn't give a shit."

"Okay. Should I come help with the dress?"

"We'll get some measurements. Harmony will probably kill me on this deadline, but she owes me." Katherine shot me a mischievous smile.

I wondered what Katherine had done that made Harmony owe her.

English had a full list by the end of our lunch. It was an overwhelming amount to do, and I now understood why at least a year was put between the engagement and the wedding. That wasn't going to happen here. It wasn't possible to happen at any point, considering my father.

"Oh, and one last thing," Katherine said, tapping English's list. "An engagement party."

"There's no time," English argued.

"What would be the point anyway?" Lark asked. "They're not actually engaged."

"They have to tell the world *sometime*, and we should have her drinking the entire time, so we dash the rumors that she's pregnant," Katherine said. I blanched. "I'll host it. We'll do it this weekend. It'll be on *Page Six* by Monday."

"Great," I muttered.

With all of that planned, the girls hopped up to go and get shit done. I was lucky to have friends who didn't look at me like I was a lunatic, but actually agreed to move the world for me. I hugged Katherine and Lark before they disappeared into a black Mercedes, leaving me and English alone.

"Well," English said, "are you going to tell me what's going on with you two?"

"Gavin wants to ... date. You know, while we do this."

English arched an eyebrow. "Do you want that?"

I bit my lip, looking down as we got out onto the New York City sidewalk. "I don't know. Maybe?"

She took my arm and pulled me aside. "Maybe or yes?"

"Yes," I whispered. "I want to date him. I want to try."

English beamed and then dragged me into a hug. "Good. Okay, good. I feel a lot better about all of this if you're happy."

"It might all crash and burn."

English snorted. "It's you. That's always a possibility. But hey, maybe you'll fall madly in love."

It didn't seem likely, but I sure liked the sound of that.

19

GAVIN

"**Y**ou're *marrying* Whitley?" Court asked with wide eyes.

"Surprise."

Sam must have heard it from Lark already because he clapped me on the back. "Congratulations, man."

"Thanks."

"Look, English told me what's going on," Court added hastily. "But I hadn't heard it from your mouth, so I couldn't believe it."

"What's to believe?"

"That someone could settle you down," Camden filled in.

"Ah, well, you know ..."

Camden arched an eyebrow in my direction. "Because that's what's happening, isn't it? Some of this is an excuse to be with her."

"No way," Court said with a laugh. He shook his head. "Come on, Camden. This is Gavin. Since when hasn't he been against marriage?"

"Since he stopped fucking everything that walked," he said bluntly.

I didn't respond to that. Just met Camden's cool look with a resolute one of my own. He wasn't ... wrong. I'd stopped fucking around last year after Court and English's engagement party. I'd sat on the sidelines at their celebration as they promised to say *I do* and realized that I had nothing. Lark and Sam were already married. Camden and Katherine had two kids and somehow didn't just tolerate each other, but also loved one another. Court and English had long been smitten, but were officially tying the knot.

All of that, and what did I had? Some blonde on my arm, whose name I didn't even remember. She'd tried to get me to bring her back to my place, but I wasn't into it after that. I'd dropped her off and gone home alone that night. And I wondered why I hadn't been able to pick up casual dating the way I had before that night.

I was a King. The eternal bachelor. I could get any girl I wanted. And yet one look at the girl with lavender hair, and I'd been willing to risk it all.

Was it ridiculous to want what my friends all had? Was it even more ridiculous to hope that Whitley came around too?

"You're really doing this," Court said, interpreting my silence as confirmation.

"He really is," Sam said.

"I am."

There was no use in denying it. Not in the minutes before our official engagement announcement would take place. If I was going to back out, now would be the moment.

And then Whitley entered our midst with my friends' wives trailing behind her. My heart stopped in my chest. She was in a long-sleeved white dress that hit her knees. The material plunged between her breasts before cinching in a ribbon belt around the middle. Her bright pink hair had been artfully put up in a low bun with tendrils framing her face. She looked like a goddess, and I wanted nothing more than to scoop her up and carry her away from all of this.

"Well, that's what we were going for," English said triumphantly.

"What?" I asked dumbly.

Whitley laughed as I drew her into my arms and pressed a kiss to her soft pink lips. "You're ... kind of drooling."

I snorted. "I would never."

"Your eyes went all dark, and you looked like you were going to caveman-throw me over your shoulder."

"*That*," I said, my voice a rasp, "is dangerously close to what I was thinking."

She giggled, and it was music to my ears. I drew her harder against me. I was *marrying* this woman. I couldn't deny that the idea was satisfying regardless. She would be mine. She *was* mine.

"All right," English said, checking her phone, "ready for this?"

"It's like having our own publicist," Whitley said, extracting herself from my arms.

English shot her a look. "You're lucky you don't have to pay me."

Whitley pulled her into a hug. "Bestie does bestie shit."

"Yeah, yeah," English grumbled.

Our friends went first into Club 360. Camden had reserved the rooftop bar for our private use for the evening. Everyone who was anyone would be there. Including a few discreet reporters who English had let in to write the correct things about our hasty engagement. All that was left was the actual announcement.

Whitley was staring down at her fresh manicure instead of up at me. Her brow was creased in concentration, and her eyes were narrowed. I wasn't used to seeing this level of contemplation on her usually playful face.

"Are you okay?"

She jerked out of her trance. "Just ... wondering if we're doing the right thing."

"You don't want to announce the wedding?"

"I know we should. Katherine explained it all. And I do want to fulfill my father's wish."

"But ..." I prompted.

"But sometimes, I wish we could do it without fanfare."

"The wedding?" I asked with a laugh. "I can't imagine anyone in my life letting me get married without fanfare."

"No," she whispered, then met my gaze hesitantly. "Us."

"Hey," I said, taking her hand. "The spotlight is for the wedding. The rest is just us, okay? We can figure this out together without all the rest of it."

"Promise?" she joked.

I held out my pinkie, and she laughed just as the door into the club opened again.

English stuck her head inside. "You two coming or what?"

"On it," I said as I offered Whitley my arm.

She put her hand on the crook of my elbow, and I escorted her outside. Everyone's eyes immediately settled on us. Shocked expressions followed us as we made it to the front of the room. I recognized at least half of the room. Colleagues and friends from Harvard and old flings. Someone had done a damn good job of making sure to include enough of the women that would be problematic all in one place. Great.

As we reached the spot to make our big announcement,

Whitley went stock-still. I glanced down at her in confusion and then followed her gaze.

Robert.

He was standing at the center of the room with Harmony at his side. Harmony glanced at him uncertainly. But Robert's eyes were solely for Whitley. Three years ago, he'd confessed his love to her, and we'd broken his heart into a million pieces. Whoever had invited him here today had a sick sense of humor.

That was probably Katherine.

But I appreciated it all the same. I probably should have gotten ahold of him before this happened, but it was too late now. We'd been as thick as thieves before things went down with Whitley, and as much as I hated to admit it, something had broken after that. We were still friends. We were cordial in public. But we'd never be the same.

A fact that I did not intend to tell Whitley.

"Hey," I whispered.

She slowly tilted her head up to look at me. My smile was megawatt to draw her attention, and it worked. She broke into a smile too.

"Ready?"

She nodded.

I turned back to the crowd, avoiding Robert's questioning stare. "Thank you all so much for coming today. Our lovely host, Katherine Van Pelt, was oblique about the reason for this party. Well, I'm glad to tell you that Whitley and I are engaged."

Whitley's smile only grew as she held her left hand forward and showed everyone my grandmother's wedding ring. "We're not ones to wait. So, look for an end-of-summer wedding invitation in the mail any day now."

Most of the crowd rushed forward all at once to issue

congratulations and look at the ring, but there were people who looked mystified by the announcement. Others, like Robert, hadn't moved at all, and he stared back at us, as if the news had punched him in the gut.

Whitley and I accepted congratulations and confirmed that, yes, we were getting married before the end of the summer. No, she wasn't pregnant. English handed her a champagne flute as soon as she possibly could. And, yes, we were beyond excited for the next step in our life.

Eventually, the crowd parted, the dance floor opened, and drinks were flowing. I pulled Whitley into my arms and swayed side to side to the music. She rested her cheek against my chest.

"That went well."

"As expected. Well, almost." Her eyes fluttered up to mine and back down. "Did you know that he'd be here?"

I had one guess who she meant. "Robert?"

She swallowed and nodded.

"No. Katherine sure is thorough."

"She sure is," Whitley grumbled. "I should have told him on my own."

"I thought the same. But it has been three years, Whit. It's not like it's the summer after he found out about us."

She bit her lip. "I suppose. I just never really talked to him about it after he laid you out at Fashion Week."

I scoffed. "I was not laid out."

"Fine," she said with an eye roll. "After he punched you in the face."

"I had a wicked bruise for two weeks after that. Very manly."

She laughed. "You're ridiculous. No punching today."

"Of course not. I probably should talk to him though."

"Yeah," she said softly. "Probably."

"Can I steal one more dance with my bride-to-be before I do the very manly thing?" I teased as the song came to an end and another started up.

She pushed me gently backward. "Go. Do the right thing. Try to come back to me with your face intact. I'm sort of attached to it."

I grinned devilishly. "Is that so?"

"Oh, put your ego away, King," she said, shoving me harder this time. "Go!"

I laughed as I backed away from her. She shook her head at me as I turned to survey the rest of the rooftop. People kept coming up to me to congratulate me.

One or two old flings didn't seem too pleased about it. I got a round of, "Who knew someone could nail you down?"

But otherwise, everyone was friendly and less hostile.

Finally, I found Robert standing alone against the railing overlooking the city.

"Hey, man."

Robert glanced over at me, and then he quickly straightened, letting a smile stretch across his face. "Gavin." He offered me his hand. "Congratulations!"

I took his hand in mine and shook. "Thank you. I'm so glad that you're here. Though I apologize that you found out this way."

Robert waved me off, ever gracious. "How else did you expect to tell me? This seems like the perfect way."

"With our history, I probably should have reached out first."

"I don't care about all of that. What's in the past is in the past. I'm really happy for you, Gavin. I'll admit that I didn't think it would all happen this fast, but I'm glad it did happen to you."

I wanted to tell him the circumstances that had made it

happen this fast, but I couldn't. Even if he was lying through his teeth, having his acceptance and congratulations made me feel a lot better. A lot less like a dick who had stolen his girl.

It hadn't happened that way at all. But it didn't help that he had actually laid me out at Fashion Week when he found out Whitley and I had slept together in Puerto Rico while they were on a break. A breakup to Whit, but apparently not to him.

"Thank you, man. I'm really happy for you and Harmony, too."

Robert's smile intensified as he turned to find his girlfriend standing next to my fiancée. Well, that was interesting.

"It's been eye-opening, to say the least. You know when it's right, don't you?"

I nodded, my eyes on Whitley. I did. I did know.

20

———

WHITLEY

Robert was fake smiling. I'd seen his real smile, and that certainly wasn't it.

He was diplomatic to a fault. It was one of his strong suits. He'd never make Gavin feel bad for what was happening even if he really wanted to. In fact, what he'd done at Fashion Week was so out of character that it was what had finally shaken me loose.

My eyes found Katherine, standing next to her husband, chatting with people I didn't recognize. As if feeling my eyes on her, she turned and met my gaze. She arched an eyebrow.

You did this, I mouthed.

Her eyes traveled to where Gavin and Robert were currently talking. Yes, I'd sent Gavin over there, but only because it was a necessity. Normally, I walked away from a relationship and never had to deal with the person ever again. That was never going to be the case with Robert. Not when I was back in New York City and we had all the same friends. I didn't mind burning a few dozen bridges on the way out. I never had. I just didn't want to burn this one. Not when I was the one who had been in the wrong.

Katherine looked back over at me and smirked like the devil she was. *You're welcome*, she mouthed back.

Damn, I loved her.

I laughed despite myself and turned my back on her. I'd been so focused on Katherine that I hadn't seen who was approaching me.

"Hello, Whitley," Harmony said.

"Hey, Harm," I said with a smile.

Harmony and I hadn't interacted that much before I left, but I always liked people who could ruffle Katherine's feathers. It had been my mission for several years. What else were friends for? But we'd definitely be working on the wedding dress going forward. Harmony helped run her mother's company, Cunningham Couture. Katherine had modeled for them in earlier years. In fact, so had Harmony before she moved fully into design.

"Congratulations. I can't wait to work on the dress with you. To be fair, she didn't tell me who you were wearing it for."

I shook my head. "That sounds like her."

"I asked, but she said I'd find out at the party." Harmony rolled her eyes. "Her flair for the dramatic has somehow increased. I thought kids would mellow her out."

"If Camden couldn't, then nothing can."

She chuckled. "Fair. So, how did this happen?"

"If you can believe it, he proposed in a limo," I said with a laugh.

"Oh, that I can believe. That sounds just like Gavin King."

"And, yeah, I don't know. I got back and moved into the

same building as him. We started spending a lot of time together, and ... it just happened."

"Huh," she muttered. "Wasn't sure either of you would settle down. No offense."

"None taken. I never plan to," I muttered. She arched an eyebrow at my present tense, and I laughed it off. "What about you and Robert?"

"Ah, the elephant in the room." But Harmony's bright smile gave away how far gone she was. "You don't mind that we're dating?"

"Why would I mind? We dated so long ago. I want him to be happy."

I had been over Robert before it ended. I wished that I'd made the decision to end it before things went downhill.

"Well, Katherine sort of set us up," she said with a mischievous smile. "It was over Christmas. I won't bore you with the details, but neither of us thought it was going to work out, and now, here we are, six months later. Better than ever."

"Good," I said honestly. I clutched her hand, glad that this wasn't half as awkward as I'd thought it would be. "That's what I want for you and for him."

Harmony beamed. "Thank you, Whitley." She squeezed my hand. "Now, let's talk about this dress. Katherine is determined to do it without you, but I would like some input."

I laughed as I put my head in with Harmony and went over what she was working on for it. It was going to be a feat to get the thing done in time. Adding a wedding dress on top of the work she already had to do was a lot to ask, but Katherine hadn't been lying when she said Harmony owed her. She'd gotten her and Robert together.

Gavin reappeared at some point, pulling me back onto

the dance floor. I leaned into him, more relaxed than I had been since we'd decided to go through with this. Maybe this would all work out, and everything would be fine.

"How'd it go with Robert?"

"He's happy for us," he said, brushing his lips against the top of my head.

I shivered at the touch. I could get used to this intimacy. "Good. Harmony too. They seem happy."

"He does seem smitten," Gavin agreed.

He twirled me around, pulling me back in close. I laughed as he moved me around the rooftop. This was not the kind of dancing I normally associated with Gavin. I was used to a lot more bumping and grinding. It was kind of fun to be whirled around the room like a princess with a partner who knew how to lead.

"I'm still not used to you dancing like this. Who taught you?"

"My mom and aunt love dancing. I'd go over to my cousins', and they'd teach us all their favorite ballroom moves. I was an escort at a significant number of Junior Leagues."

I snorted. "I cannot picture you like that."

"You didn't do big Texas rites of passage?"

"No!"

"Not even a mum?"

I swore. "Fine. I did wear a mum for homecoming. My sophomore year, I dated the Junior League president's son. She made me the most elaborate mum to wear, and I was the envy of the entire school. It was so heavy that it had straps for my shoulders. There were so many bells that it jingled, and you could hear me coming down the hall."

Gavin cackled. "Oh my god, I wish I had seen that. Wait, do your parents have pictures?"

"Don't you dare, King!"

"Ah, come on, Bowen. It's too much fun."

"It was embarrassing. I broke up with him after that and hooked up with his older sister. I was lucky my mom never found out."

"Heartbreaker."

"That's me."

He bent down and stole a kiss.

I startled. "What was that for?"

"Because you're cute."

I narrowed my eyes. "That's not a reason."

"Sure it is," he said easily and then tugged me back out into the dancing.

The best part about being around Gavin was that it was always a riot. I'd always heard that opposites attract, but in this instance, I'd never been more attracted to someone who was so like me.

We danced the night away, drinking with our friends and making the rest of the party laugh with our antics. It was a better night than I'd anticipated. No one seemed skeptical about our arrangement. They all accepted it as if they'd been waiting for it to happen.

One woman, who I only had a vague recollection of, even pulled me aside at the end of the night to say, "I'm so glad that you two have stopped pretending like you're not together."

I gaped at her in confusion. Had everyone thought that we were suited and just never told me?

Gavin went off to have a drink with Court sometime after that, and I found myself alone for the first time all evening. I'd sent Gavin after Robert earlier to smooth things over, but it felt like my turn. He'd been happily at Harmony's side all night, and now, we were both alone. I strode over to where he sat in one of the near-empty booths.

"Hey, you," I said, sliding into the seat across from him. "Warm."

Robert's gaze shifted quickly to me and back to the party beyond. "It is. Summer is officially here in the city."

"How have you been? You and Harmony seem to fit together."

His face split as he searched out his girlfriend, who was standing on the other side of the room with English and Lark. "We do. It's a happy coincidence. Much like you and Gavin."

"You're not mad?"

He finally looked me fully in the face. "Of course I'm not mad. It was wrong of me to react the way I did when I first found out about you two. I'd always known how Gavin felt about you. I should have expected it."

"What do you mean?"

"Well, you know, he's always been in love with you."

I laughed.

He didn't.

"Gavin didn't love me back then. We were a fling, Robert. I assure you, it was nothing like that."

Robert shot me a skeptical look. "You know, I asked him about you before you and I got together."

"I didn't know that."

"Oh, yeah. He was into you. I knew before anyone. I asked if he was ever going to make a move or if I could."

"He never made a move. So, you must have been off base."

"Nah. He laughed it off and gave me his blessing. Said neither of you would ever settle down, but good luck to me."

Robert shook his head. "I should have taken him at face value. Since you never would settle down with me."

I winced. "That had nothing to do with you."

"I know. Trust me, by now, I know." He shrugged and leaned back into his seat with a sigh. "You and Gavin are perfect for each other. So, if you've finally figured that out, I'm glad you're both agreeing to settle down."

Something like panic settled in my bones at those words. But I quickly laughed it off. Gavin hadn't loved me then. He wouldn't have told Robert to go for it if he'd been that into me. We were trying this out now, and I could admit that I was deeply enjoying what exactly being with Gavin King meant.

But that didn't mean that pesky L-word had to get involved in all of this. I'd never said it to anyone. I couldn't imagine Gavin saying it to anyone either.

Robert just grinned at me. "Truly, Whit, I'm glad you're happy."

"Thanks." I stood, prepared to walk away from the conversation. Then, I closed my eyes, sighed, and turned back to him. "I am sorry about what happened before. I didn't want to hurt you."

"Thank you. It's okay. We're both past that now, but I appreciate it."

I smiled down at him and then left with a huge weight lifting off my shoulders. I'd spent my whole life burning bridges. It was nice to know that I hadn't completely fucked this one up. That we could all still interact after this.

Gavin wrapped his arms around me as soon as he found me. "What were you two getting up to?" If I didn't know better, there might have been worry in his voice.

"Nothing," I said, taking his hand and tugging him toward the exit. "Let's get out of here."

"Oh?"

I arched an eyebrow at him. "I believe we're newly engaged, and that means we can leave anytime we'd like."

He laughed and let me drag him away. We were in a car, heading toward our building soon enough, and then out onto the New York City streets again.

"Your place or mine?" I teased.

"Mine," he growled, dragging my lips against his as he crushed me against the mirror in the elevator.

I fumbled for the buttons and pressed his floor as we made out while riding up to nearly the top of the building. He lifted me up, wrapping my legs around his waist as he carried me across the hall to his door. He inserted the key, twisted the knob, and let us inside.

Clothes were strewn all over the floor on the way to his bedroom. His hands were in my hair. His lips on my super-heated skin. Breathless, back-arching, toe-curling moments passed as he got me into the room. His cock was in my hand. I pumped him as he groaned against me. Our lips met, wet and desperate. The last couple of hours had risen our desire to a crescendo.

Finally, he gave up with the teasing and turned me around, pressing me down into the mattress. I groaned as his fingers found the entrance of my pussy. He slipped two inside with ease.

I moaned as the words, "So wet," slipped free from him. "Please."

Foil tore. A silent moment of anticipation as he rolled a condom down his length. Then, he thrust his way inside my welcoming body. I cried out. He hadn't been gentle, and, fuck, I didn't want him to be.

His hand fisted into my hair, arching my head backward and giving him better leverage to drive deeper into me.

"Is this what you wanted?" he asked into the darkness.

"More."

And he gave me more. Until we were both sweaty, panting messes. Until I was so close to climax that I was seeing stars. Until there was nothing but want, need, and desire. This was just a dream of a second, of infinity. Nothing more, nothing less than eternity stretching out as he stretched me out.

Then, we both tipped into that deep abyss and gave over everything to that need. My walls contracted so hard that it was nearly painful as everything shuddered with relief. Gavin roared with his pleasure, emptying himself deep inside of me.

I gasped when he slid out a moment later and collapsed forward onto the bed. Gavin returned soon after and lifted me under the sheets, holding my still-trembling body.

He trailed kisses down my neck and across my shoulder. "You were perfect."

"Mmm," I groaned, halfway to sleep.

"My little pixie."

I snuggled deeper against him as the day slowly came back to me. "Gavin?"

"Hmm?"

"Did Robert ask you if he could date me before we dated?"

He stilled momentarily. "He did. Did he tell you that?"

"He said that you loved me, and he knew it. So, he asked your permission."

Gavin was silent a beat too long. "Well, it wasn't permission. So much as he told me he was going to ask you out if I didn't man up and do it first."

"But you didn't."

"No, I didn't." He ran a hand up and down my back. "Would you have taken me seriously back then?"

"Hmm," I said, as if contemplating it. Thinking of the Gavin King who was as wild and unrepentant as I was assured me that it wouldn't work. He didn't seem that way right now though. "Probably not. I didn't take much seriously."

"Yeah," he said softly. "That's what I figured."

"Love complicates things anyway," I told him.

"Indeed."

"I've never told anyone I love them," I admitted into the darkness. "Have you?"

He pressed a kiss into my shoulder blade. "No."

I relaxed at that word. We were the same. And that was for the better. We understood each other. I didn't want to complicate this. I wanted it to be as perfect as it was right in this moment.

I was almost asleep when I swore I heard Gavin say, "But I intend to tell you."

But I was sure that couldn't have been right.

PART IV

CHASING RAINBOWS

21

WHITLEY

"Dr. Bowen," the receptionist called, stepping into my office, "your fiancé is here."

Her cheeks dimpled with excitement, and she looked a little dazed. Gavin must have worked his charm on her.

"Thank you, Lucinda. I'll be right out."

I put off what I had been working on, grabbed my purse, and stepped into the hallway. My boss, Dr. Kevin Varma, entered from the next office over.

"What is this I hear? He's here? Do I get to meet the fiancé finally?"

"He's here," I confirmed. "Try not to scare him away."

Varma laughed. "I haven't scared away any of my sons-in-law, and this one will be as good as my son as well. As you are my daughter by everything but birth."

I glowed at that assessment. It was one of the reasons that I'd moved home. Yes, he was paying me an astronomical amount, but I felt like family here.

"Fine. Come on. Let me introduce you."

I strode down the hallway and out into the waiting room. Gavin stood there with a bouquet of summer flowers in a riot of color to match my new hairstyle. I'd gone for an almost mermaid level of rainbow. Teal moved into blue, moved into green, and down into a deep dark purple to my cotton-candy pink. I loved it. The fact that Gavin would think to get me a bouquet of roses in the same color pattern made my heart do an unexpected flip.

"Hey, stranger," I said with a grin.

He'd been in Midland for the last couple of days for work, and I could admit that I'd missed him. I'd *really* missed him.

He tugged me in close and brushed a needy kiss on my lips. "Hey, you. Miss me?"

I snagged the flowers from him. "Maybe." I held the flowers to my nose to hide my secret smile and turned to Dr. Varma. "Gavin, I've been meaning to introduce you. This is Dr. Varma."

"Please call me Kevin," Dr. Varma said, offering his hand and shaking Gavin's energetically. "It is a pleasure to meet you. It is a great honor to meet the man who thinks that he can tame a lion."

We both laughed. "He's not taming me."

"I truly am not," Gavin said easily. "I like her just the way she is."

"Bless you," Kevin said with a chuckle. "You will always have your hands full."

Gavin winked at me. "I intend to."

I flushed and tried to roll my eyes through it. "You two are obnoxious."

"She likes us that way," Kevin said jovially. "Now, I assume you're here to take her to lunch. Hand me those flowers, and I will find a place for them."

I passed them to him. "Are you sure?"

"Get out of here before I change my mind. I remember being young and in love. Go."

I held my hands up in surrender and followed Gavin to the elevator. "You know, you could have sent a text that you were back."

"What? And miss getting to make your receptionist nearly faint? And meet your boss? Please. This was way more fun." I poked at him, and he snagged my hand, kissing it. "Act like you don't like it."

But I did. I did like it. We'd only been officially dating for a few weeks. I'd only been back in New York for a matter of months. Still, my world felt upside down. Yes, we were having a fake wedding. But the very *real* dating, the very *real* wooing, was utterly unexpected. I liked every bit of that.

Gavin stopped at a sandwich place, and we grabbed things to go, heading into Central Park.

"While I have you," I said after chewing a nice giant bite of my lox on an everything bagel, "I have some things we need to nail down."

"Oh? Like you?"

I rolled my eyes at him. "I wish. That'd be more enjoyable than wedding planning."

"I thought the girls were in charge of most of it."

"They are. Most of it. Which means I still have some decisions to make."

The only thing we'd really talked about for the wedding before he left for Midland was how we were going to pay for it. I insisted, since it was my wedding, I would foot the bill. Plus, my parents had a wedding fund for me. But he scoffed at the suggestion and said he was paying. No questions.

It was a tremendous argument, but in the end, he won. I didn't even know how it had happened. I never let anyone win in an argument, and yet Gavin had. He'd pushed me into this with the fake proposal. He'd suggested we go through with this. He was more at fault than I was for this turning out this way. And anyway, he had more money. Like a lot more money. And he argued, if I didn't let him, he would probably pay everyone before I could get there.

So, I'd conceded. Bastard.

"Okay, English already decided on the color pattern. We're going to figure out bridesmaid dresses. I'm having English as my maid of honor, Katherine and Lark as my bridesmaids. You'll need three groomsmen."

"Done. I'm going to have Court as my best man, Camden and Sam as my groomsmen."

I checked that off my list. I'd already figured but thought I might as well ask.

We went through the rest of the long list English had given to me. It was easier, walking through the gardens and sitting by the lake, discussing it with Gavin, than doing it at home, alone. It was definitely more fun.

"Okay, last item," I told him. "We need to figure out a prenup."

He did a double take. "What?"

I blinked. "What?"

"*What*?" he repeated.

"I don't know what you're what-ing," I said with a laugh. "A prenup. You know, a legal document that says the money you had before the wedding and the money I had before the wedding stay separate if we divorce."

"I know what a prenup is. I've never met a woman who wanted one."

I arched an eyebrow at him. "I don't want your money."

"I know, but ..."

"But what? A prenup is just a legal agreement that we're not going to be dicks about the money we made before we decided to make our own shit legal. It's not a big deal. Why do people make it a big deal?"

"Guess I was only dating gold diggers," he joked.

But I could see that he was actually put out by this. He'd been made to think that even asking for one was a horrible idea. I could see it all over him.

"Did Margaret and Locke have one?"

"Yeah, but ... that was different."

"How?"

He shrugged. "It doesn't matter. You're sure about this?"

"I'm frankly shocked you would marry someone without one."

"No, no, I want one. I'd just never thought that someone I was marrying would suggest it."

I shot him a mystified look. "You really have been dating the worst sort of people, haven't you?"

He grinned and tugged me in for another kiss. "Not anymore."

I swatted at him, but that thing happened in my stomach again. "Oh, shush. Do you want me to get a lawyer, or do you have one on staff?"

"I know a guy."

"Good. Do the thing, so I can mark it off the list."

"Yes, ma'am."

"Don't *ma'am* me," I said, wrinkling my nose at him.

He laughed and threaded our fingers together as we headed back toward his work. "You can call me sir." He winked at me. "In bed."

"Yes, I gathered that's what you were referring too," I said with a shake of my head. But I was smiling ... and considering it.

When we made it back to my work, Gavin drew me in for another long kiss. "I missed you while I was gone."

"Well, I am very missable."

"You are. And my mom and aunt say hi. They're excited for the wedding. Mom wanted to throw you a bridal shower in Midland, but there's not a lot of time."

I bit my lip. "Is it a faux pas to accept a bridal shower for a fake wedding?"

"It's still a real wedding, Whit." He curled a lock of rainbow hair around a finger. "I'd take you with me if you wanted to do it."

"Put it on the list." I hadn't thought about things like bridal showers. I loved his family. I'd rather do one there than with my family and their friends.

"We could go to Dallas after that to check on your dad too," he suggested.

I swallowed and nodded. "Okay. Maybe."

"And I have another request."

"What else?" I asked with fake exasperation.

"The opening of the summer season in the Hamptons is next weekend."

"So?"

"So ... Camden has a house, and normally, I show up whenever I can get drunk. But I thought we could go. Think a vineyard event and a cupcake gala for LGBTQ+ youth and beach parties."

I snorted. "That's not really my scene."

He leaned into me and ran his thumb along my bottom lip. "Bonfires and late-night pool dips and sex in Camden's mansion."

"Now, you're speaking my language."

"It could be fun. Just me and you and the high society of Manhattan on vacation."

"You have a way of making it sound appealing and

ridiculous." I touched my hair. "They're all going to sneer at the rainbow."

"So what? Like we care what anyone else thinks. Come get drunk and have lots of sex with me all over the Hamptons."

I couldn't help it. I laughed. "Fine. You win. I'll go with you. But if someone acts like a bitch, I'm probably going to get in a fight."

"And I'll be there to back up my feisty little pixie. But since we're staying with the king and queen of the Upper East Side, no one will say anything ... to your face at least."

"Real reassuring, King."

"You've already agreed. Pack a bag. We're going."

"Fine."

He kissed me again, long and hard. "I like winning. It's fun."

"Get out of here before I change my mind."

Still, he kissed me again. "I really did miss you."

Then, he stepped back onto the sidewalk and headed to work. My stomach flipped traitorously.

What was Gavin King doing to me?

22

GAVIN

Opening the social season in the Hamptons was a pastime that I didn't think could be improved. Then, I stashed Whitley Bowen in the passenger seat of my black Jaguar convertible with the top down and blasted music, and we sang at the tops of our lungs the entire way out of the city. Her sweet voice the tune for the drive. Her mermaid hair blew wild and free as we turned toward the Hamptons.

"You've really never been here for the start of the season?" I asked her as we crawled through the busy streets in Friday afternoon traffic.

"Never. I've been out here a few times over the summer, but I usually decide to work instead."

"You'll love it. Bringing Manhattan to the Hamptons is always a treat."

"If it's all the same people, I don't get what the big deal is."

"Mostly to escape the oppressive city heat and retreat away from the peons."

She snorted. "You're an elitist dick."

"Joking," I said with a wicked grin. "It's just nice to go to the beach and party away from work."

"Fair." She stuck her hand out the side of the window and wove it through the air. "It is beautiful out today."

My gaze swept over her. She *was* beautiful. Over the last couple of weeks that I had gotten to spend alone with Whitley, my already-unprecedented need for her had only grown. The look on her face when I spent a few days out of town had proven to me that she felt the same. Even if she wasn't ready to admit as such. She'd told me she missed me, and that had felt like a step in the right direction.

When we finally reached our turn, I pulled off the road, drove up to the gated house, and entered the code. The gates slowly withdrew to reveal the Percy property. I'd long since given up on being awed by the extravagance of the Upper East Side, but this house was giant, even for a Texas home. In the Hamptons, it had to be worth tens of millions.

I parked out front and popped the trunk. Whitley took her time, surveying the house as I dragged our two suitcases out of the back. I snapped the trunk shut, and she jolted back to reality.

"I can take mine." She held her hand out.

"Don't worry about it. Get the door."

She jogged forward and pushed open the enormous door that led into a foyer. Katherine and Camden must not have been too far in front of us because there was still staff running around, preparing rooms and finishing their dusting. Katherine looked annoyed as she held her son, Beckett, in her arms. Their two-year-old daughter, Helena, was the spitting image of her mother. She held the hand of their nanny and turned with excited eyes as Whitley and I came inside.

"Aunt Whit!" Helena said, throwing herself into Whitley's arms.

"Hey, punkin." Whitley hoisted her up onto her hip and bounced her. "How are you getting this big? I can barely hold you."

"Tell me about it," Katherine grumbled. "They both are growing so fast. That's what I get for having Camden's giant children."

Helena just beamed. "I'm so big because I have a giant brain, and I'm going to be a genius."

"Is that so?" Whitley asked. "What are you going to do with your genius? Are you going to be a doctor like your aunt Whit?"

Helena wrinkled her nose. "I don't like blood."

"Oh, that is a requirement generally."

"I could be an astronaut!"

"You could," Whit agreed.

Camden stepped into the foyer like a thunderstorm with a phone pressed to his ear. He waved at us and then kissed his wife. "Can you handle the rest of this? I have to take this call."

"Of course."

"Daddy!" Helena called.

Camden grinned, taken with his daughter. He pressed a kiss to her cheek as well and then disappeared down the hall. Helena's bottom lip stuck out as her daddy left.

"Daddy should come play!" Helena decided.

Katherine smoothed her dark hair. "Daddy has to work. You can go play with Nanny Kimberly or see if you can cajole Aunt Whit into it."

Helena dropped down, wobbly on her two feet, and looked between Kimberly and Whit. "Both!"

Kimberly smiled at us. She was young, maybe her early

twenties at most, with shoulder-length blonde hair and kind, clear eyes. She didn't seem to be the kind of person Katherine would be okay with hiring.

"I can take her upstairs. You don't have to come," Kimberly told Whitley.

"I want to." Then, Whitley had Helena's hand in hers, and they traipsed upstairs.

"All right," Kimberly said. "Would you like me to take Beckett too?"

Katherine shook her head. "I'll hold him. He's almost asleep anyway. If I disturb him, who knows if he'll go down?"

"As you wish." Then, she followed Whitley and Helena upstairs.

"She seems nice," I told her. "A little pretty for a nanny position."

Katherine shot me a devilish grin. "Are you insinuating that my husband has wandering eyes?"

"Not if he wants to keep all of his limbs."

Katherine's smile only widened. "Well, at least you know me. Anyway, Camden has never had interest in the help. Unlike some people." Her face was suddenly furious, and then it disappeared when she looked down at her son. She ran her hand over his tuft of hair. "I trust him."

Which was bold, considering their past problems. But I was happy for them. They seemed to be doing better than ever.

"And you and Whitley?" Katherine asked. "Are you keeping your hands to yourself?"

"With Whitley? Definitely not. She's in my bed every night."

"Good. Keep it that way, King. Or you'll find yourself without certain parts as well."

I winced at those words. "No worries there."

Katherine shot me an assessing look. "You're serious about this, aren't you?"

"Yes," I told her at once.

"Hmm," she said.

"What?"

"Whitley is going to need some convincing. She's been hurt too many times by every person in her life. That laugh and the crazy stories are defense mechanisms. I hope you've realized that."

She arched an eyebrow, and I nodded. I had noticed that. The *bad girlfriend* bit wasn't even close to reality in the weeks we'd been together.

"Do you feel like you're up to the task? Because if you hurt her ..."

"I won't." I couldn't even fathom it at this point. We were finally on the same page. I didn't want to do anything to disrupt that. "I won't," I repeated more firmly.

Katherine nodded, taking that as the promise it was. "I'm going to try to get Beckett down. You have your regular room upstairs. We'll head to the vineyard in a few hours. Feel free to use the house like it's yours."

She headed into the first-floor master bedroom. It was strange to see Katherine as a mother, and it also somehow made perfect sense. Before I'd seen her with her two children, I never would have suspected she'd make a great mother. She'd never been the mothering type, but she was absolutely a great mom. And Camden, despite his years of abuse from his own father, was just as amazing. Their love for their children was unconditional.

I hauled the bags upstairs and deposited them into a suite, then went in search of Whitley. She was in the nursery, having a tea party with Kimberly and Helena. I watched for a few minutes, admiring the way that Whitley seemed entirely invested. She glanced up once and saw me watching and then grinned.

I waved her off and headed back to the room. A half hour later, Whit found me on my laptop at the desk in the corner. She wrapped her arms around my neck and pressed a kiss to my cheek. "Hey."

"Hey. How was the tea party?"

"Delightful. Helena is a ball of joy. She wants to come to the vineyard and drink grown-up drinks. Or so she told me."

I laughed. "That sounds right."

"Do you need to work more?"

"No, I'm off the rest of the weekend. Want to tour the house and raid the fridge before we have to go?"

"Absolutely."

I took her hand, and we ran back down the stairs like we were kids. Whitley had stayed at the Kensington house before, but never the Percy home. I did the tour, culminating with the massive pool and hot tub. We took drinks out by the pool and basked in the sun.

"Maybe I could get a house out here. It's the perfect escape."

"It'd be an outrageous expense. The Percys have had this home for generations."

"Well, then I'd be getting it for future generations, right?" I reached for her hand and pressed a kiss to her palm. "Wouldn't you want to come here with me?"

Her eyes went distant for a moment. As if she were thinking about that inexplicable future. Then, they snapped back to reality, and something like fear rocked through them. I was talking about a future that I wanted her to be in. That must have been terrifying.

"I would," she finally said. "I like it here. I always enjoy the water."

There was a *but* on the tip of her tongue, but she never voiced it because Katherine interrupted us by saying it was almost time to go.

We changed into something more presentable for the vineyard. I offered to drive, but Camden insisted we take his black Range Rover. Camden wasn't the type of person who let anyone else have control. I never knew how he had a driver in the city, except that it was a necessity with traffic. No way was Camden Percy taking the subway.

The vineyard was already packed when we arrived. A long table was laden with a vibrant display of flowers. Each place setting had a name written on it for dinner. Fancy wine vintages were offered upon entrance with a tasting of their latest varieties from the vintners available at tables around the venue.

Whitley and I each grabbed a glass—hers white, mine red—and then found our place settings. I startled when I saw that the setting next to mine read *Margaret King*.

"Maggie is here?" I asked in surprise.

"She is?"

I pointed at the table setting as my eyes scanned the room. My cousin was back from the honeymoon—a week on the Amalfi Coast at a five-star villa. But I hadn't seen her since her arrival in New York City, where she now lived full-time with Locke.

"Oh, there she is," Whitley said.

I followed her finger and reared back in confusion. She was with a Locke, but not the one she'd married. Micah Locke stood at her elbow. She laughed at something he said, and he grinned like the weaselly predator I knew him to be.

"That is not Locke," Whit pointed out.

I narrowed my eyes. "No, it's not. Let's go say hi."

Whitley took my hand, and we walked across the vineyard lawn toward my cousin. Margaret startled when she saw us heading toward her. Then, her smile brightened, and she detached herself from Micah's side. She collided with Whitley, giggling and jumping in a circle.

"Oh my god, you're here! I had no idea!" Margaret gasped.

"I'm so glad to see you. Tell me everything," Whitley said. "How was the honeymoon?"

"To die for! Everyone should take a trip to the Amalfi Coast. You'll never want to leave."

"Speaking of, where is your husband?" I asked.

Maggie sighed. "Olympics are two years away, and he took two weeks off for the wedding and honeymoon. He has no time for all of this." She waved her hand at the vineyard. "He needs to be practicing. Qualifiers are coming up faster than anyone could ever imagine. They'll be here in the blink of an eye."

"And that's why you're here with Micah?"

"He was generous enough to offer to take me. Let me introduce you to my friends." She took Whitley's hand and headed toward a gaggle of women nearby.

Micah had just extricated himself from his conversation and was heading my way. He looked nothing like his athletic older brother. Though I knew he'd swam for years too. He'd even gone to college on a swimming scholarship, but at some point, he had gotten tired of the comparisons to Merritt and quit. He worked for the Locke family business now.

"King," Micah said with a glance at Margaret before back at me. "Didn't know you'd be here."

We shook hands, but I got a weird feeling about all of

this. If we were anywhere else, I might take him aside and demand answers. But we were at the start of the season, and there were too many people around. Already, attendees were flocking to Whitley, complimenting her mermaid hair, congratulating her on our engagement, and begging to see her ring.

I decided it didn't matter at that moment. My cousin's story was as complicated as mine was. And if I was going to pretend, then she could too. I just wanted a good time with my fiancée—fake or otherwise.

23

WHITLEY

The next evening, I'd just finished getting ready when I heard English downstairs. I threw on my strappy heeled sandals and hurried downstairs to find English standing there in a long yellow dress.

"You made it!" I cried, pulling English in for a hug.

They were staying at the Kensington house but hadn't been able to make it to the vineyard last night because of some last-minute wedding fiasco. I'd offered to stay, but she'd insisted Gavin and I go to the Hamptons.

"We made it," she said. "Wedding fiasco averted."

"What happened?"

English rolled her eyes. "Nora came into town for a meeting, but when we went through the list of vendors I was working with, we discovered that the old wedding planner had canceled them all."

I gaped at her. "What?"

"Yep. She was less than thrilled that I wasn't using her anymore, and this was her parting gift on the way out."

"Jesus."

"Yes, well, Leslie and I have never been so united."

English had a chilling smile on her face. "Fucking over the mayor of New York was probably not her best move."

"Definitely not, but at least you could tell Leslie *I told you so*."

"Oh, she did," Court said as he strode into the room. "Fabulously, I might add. With real gusto."

English gave him a clever grin. "When I'm right, I'm right."

"I very much doubt my mother will ever forget it."

"She shouldn't." She rose onto her tiptoes and pressed a kiss to her fiancé's mouth.

"And you too, if you know what's good for you," I added.

Court shot me a grin. "Cheeky little shit today, aren't you, Whit? Where's *your* fiancé anyway? I'd like to remind him the same thing and see how he takes it."

"My fiancé already knows who calls the shots."

Court laughed. "That right?"

English elbowed him in the ribs. "Don't antagonize her."

"*Me* antagonize *her*?"

I chuckled as the rest of our party appeared in the foyer, dressed for the gala tonight. Katherine was in a blood-red dress while Lark was in a forest green. The guys were all in crisp black suits.

And then there was me, in a seafoam dress that swirled around my feet like I was a mermaid just stepping out of the water.

Gavin's russet hair shone as he caught sight of me, and his eyes lit up like Christmas morning. "Damn," he groaned.

Then, he swept past his friends and scooped me up, twirling me in place. I swatted at him, as if I didn't enjoy the spectacle.

But it was Camden Percy, of all people, to comment on it. "I'm glad you have stopped pretending you're not dating."

"We weren't pretending ..." Gavin interjected.

Sam gave a disbelieving guffaw.

Court clapped him on the shoulder. "Keep telling yourself that."

Katherine gestured to the door. "Now, let's go before the children realize we're leaving."

Everyone laughed, and we piled into two cars and drove to the seaside venue. We were greeted at the entrance to the glass building with flutes of champagne and little finger food.

I took a cucumber sandwich with reluctance. "I thought this was a cupcake gala."

Gavin snorted and gestured off to the left, where I discovered an entire sculpture of the glass building we were currently standing in, made entirely of cake and cupcakes.

I gawped. "Holy shit."

"You can have cake to your heart's content. But first, dinner."

We were seated at a table with all of our friends. I spotted Margaret at a nearby table in a bright pink dress. Micah Locke on her arm again. They were laughing, and she was making friends with every person nearby, as she had done the previous night.

She hurried over to plant a kiss on my cheek. "Cousin," she said with a laugh.

"Hi, Maggie," I said, turning in my seat to face her. "How was your day?"

"Oh, delightful. The Lockes have a house not far from here. We mostly hung out by the pool all day."

"Sounds nice."

"Also," she said almost conspiratorially, "I heard someone is having a bridal shower back in Midland."

I glanced at Gavin, and he groaned.

"I hadn't confirmed it yet, Maggie."

"Well, Mom told me she was already in full planning mode and that I'm expected to be there. Can I fly with you?"

My cheeks colored. We'd discussed this, and I'd told Gavin to put it on the schedule, but I hadn't really heard that he'd moved forward with the idea.

"You still want to do it, right?" Gavin asked hesitantly.

"Of course she wants to do it," Margaret said, speaking over him.

Gavin arched an eyebrow, and I nodded quickly.

"Yes, let's do it."

"All right," he conceded. "Then, sure. You can fly home with us."

"Excellent. I can't wait," Margaret said. "I'm going to head back to Micah." She waved her fingers at me and then disappeared.

Gavin practically pressed his lips to my ear to ask, "Are you sure?"

On one hand, maybe it was shitty to accept gifts for this wedding. It wasn't real, and it was happening in such a short period of time. But on the other hand, maybe I *wanted* to go. Not that I knew what to think about that, except that I adored his family. I'd never had people in my life like that.

"I'm sure," I finally told him.

He kissed my cheek, and his smile was all genuine. I realized that I liked that too.

A few minutes later, dinner was served, and we all ate the delicious meal prepared by the venue. Cupcakes came later. I couldn't decide between three decadent flavors, and Gavin insisted we get them all. Chocolate chip cookie dough ended up being my favorite. I'd never had it in a cupcake before, and it tasted so much like ice cream that my taste buds were confused that it was cake.

After dinner was cleared, there were a handful of speeches, and then Gavin pulled me onto the dance floor. Again, I had a bunch of people come up to ask about my hair and who my stylist was.

Katherine laughed beside me when one person came back to ask again. "This is fascinating."

"That people like my hair?"

"No, I like your hair. I'd never wear it, but it's so you. It's ridiculous to think that anyone else has a sufficient personality to carry it."

I blinked. "That sounded like a compliment, Katherine."

"Maybe it was."

"Careful, or I'll think you're hitting on me," I told her with a playful wink.

Katherine was obviously straight, but I liked teasing her all the same. I mean, if she had even an inkling of playing for the other team, I would know and be there so fast.

Katherine shot me a bemused look. "See what I mean? Sufficient personality."

"Well, I can't deny that."

"And you and Gavin?"

"What about us?"

Katherine arched an eyebrow, and her lips quirked. "You know exactly what I mean."

I glanced around the room, finding him easily, as he was in a deep discussion with a group of other businessmen. My gaze softened. "I like him. It seems crazy since we were such close friends for so long. I never thought either of us would be serious enough to even try this."

"He seems awfully serious," Katherine added.

"He does. Doesn't he?"

"Yes. How do you feel about that?"

"I thought I'd be terrified, but I sort of like it."

Katherine scowled. "You like how much he likes you, or you find you like him as much as he likes you? Because the first is dangerous territory, Whit. I don't want you to lead my friend on any more than I'd let him break your little damaged heart."

From anyone but Katherine, that would be an insult. But I took it at face value. That was where all of her words came from. And I considered them just as seriously in turn.

"I'm going to Midland with him for a bridal shower."

"Really?" Katherine asked, a note of surprise in her voice.

"I *want* to go. I love his family."

"And him?"

I bit my lip. "Well, I don't like it when he's gone. And I've been having these ... weird feelings."

"Describe them."

"Like, you know, when you hit a big dip in the road. Like swoops in my stomach."

Katherine's grin turned feral. "Butterflies."

I laughed. "No, no, it's not like that. It's like tidal waves. Sometimes, when he says something or kisses me, it's like everything rocks on the open sea."

"Because you like him."

"Yes," I whispered.

"Good." She nodded and patted my shoulder twice. "Good. Now, try not to run away scared, okay?"

Katherine looked me up and down to see whether or not I was being serious. Then, she nodded, as if satisfied, and headed toward her husband, who was walking in our direction.

I didn't know exactly what she must have seen, but it must have convinced her that I wasn't going to run this time. I didn't know what that meant either. But I couldn't actually run anywhere when we were officially getting married in a few weeks. Doing this for my dad was important, and anyway ... I liked my time with Gavin. I liked Gavin.

I sighed and shook my head. Katherine was getting in my head. I didn't need to worry about all of that yet.

I lifted the bottom of my skirt and headed toward the bathroom. The place was massive, and after doing my business, I decided to step outside. Most people were still inside, enjoying the air-conditioning. It was shockingly warm today, even with the sea breeze blowing in off the water.

Pulling my hair off of my back alleviated some of the heat, but it wasn't enough. I was going to have to return to the cooler temperatures as well. As I turned the corner though, I saw a flash of pink.

My brow furrowed as I stepped forward. That looked like Margaret's dress. But why would she be hiding around the corner?

Then, I saw *exactly* what Margaret King was doing.

Micah Locke had her pinned against the side of the building. Her leg was hitched up around his waist, and they were kissing like their lives depended on it.

A gasp escaped me, and I reared back. My hand flew to my chest. My eyes going wide.

Micah jumped back from Margaret, as if he'd been scalded. Margaret looked at me in a state of horror. She'd been married to Merritt Locke for a matter of weeks. They'd just returned from a week on their honeymoon. And now, she was making out with his brother.

"Uh, what the fuck?" I spat.

Margaret leaped forward, pushing Micah behind her. "Oh my god, Whitley. I can't believe you saw that. Please, please, please don't say anything to anyone."

"That's his brother!"

"I know. I know," she said quickly, stumbling forward slightly. Maybe she'd had too much to drink. "It shouldn't have happened, and it'll never happen again. Just please don't tell Gavin."

I glared at her and then to Micah. "Well, what do you have to say for yourself?"

Micah looked between me and Margaret, as if he had no idea what to say. "We're drunk. It was a mistake."

"Then, maybe you shouldn't be staying at this mistake's house," I snapped at Margaret.

Margaret looked close to tears. "You're right. I don't know how this happened." She dabbed at her eyes. "Are you going to tell Gavin?"

"Are you going to go home and tell your husband?"

She bit her lip and nodded. "Yeah. I ... I'll tell Merritt. He'll forgive me. But ... I just ... I don't want the rest of my family to know."

I clenched my hands into fists. I wanted nothing more than to let everyone know what an idiot she was. I'd left relationships for way less than this. I couldn't believe she'd done something so stupid. And Micah seemed ... unrepentant at best.

The whole thing made my head spin. But it also wasn't my place to tell her family what she'd done. If it had happened to me, I would have glitter-bombed the house and let every person know what a douche they were. But ... I was marrying into this family. Whether real or not, this would complicate matters.

"Fine," I grumbled. "But get out of here and go home and text me what Merritt says. I'm not going to be an accomplice to your cheating. If you don't tell him, I will."

Margaret's face paled. She must have seen how sincere I was. "Okay. Yeah. I will. Thanks, Whitley."

I nodded and then hurried away from them, leaving the shattered pieces of their deception behind me. It made me sick to even know about it. Like something slimy was on me. And it was hard to shake, even when I got back to the party and into Gavin's arms once again.

24

GAVIN

Whitley looked flustered when she returned to me. No amount of gentle cajoling could get her to explain what had happened. She just laughed and played it off, quickly changing the subject.

I didn't know what it was about.

But it couldn't be good.

She was stiff in my arms the rest of the night. As if uncomfortable to be there, when she'd been nothing but overly willing since we'd agreed to date. Whoever had said something to her, they'd certainly be hearing from me when I found out what they'd said.

Even Court noticed.

When we finished for the night and were heading back toward the cars, Whitley clung to English's arm and was whispering furtively in her ear.

"What's up with that one?" Court asked.

"I wish I knew," I told him.

"Thought you were getting along."

"We were."

I followed Whitley as she and English took off ahead of

us. English gave her an alarmed look, glanced back at me, and then pulled her closer to her.

Great. Just great.

What the hell was that about?

"So, what did you do?"

"Do?" I demanded. "I didn't do anything."

Court snorted. "I highly doubt that. What else could have happened?"

"I don't know."

I'd thought she was being strange, but I hadn't put much more thought into it. There had been at least one or two ex-flings at the event. It was an occupational hazard at this point. I had been a serial dater, but Whitley knew that, and she'd never cared before.

"I'm sure I had a few exes there."

Court laughed and clapped me on the back. "You must truly be that deep with Whit if you didn't even notice who else was there."

"Who was there?"

"Marissa."

"Who?" I asked, mystified.

Court shook his head. "Fuck, dude. The model you took to my engagement party."

"Oh. Right. No, I remember her." I did remember sending her home and never talking to her again. "What about her?"

"She was eye-fucking you all night."

"So? Whitley isn't going to be upset about that."

"Maybe not, but she was part of the group of people you were talking to for at least a half hour earlier."

I blinked. I had no recollection of this. "What are you talking about?"

Court just shook his head and pointed at the car. "Get in. You're a goner."

I wanted to ask more questions. Did Whitley think that I'd been hitting on someone else? That didn't sound like Whitley. Not when our relationship had started by pointing out the attractiveness of everyone else in the room.

That was beside that point. I hadn't even noticed Marissa in the crowd or apparently her being in my vicinity for a long stretch of time. Surely, it wasn't something this ridiculous. I'd have to clear this up with Whit because I hated the sudden strain when everything had always been so easy with us.

I piled into the car, taking the backseat next to her. I slung an arm across her shoulders, and she settled her head against my chest. Nothing seemed out of the ordinary as we drove the narrow lanes back to the Percy house.

Katherine and Camden hurried inside to see the kids. Whitley was hot on their heels when I grabbed her hand.

"Hey," I said, pulling her against me. "Come down to the beach with me."

"I'm kind of tired," she said with a yawn.

"We'll bring blankets. You can nap out there."

She bit her lip. "I was just going to pass out."

"Come on," I said with a laugh, tugging her closer and running my thumb across her bottom lip. "What happened to having sex with me all over the Hamptons?"

She rolled her eyes at me, but I watched the tension leave her shoulders. "You sure know how to charm a girl."

I flashed her a wicked grin. "What can I say? Charm is my middle name."

Her lips tilted upward and she had a devious look in her eyes. "Fine. But let me change first."

"Nope," I said, drawing her toward the back door. "Booze

and blankets are all we need."

She opened her mouth to object, but I was already rummaging through the hall closet. I found two giant blankets, and she took one out of my hands. I used the other hand to loosen my tie as we headed into the kitchen. I dumped a few beers into a cooler and hoisted it over my shoulder.

Then, I took her hand and headed outside, past the pool and down toward the sand beyond. I spread the blankets out. Whitley hiked her dress up to her knees and sank down. I dropped my jacket, rolled my sleeves up to my elbows, and took the seat next to her.

I passed her a beer, which she took gratefully. While we both took swigs of the drinks, our gazes swept out to the dark sea beyond and the clear view of the stars. I could never see the stars in the city. The Hamptons still weren't close to what I could see from Texas, but it felt a sliver closer to home. Big, vast, and eternal.

"This is nice," she said finally.

"Thought you might like it."

She shot me a rueful smile. "I really was tired. I could curl up right here and sleep the night away."

"You might wake up with sand all over you," I said with a laugh.

"Worth it."

She moved her rainbow hair over to one shoulder and then lay fully back on the blanket. Her eyes were still wide open, staring up at the endless night sky. I couldn't tear my eyes away from her. There was a whole wide world out there, but she was the most beautiful thing I'd ever seen.

"You're staring at me," she pointed out.

I chuckled, ditching my finished beer and coming onto my side next to her. "Wondering how I got so lucky."

"You fake proposed."

"This doesn't feel fake."

"No," she whispered, but she sat up, hugging her torso.

I sighed and sat up too. "What's going on? You've been off for hours."

"Nothing," she said automatically.

"Is it about … Marissa?" I asked hesitantly. "Because I didn't have feelings for her on the one date we went on and didn't even notice her tonight until Court mentioned it."

Whitley shot me a strange look. "Who is Marissa?"

I shrugged. "Some girl I went on one date with."

"Why would I care about her?"

I laughed. "I really have no idea. That's what I get for listening to Court Kensington. I told him you wouldn't care. You'd probably be the one to point out who the hot people were in the room."

"That does sound like me."

"Well, good. I thought I was losing my mind when he mentioned it. I swore I knew you better than that."

She tilted her head, as if contemplating exactly what to say to that. "You're not looking at anyone else?"

"What?" I asked in disbelief. "Of course not. Are you?"

"No, but we really hadn't said …"

"I told you I wanted to try this. I didn't think I had to get more exclusive than a ring on your finger."

She nodded, a pure Whit smile on her face. "Fair."

"So, are you going to tell me what's been up tonight?"

"I don't know, Gavin. Something weird happened, but I shouldn't have let it bother me that much." She bit her lip and looked down.

I wanted to ask what *exactly* had happened, but I wanted her to get it out in her own time. I squeezed her side and pressed a kiss to her temple. "What's going on up there?"

She leaned her weight into me again, as if she were surrendering to this conversation. "I can't stop thinking about my dad."

She hadn't said more than a word about her dad since that night she'd first found out about his diagnosis and cried in my arms. It was as if she had to compartmentalize what had happened so that she could survive. I didn't blame her one bit, but I was happy to talk to her about it.

"I've been purposely not thinking about the *why* of our sudden marriage. It's easier to check lists and make plans than to think about what comes *after*."

"That's understandable."

"Is it?" She looked so small. "It feels like I don't want to look at what's happening. I don't even want to talk to my parents. I don't want to find out what's going on. There's no way for me to fix it. Even if I'd gone into the right medical field."

"Where you'd have been miserable," I reminded her.

Her eyes met mine again, and she softened. "That's true. I chose what I liked, but there's so much what-if."

"You can't live in a what-if world. You can only live in reality."

"That's no fun. I want to be a fairy princess and use magic to make all my problems go away."

"Does that make me your dark fairy prince?"

She rolled her eyes. "No. You're a King, obviously."

Then, we both burst into laughter. The mood lightened considerably. Whatever lingering weirdness that had clouded our interactions was dispelled. I didn't know what had happened at the gala tonight, but my Whitley was back.

As I leaned her back into the sand, kissing her breathless, I was glad for whatever had brought her into my life again.

25

WHITLEY

ood news and bad news.

Good news: Margaret told Locke. So, I didn't have to.

Bad news: That meant I couldn't tell Gavin.

I had never been a good secret keeper. Especially not from someone I was actively sleeping with and spending almost all of my waking moments with. I'd gotten away with talking about my dad in the Hamptons to cover my unease about his cheating scumbag of a cousin, but I wasn't going to lie to him either. No matter what I'd promised Margaret.

Luck won out though. I wasn't sure if Margaret was too embarrassed by what had happened or worried that her family would find out, but she backed out of my bridal shower. Gavin thought I'd be sad when he told me the news, but I could barely hide my relief.

"She said she wanted to hang out with Locke this weekend instead," he said with a shrug. "Newlyweds, you know?"

"Good," I said automatically. "She should."

She needed to do a lot more to repair her marriage than

stay home one weekend, but it wasn't my marriage to deal with. I would have left her ass so fast and blown up her entire life on the way out.

But that was the old Whitley. I was trying for something new here. And it was fucking hard to keep my mouth shut and let people deal with their own bullshit.

With Margaret's absence, the flight to Midland was bliss. I'd been dreading being in her uninterrupted presence for four hours. I wasn't sure I would have been able to keep it together on that flight if she'd been there. He'd already suspected something was wrong anyway. And now, I got Gavin all to myself.

When we landed on the tarmac, it was a boiling hundred degrees. Gavin insisted on wheeling both of our bags toward the awaiting black car. He'd gotten us a room at the same hotel we'd stayed in for the wedding.

I changed into a white tulle dress, going full tilt for the theme, and did a twirl for him. "Well?"

He rose from the chair he'd sunk into earlier to answer an email. "Is this anything like your dress?"

"I have no idea. I haven't seen it yet."

He laughed. "What? How is that possible?"

"Katherine and Harmony are working together. Harmony designing and Katherine … giving her input."

"That's the most Katherine thing I've ever heard."

"I did give them all permission to take over. I have a fitting sometime after we get back. So, I'll see it then."

"What if you hate it?"

I shot him a skeptical look. "Between Katherine and Harmony? There's no chance I'll hate it."

He stepped forward, sliding his arms around my waist. "Well, I'll like it either way. I like this one. You could just wear this."

"One, I would not deprive Katherine the opportunity to be in charge. Two, this is just a fun dress. Not wedding material anyway."

"Whatever you wear is wedding material."

Then he kissed me, so I had no opportunity to respond. My brain sputtered at those words, short-circuiting as I tried to process them. And for some reason ... I wasn't even upset to hear them. In fact, something shifted in my stomach again, almost like pleasure. Did I want Gavin King to think I was marriage material?

"If we didn't have somewhere to be," Gavin said with a grin when he pulled back.

"Do we have somewhere to be?"

He laughed. "Unfortunately. Come on. I got a text from Trey that they left a car for me downstairs."

I pouted but relented when he pulled me toward the door.

We took the elevator downstairs and out into the Texas heat. I was already fanning myself as we stepped outside to find a black lifted truck waiting for us. Gavin shook his head.

"Of course he did," he grumbled under his breath.

"Please tell me that he left you a hat too."

Gavin popped open the front door, and to my delight, a cowboy hat was waiting for him. "Fuck."

"Put it on. Put it on!" I cheered.

"You're serious? You want to see me in this thing?"

"Hey, I'm hot for cowboy." I winked. "Plus, I have to take pics to send to all of our friends."

"No fucking chance," he said, but he put the hat on as soon as we climbed inside.

I did take a picture of him in the hat and then immediately made it my contact picture for him. "There." I showed him what I'd done. "Now, a cowboy will show up every time you text or call me."

Gavin looked at the picture and sighed. "Fine. You win."

"I like winning."

"Don't I know it." His signature smirk returned. "Maybe if you're lucky, I'll let you see me in just the hat."

I nearly choked. The visual he'd delivered was unparalleled. I'd never known how much I wanted that until just then. I shifted my leg over top of the other to hold back the pulsing from my lower half. We definitely should have had a quickie before heading over to his aunt's.

He grinned wider and moved his hand to my bare thigh. As his hand crept ever higher, I swatted at him.

"Not fair."

He laughed. "Oh, come on. I can tell you want it."

"I wanted it back in the hotel room, not in the car."

"As if it'd be the first time you hooked up in a car."

"No, but we are three minutes from your aunt's house."

"And?"

"You're the devil, Gavin King."

He smirked and slid his hand up higher. "At your service."

I swatted him away again, but he grabbed my hand this time and linked our fingers together. My heart thumped noisily in my chest at the gesture. It was so loud that I swore he could hear it. But he just shot me that lopsided grin and then kept my hand secure in his. Like I was his. Like we belonged like this.

I let my giddy smile show as we pulled up to the insane King mansion on the outskirts of Midland. Even though I'd seen the three-story structure on our last trip here, somehow, it seemed even more ostentatious than before. The white roses were everywhere, lush and lovely.

Gavin parked out front, and then we both hopped out of the truck. Malcolm, Trey, and Nate were standing outside, each with a beer in hand.

Nate leaned against the front railing and whistled. "Well, well, well, what do we have here? Does Gav finally remember his roots?"

Trey laughed next to him. "I left it, just in case."

Malcolm drained the rest of his beer and set it down on the railing. He strode down the steps and met us at the entrance. He offered his hand to Gavin and tipped his own hat at me.

"Pleasure to have y'all back in town."

Gavin grinned. "Glad to be back."

Mal's eyes found mine, and I froze under his intense gaze. The first time I'd met him, I'd known he had this unmistakable energy. Like the room was charged around him. Like *he* was in charge of everything around him. And I felt it again then. As if he could see beyond what Gavin and I were to the core of our relationship. Then, he cocked a smile in my direction, and I relaxed. We'd been weighed and judged, and he approved. Somehow, Malcolm's approval meant something.

"Come on inside, Whit," he said, gesturing to the front door. "The ladies have taken it upon themselves to throw quite an event for you. Don't mind us as we steal Gavin."

I arched an eyebrow at Gavin. "What trouble are y'all getting into?"

"Don't you worry about that," Malcolm said. "We'll take care of him."

"We're going riding, aren't we?" Gavin guessed.

"Hell yes," Nate said.

"We'll see you after," Trey said with mischief in his eyes.

I laughed and waved Gavin away. A day of drinking and

horse riding with his cousins was probably just what he needed now that he was away from the city.

"Have fun."

I strode inside to find the house even more magnificent than last time. White, gold, and silver balloons delivered an incredible archway with *Congratulations, Bride!* in big gold letters with a massive inflated diamond ring. Flowers covered every other available space. As if Gavin's aunt Susannah had taken her entire garden and brought it inside for the event.

Susannah was the first to greet me. "Whitley, you made it! We're so happy to welcome you today."

Tears pricked uncomfortably at my eyes as she hugged me. I'd felt immediately like I belonged with Gavin's family when I met them the first time. But I'd been the fake fiancée then, and now ... well, now, I wasn't quite a fake bride-to-be. Things were starting to feel really *real*.

Gavin's mom, Julianne, pulled me into a hug next. "My future daughter-in-law." She put me at arm's length. "You're more beautiful every day."

"This hair," Susannah said, gesturing at my rainbow hair. "It suits you."

"You're not a natural blonde, are you, honey?" Julianne asked about the color I'd been the last time I was here.

"You'll be shocked to hear that I'm not a natural rainbow either."

Both women laughed and gestured for me to join the group. I took a seat next to Margaret's younger sister, Cora. She beamed at me and showed me the paper plate she had in her hand.

"It's for your rehearsal bouquet," she explained. "I'll add all the ribbons from the gifts to it, and then you'll walk down the aisle at the rehearsal with this bouquet."

"What a cute idea."

Cora grinned. "I'm glad to be here. Especially since Maggie canceled at the last minute."

My smile wavered. "Yes, that was unfortunate."

"That's Maggie."

Susannah put her hand on my shoulder. "Can I get you refreshments or anything before we get started? I'm just so happy that you let me do this. I love to throw a big party. And you already feel like family."

"Thank you, Susannah. That's so sweet."

"Not that she gave you a lot of time, Sue," Julianne said with a laugh. "This is a quick wedding."

I flushed at the comment. "Well, when you know, you know, right?"

"That's right. And how couldn't someone know with your son, Jules?" Susannah asked, cocking an eyebrow.

They exchanged looks that said they had already talked about this and agreed not to bring it up.

"We're beyond excited. No matter the timeline," Julianne said.

Susannah nodded once. "Now, refreshments?"

<hr>

The bridal shower was way longer than I'd thought it would be, but I had a good time and got more gifts from the women Susannah had invited than I ever could have imagined. Everything would have to be packed and shipped to New York. Something Susannah insisted on taking care of.

Cora tugged me away from all of her mother's friends and out onto the back patio. "Phew! Glad to be done with that."

"Oh, come on. It was fun."

"Yeah, but not when the boys get to be off drinking at the barn." Cora grabbed my arm. "Let's go."

"Go where exactly?" I asked as I hurried after her.

She grinned at me and then rushed over to the stables. "You know how to ride, right?"

"I have been on a horse."

"You can take Mom's horse, Tabby. She's real easy tempered. It'll be fine." She gestured to a bin. "We keep extra stuff over there. I'm sure there're some boots that will fit you."

As she began to saddle the horses, I went through the boots until I found a pair that were just a little big, but I had small pixie feet, so that wasn't surprising. I also found a pair of leggings, which I slid on under my white dress. Cora was already in biker shorts, so she was good.

Cora helped me onto Tabby's saddle, and then we were off. I had some experience with riding, but I was far from accomplished. Thankfully, Cora was right about Tabby. She followed along behind Cora, and I didn't have to do much of anything.

The trail ran through a copse of trees before leveling out to the flat West Texas shrubbery that I was more accustomed to.

"Sort of beautiful out here."

"You get used to it at least," Cora said with a laugh. "Sometimes, we take the horses out to the state parks, and I'm always so mesmerized by all the greenery. Wish we had it here too."

"I get that. I live in a giant steel city."

"True. But you and Gavin must love it up there. I can't imagine him moving back."

"Me either. He belongs up there." Then, I bit my lip. "But he sort of belongs here too."

"He's a chameleon. He can belong anywhere."

That was a trait we had in common. It was a little disorienting to hear someone voice it out loud.

Cora glanced over at me. "Do you see much of Maggie?"

"Uh, some. We saw each other in the Hamptons."

Cora shook her head, bit her lip, and then seemed to come to a decision. "Does she seem ... happy?"

"Uh ... why do you ask?"

"Well, you know," Cora muttered. She glanced over at me nervously once. "I'm sure Gavin told you, right? About the arranged marriage?"

Somehow, I managed not to sputter in shock. Arranged marriage? Locke and Margaret had been *arranged*? Fuck.

Well, that explained ... a lot. Like why she was hooking up with his brother. And why she hadn't seemed to care when I forced her to tell Locke what was going on. And pretty much everything else.

But why hadn't Gavin told me?

"Shit. He didn't tell you?" Cora asked, correctly interpreting my silence.

"Not exactly."

"Shit. I wasn't supposed to say anything, but I've been so worried about her. She agreed to go through with it but, in classic Maggie fashion, didn't think any of it through, and she won't respond to my messages when I ask."

"Wow. Well, that's a lot. I'm sure she's just adjusting to her new life."

Which was the understatement of the century, considering what I'd seen Maggie getting involved in.

"Probably. Will you look out for her? I think she's maybe in over her head."

"Yeah. I'll do what I can."

We lapsed into silence as my thoughts roared with unanswered questions. Thankfully, after a few more minutes, when my legs were just beginning to get sore, a barn became visible on the horizon. A speck and then a house and then a colossal structure in the middle of nowhere, illuminated from within by bright lights, with a few hitching posts on the outside.

Cora dismounted once we reached a post, and after Cora helped me dismount, she tied the horses up.

"We used to come out here all the time as kids," she said, drawing me toward the barn. "Now, it's like a man cave. You'll see."

She tugged the heavy door open and revealed the massive interior of the barn. There were two pool tables at the back of the space, a full kitchen and bar on one side, along with darts, a dance space, and multiple enormous televisions for watching the game. Not to mention, a fully fitted loft up a short flight of stairs.

The guys turned in unison at our entrance. Gavin's face lit up at my appearance, and he extracted himself from the game of pool he'd been playing to pick me up around the middle and kiss me hard and fast.

I laughed at his exuberance while his cousins whistled.

"Rack 'em up," Cora said with a keen grin. "I'm in."

"Fuck. We're all finished," Nate grumbled.

"You're the one who taught me," Cora reminded him.

"Yeah. Clearly a mistake."

I laughed with everyone else, but Gavin still had eyes only for me.

"Hey, can we go somewhere private to talk?"

He shot me a quizzical look but nodded before taking my hand and leading me out of the barn. We headed over to the horses. Gavin fished an apple out of a bucket and fed it to the horse he'd ridden over here.

"Everything all right?" he asked, concern suddenly coming into his voice.

I couldn't hold it in a second longer. "Why didn't you tell me that Maggie and Locke's marriage was arranged?"

Gavin froze. "Who told you?"

"Cora. She was concerned for Maggie. And for good reason, considering I saw Maggie hooking up with Micah Locke in the Hamptons! I made a huge deal out of it. She had to tell Locke what happened. It's probably the reason she isn't here. I had no idea it wasn't a big deal since she begged me not to tell you."

Gavin's green eyes went shockingly dark. "She did what?"

I opened and closed my mouth. I'd been so sure that the arranged marriage meant the relationship was fake. Katherine and Camden's had been arranged and fake for so long. That was my metric. Maybe this was different.

"Is that why you were upset at the Hamptons? That's what you couldn't tell me?"

"Fuck, I shouldn't have said anything. I'm so confused. Gavin, what is going on?"

He sighed and pulled me in closer. "Maggie and Locke *are* arranged. Our families set it up, but as far as I knew, it was a real marriage still. I certainly didn't think Locke would approve of her sleeping with Micah." He brushed a stray lock of my rainbow hair out of my face. "Why didn't you tell me? You've been dealing with this all alone?"

"She begged me not to tell you. But why didn't you tell me about the arranged part?"

"Just the family knows. And I suppose, now, you *should* know since you'll be family soon." His smile returned at that.

"Yes. Your mom and aunt seem smitten with that idea."

"They're not the only ones," he said, tilting my chin up to look into his eyes. "I'm quite fond of you myself."

"Oh, are you?" I asked with a grin.

"Indeed."

And seeing him look at me like that sent shivers straight down my spine. I was his. Completely and unequivocally. In that moment, not a single thing about this was fake.

"Gavin," I said hesitantly, "I don't want us to be like Maggie and Locke."

His thumb tracked against my bottom lip. "And what do you want?"

"I want it to be real," I whispered.

His lips brushed against mine as he breathed the truth into me. "It is real."

26

GAVIN

The time with my family ended too soon. As we got back on the private jet to fly into Dallas to spend the holiday weekend with Whitley's family, I could feel her anxiety increase with every traveled mile.

"Maybe we should have celebrated the Fourth of July with your family," she muttered as we landed on a private airfield in south Dallas.

"But your brother invited you personally."

"I know." Her eyes darted around, as if she expected her family to jump out of the bushes to embarrass her. "Just ... try to keep an open mind. My family isn't like ... your family."

I grabbed her around the middle before we got to the awaiting car and kissed her deeply.

She laughed as she drew back. "What was that for?"

"To remind you that I'm right here. I'm not going to be scared off, Whit. It's going to be fine."

"You say that now," she said with an eye roll and then opened the car door.

Nothing I said the entire drive to her family's home in

Dalworthington Gardens could ease her mind. She was practically bouncing in her seat by the time we were in the city.

"Are those ... cows?" I asked in surprise. "Aren't we within city limits?"

"Yes. Dalworthington Gardens was started as a farming center by the federal subsistence homestead program in the '30s. It's the only active colony still in existence, and as long as the land is in continuous usage, we can still use it for livestock," she said, as if reading from a brochure of the town. "My family was one of the first settlers, and we've had the use of the land ever since."

"Fancy."

She snorted. "Hardly. It's just a quirk of my heritage that my family is really proud of." She shrugged as her gaze swept across the land, seeing more than the suburbs and farmland in her history.

I, however, craned my neck to look at the place that had created yet clearly not contained my little spitfire. Then, my eyes rounded. "Does that say Bowen Street?"

She sighed heavily. "Uh, yeah. That's named after my family."

"The Kings don't have a street in Midland." My grin widened. "You're way fancier than us, Whitley Bowen."

She rolled her eyes dramatically. "Lord help us."

The car turned off Bowen and onto a paved lane, lined with giant oak trees. It was like something out of a movie. The house at the end of the lane was modest and well cared for. The grass was manicured, the trees immaculate, and everything about it said that someone had put a lot of love and care into the surroundings. I appreciated that.

Though I could see how a place like this would be suffocating for someone like Whitley.

We piled our luggage onto the walk as her mom opened the front door and rushed down the steps.

"You made it," she said cheerfully.

"We made it," Whitley confirmed.

"Walter is just inside. Can I help with the bags?" Cynthia asked.

"I have them," I assured her.

She beamed at me as if I was everything she could have ever wanted in a son-in-law. It was slightly unfair that I'd done nothing to earn that praise, except an accident of birth, but it could be worse.

Cynthia put her arm around her daughter and whisked her toward the house. Whitley looked back at me once in alarm, but I waved her off.

"I'm right behind you."

She looked relieved and followed her mom inside. I carried both of our suitcases up the stairs and into Whitley's childhood home. It had been updated recently with modern finishings, but it couldn't mask that the house had been built decades ago. I dropped the bags in the front room, and my eyes were immediately drawn to the mantel, where dozens of picture frames were filled.

Whitley was saying something to me, but I headed over to the mantel and found Whitley and what must have been her brother, Wyatt, looking back at me over and over again. No matter how difficult her upbringing had been, her parents loved her. Even if that love seemed to be conditional.

"Oh god," she groaned, trying to yank me backward. "Don't look at those. It's so embarrassing."

"Is this you?" I picked up a frame from the mantel with a picture of a young curly-haired brunette, smiling with braces and glasses as she held a baseball bat. "You played baseball?"

Whitley snatched it out of my hand. "Softball."

"She was so good too," Cynthia said. "Wyatt played baseball, and she wanted to be just like him at that age."

"Ugh," Whitley said, replacing the picture. "We don't talk about those years."

"How long did you play?"

She groaned. "Three years. They wanted me to play on the high school team, but I was over it by then." She shrugged and met my eyes. "I wanted to sing."

Her mother sighed behind her. "She might have gone to college on a full scholarship for softball if she'd stayed with it."

"Instead, I had academic scholarships," Whitley muttered under her breath.

"Which we were proud of," her mother said quickly.

I picked up another picture. A young Whitley, maybe four or five, standing in a tutu and holding a bouquet of roses.

"You were adorable."

Whitley shook her head. "Is Dad almost ready? We should go."

"Let me check on him."

Cynthia disappeared to check on her husband, leaving us alone in the living room.

"So, you were a natural brunette."

"Don't remind me."

I fingered the rainbow ends. "I like it however you wear it."

"I haven't had my natural brown hair in ages. I don't even know what I'd look like with it."

"You'd be as beautiful as ever," I assured her, planting a kiss on her lips.

A moment later, her father appeared in the doorway. He looked frailer than the last time we'd seen him. Just over a month had passed, and the difference was striking. Whitley's face crumpled at the sight of him. She'd been trying not to think about her family and the tumultuous relationship she had with them, but seeing him like this only a month later had to be discomfiting.

"Ready to go, sweetheart?" he asked, pulling Whitley into a hug.

"Are you sure you want to go?"

"It's the annual Fourth of July festival. Of course we're going to go."

Whitley didn't argue with him, just followed her parents out to the car. We piled into the backseat, and a few minutes later, we were parked in front of a colossal white structure that was the local country club.

Whit had warned me what we were going to do here, but I hadn't known what to expect. The building was enormous, and the small festival I had anticipated was a huge carnival—complete with rides, food, and games—with people already camping out on the golf course to watch the fireworks.

Before we took two steps toward the festival, two young ginger children barreled away from their parents and collided with Whitley. She laughed and sank down to their level.

"Aunt Whit!" they both cheered.

She hugged each of them tight. "It's so good to see you." Her smile was infectious as she looked up at me. "This is Wesley and Wynona." Then she gestured to me. "And this is Gavin."

Wynona eyed me warily, but Wesley stuck his hand out like he was a proper gentleman. I shook it just as dramatically.

"Hi. I'm going into the second grade."

"Pleasure to meet you."

"Are you going to bring Aunt Whit here more often?"

Wynona perked up at this, slinking out from behind her brother in anticipation of my answer.

"I would be delighted," I assured him.

Whitley laughed, ruffling Wesley's impeccable hair. He ducked, as if offended by the gesture.

"You two are going to be coming to New York soon for our wedding."

"Is that like California?" Wynona asked softly. "We saw you in California."

"It is nothing like California," Whitley said with a laugh. "But you'll like it all the same. There's so much to do. Plus, you'll be our flower girl."

Wynona's eyes lit up at that. "I can do that!"

"And I will be the ring bearer," Wesley said proudly.

"That you will," a voice said, now that their parents had finally caught up with them. The voice belonged to a woman nearly as short as Whitley, which was a feat. She had long ginger hair and a kind smile. "Hi, I'm Carrie."

I shook Carrie's hand, and then Wyatt appeared at his wife's side. I could see the immediate resemblance to my Whitley in his features. Except that he'd apparently gotten all the height in the family. He was only a few inches shorter than me as he extended his hand.

"You must be Gavin," Wyatt said.

"That I am." We shook once, firm. "It's good to finally meet you."

"Anyone who makes Whitley happy is welcome here," he said easily. "Shall we? Mom? Dad?"

They both nodded, and as a family, we headed into the bustling festival. We ate funnel cake and caramel apples. I convinced Whitley to ride a spinning ride that made us both very nearly sick. At the end, I played the ring toss until I won Whitley a fluffy pink teddy bear. She held it tight to her chest as we meandered the grounds together.

My heart soared as I saw her anxiety about the afternoon dissolve away. She took my hand and rested her head on my shoulder.

"This has been fun," she admitted. "I wasn't expecting it to be fun. No one has been horrible to me."

"Just wait ... there's still time."

She snorted. "Fine. Fine. I do need to find my mom. She said that some of the ladies at the country club wanted to give me something." She wrinkled her nose. "I want to tell her no, but I just ..."

"What?"

"They did me wrong so many times. Maybe they don't even deserve all of this from me, but I don't want to live my life with regrets. And I'd regret not seeing this through for my dad. No matter what our history is."

"That's very mature of you."

She poked me in the side. "Don't make fun of me."

I snatched up her hand and brought it to my mouth. "I'm not. I'm serious. It's good that you're reconciling as much as you can right now. There's not a lot of time. Just because you don't have what I have with my family doesn't mean you can't have something."

She sighed. "I just feel like ... like I'm letting Safia down by being okay with them."

My heart skipped at the mention of her ex-girlfriend. I'd

known they were serious, but we hadn't talked about the relationship much. With Whitley, when something was over, it was dead and buried. To have her mention it ... she must have been very vulnerable.

"Your father is dying. I never knew Safia, obviously, but I can't imagine you dating someone who wouldn't acknowledge the importance of that."

"Yeah. She had a kinder heart than me."

"I very much doubt that. Look at all you're doing here."

"But I can't put the past behind me."

"You don't have to. You don't have to forgive and forget. You have to move forward."

She nodded once and leaned up onto her tiptoes to steal a kiss. "Thanks, Gavin."

My heart leaped at the look in her eyes. I wanted to tell her how I felt. I wanted to tell her right then and there. To pour my heart out to this little pixie. She was mine. All mine. And I couldn't stand another second without her knowing.

But then she pulled back, and the moment passed.

I buried the words that I'd almost spoken. The words I wanted to say, but I refused to frighten her. And I watched her walk away to find her family once more.

27

WHITLEY

I tromped up the hill toward the country club. Night was falling rapidly as the sun began to set on the horizon. Soon, we'd have to find our seats on the hill to watch the fireworks, but for now, I was supposed to meet my mom.

I was halfway there when footsteps sounded behind me. I jerked around. My New York instincts taking over. But all I found was my brother jogging toward me.

"Jesus, you scared me. What are you doing?" I asked, falling into step beside him.

"Sorry about that. You should watch taking the Lord's name in vain here. Someone might go apoplectic."

I rolled my eyes. "We're way past that for me."

He laughed. And suddenly, we were kids again. My big brother, the perfect model older brother, who did everything right, and his wayward little sister. It felt right in its own way, even if the dichotomy was unfair.

"I'm surprised you came back," he said.

"You and me both."

"Especially with a King at your side."

"Wasn't exactly planned."

"That's not how Mom is spinning it."

I groaned. "What is she saying?"

"You know. The same old, same old. It's why I couldn't believe you were here. And that you've kept your mouth shut so far."

I arched an eyebrow. "Should I be pitching a fit?"

He shot me an even look. "After what happened in LA, I wouldn't blame you."

I stopped at the top of the hill and looked out across the festival below. "I'm still not happy with them. What they did was horrible, and I've never gotten an apology." I sighed. "I really don't expect one either. And if Dad wasn't dying, I probably wouldn't be standing here right now."

But I didn't have to forgive and forget what had happened. I didn't have to do anything but live through this moment. I couldn't change what had happened with Safia, but I couldn't change that my dad was sick either.

"How's he doing anyway?" I asked before he could respond. "Really doing?"

Wyatt's shoulders drooped. "I don't know. He won't say much to me. He's keeping his head up and pretending like nothing is wrong. Mom told me the immune therapy seems to be helping, but he's too proud to admit any of it to me."

"That's so frustrating. Why does it have to be a secret?"

"I honestly think he's just trying to get through to this wedding."

I dropped my head as the weight of it all crashed down on my shoulders. This wedding. Which had started out fake and was getting more and more real as the days went on. A reality that I couldn't even deny that I liked. I wanted what Gavin and I had to be as real as it felt to be in his arms. It didn't alleviate some of the guilt though that it had all started out as a lie.

For a moment, I wanted someone else to know. Someone who was dealing with all the same stuff with my parents as me. Someone who had known me my whole life.

"About the wedding ..."

Wyatt frowned. "Please don't tell me that you're breaking it off. I don't think I could keep Mom together if you did."

I shook my head. "What? No, Gavin and I are getting married."

"Okay, good. I just ... you know ... I never thought you'd get married. I couldn't believe it when Curt told me that he'd seen you in Midland."

"So, that is how Mom found out!"

"Well, no. I wanted you to be the one to drop that bomb on her. But someone at church got to her first. I had to act surprised when she told me."

"Jesus," I grumbled.

He cracked up and shook his head. "So, what about the wedding?"

"Gavin and I ... it's not ... it didn't start out ... real." I stumbled over the words, unsure of how to get them all out.

Wyatt's brow furrowed. "What does that mean?"

"Like, I was covering for him. He'd told his family that he had a girlfriend and well, I'm a bad girlfriend. So, I went to the wedding as his fake fiancée. We were going to break up when we got home and then when Mom and Dad showed up, we decided to go through with it for them."

Wyatt seemed to take a moment to consider this. "That is such a Whitley story."

I laughed and smacked his arm. "It's true. The whole relationship was fake."

"But it's not fake anymore," Wyatt said. His eyes shifted down to the festival again. "I know you, Whit. I've known you your whole life. You've never looked at anyone the way you look at Gavin King. If you don't love him, I don't know what love is."

I flushed at the comment. At the ease with which my brother saw right through me. "I ... I ..."

"Just because it's the person our parents want for you doesn't make him the wrong person."

"I didn't say that," I said defensively.

He laughed. "Yeah, but I know you. He's good for you. You two look so happy together. I haven't known him long, but I can tell, Whit. There's a reason you agreed to go through with this with him. And there's a reason you're going to stick it out." He touched my arm. "Just let yourself be happy, okay?"

"Okay," I whispered as tears came to my eyes. I hastily swiped them away. "Thanks."

"What are big brothers for?"

"Generally? Being a dick and beating me up in middle school."

Wyatt laughed. "Hey, you're the one who stole my high school girlfriend."

I shrugged with my hands out at my sides, giving him my best look of innocence. "Some people just have more game."

He rolled his eyes. "Get inside. You're ridiculous."

I waved him off and headed inside to find my mom. I was glad that we'd had that talk even if it hadn't gone at all how I'd expected it to. At least he'd kept me from obsessing about what my mom had in store for me.

When I stepped inside the country club ballroom, I was surprised to find it empty, save for my mom. Some part of me had been expecting her to throw some big, elaborate party with all the women that I'd hated growing up. But it was just my mom, holding an envelope and a small box.

"Hi, sweetheart."

"Hi, Mom. What's this?"

She smiled down at the box and then back at me. "I wanted to throw you a party, but with the festival, there wasn't time. Plus, I didn't think you really wanted one."

"I didn't," I admitted. Not that I'd thought she'd accept that.

"Also, I saw how small your apartment is in the city. Even when you move in with Gavin, you won't have that much space. What's the point of having *things* when you have nowhere to put them?"

I stalled in place. "That was … thoughtful."

My mom laughed softly. "I can be thoughtful sometimes, dear."

I didn't respond to that. It would only result in an argument, and I could see my mom was trying not to fight.

"So," she said softly, "I did this."

She passed me the envelope. I tore it open and found a letter, signed by dozens of women. I recognized at least half of them. Inside was a check written to me for five figures. My eyes bulged.

"Mom!" I protested.

"It's from all of us. In lieu of a party … and since I'm not paying for the wedding," she said quickly, "I wanted you to have this."

"It's way too much. Dad needs it for his treatment. You need it for after …" But I couldn't get the words out.

And my mom choked on the sound of *after*. She dabbed at her eyes. "His insurance is covering most of it. I'll have life insurance for … after." She pressed the check back into my hands. "You need this for now."

I deposited the check into my purse. "Thank you," I said

even though I had no need for my mother's money. I knew how much it meant to her to be able to provide.

"And this," she added, handing me the box, "I'm hoping you'll wear it on your wedding day. Your ... something old."

I flipped the lid on the red box and found a diamond studded tennis bracelet that I'd seen my mom wear every day growing up. "The one Grandpa got for you for your wedding day?"

She nodded. "It was new when I wore it, and now, it's old for when you wear it."

"Mom," I whispered, slowly closing the lid, "would you have given me this if I were marrying someone else?"

She bit her lip and looked down at the box still in my hand. "If you're asking about Safia, then ... yes."

She met my gaze, and I saw tears there.

"I want to believe you, but you *left*. You *left* instead of staying in California and getting to know her."

"I know. I thought I was making the right decision at the time. My church would still say that I made the right decision. But not talking to you for months after that? Not being involved in your life? Not even being a person that you wanted to tell that you were engaged? I don't want to be that kind of mother." She sniffled, wiping at her eyes. "With your dad so sick ... I've had a lot of time to think about what happens after. What he's going to miss out on. It's changed my perspective." She clasped my shoulder. "I want to be in your life."

Maybe it wasn't perfect. Maybe it wasn't the proclamation that she was suddenly fine with having a bi daughter. It was still more than I'd ever thought I'd hear from my mom. A fresh start to figure out what our relationship could be in the wake of this new understanding.

So, I hugged my mom and promised to wear the

bracelet. She smiled back at me, and we headed down to the fireworks together.

Gavin was seated on a quilt between Wesley and Wynona, who were both animatedly discussing every ride and game they'd played that day. They both had light-up swords of some kind and randomly smacked them against each other across Gavin's lap. He just laughed, egging them on all the while. Carrie and Wyatt sat in chairs directly behind them with Dad seated heavily in another chair. Mom sank into the seat next to him and immediately began fussing over him.

"Well, isn't this cozy?" I said with a laugh. "Where am I going to sit?"

"Next to me!" Wynona insisted.

"No! Me!" Wesley chimed in.

"That's my cue," Gavin said as he vacated his seat, and I plopped down between the children.

Gavin took the seat on the other side of Wesley, where he could lean over and link our hands together.

He whispered, "Everything all right?" and nodded at the box I was carrying.

I nodded. "I'll tell you later."

With the sun finally setting, a firework burst into the sky, and silence fell over the awaiting crowd. Gavin kissed my cheek and then turned his face up to gaze at the night sky. We sat there for a half hour as colors and loud noises and shapes were displayed over and over again. It was magical as the display came to a close with a cacophony of sound.

Wyatt and Carrie herded the yawning children back toward the cars, and we followed behind them. We said good night and then piled into the back of my mom's car. A half hour later, after we managed to get stuck in fireworks traffic, we were back on the farm. We said good night to my parents and then trudged our way to an upstairs bedroom.

"Which one was yours?" Gavin asked.

"That one," I said, pointing to a room filled with my mother's crafting equipment. "She changed it as soon as I went away to college. Always wanted her own craft room."

I opened the next door. Gavin had deposited the suitcases here earlier in the day. They were pushed against a wall, and the king-size bed was inviting.

"This used to be Wyatt's room, but just the guest room now."

He toed the door closed behind him. "So, what happened with your mom?"

"She sort of apologized for how she'd acted, and she gave me the bracelet her dad gave her on her wedding day."

His eyes sparkled in the dim light. "That's big, Whit."

"It was."

Though I could hardly think of what my mom had said and was still focused on how clearly Wyatt had seen into my heart.

I'd never loved anyone before. I'd never used those words. They always felt cheap. Like people just said them to show affection and not when it was real. All I knew was that I didn't want to go another second without Gavin. And I was looking forward to that moment when I walked down the aisle with him.

Was that love?

Did I *love* Gavin King?

He grinned at the look on my face and then drew me toward him. At the first touch of his lips on mine, the day was swept away. I dragged him closer to me.

"We're going to have to be quiet," I groaned.

"We can be quiet," he said as he walked me backward toward the bed.

His hands slid under my skirt, dragging along my bare legs. I wrenched at his shirt, desperate to get him out of it, to feel his body against mine. My back made contact with one of the posts on the bed, and a squeak escaped me.

"Shh," he murmured as he claimed my mouth again.

My panties hit the floor, and I kicked out of them as I worked his belt loose and dragged his pants down.

"Fuck," he groaned as my hand slid into his boxers.

"Shh," I reminded him teasingly.

He arched an eyebrow at me and then gripped my thighs with such force as he lifted me off of the ground. I inhaled a gasp as I wrapped my legs around his waiting waist.

"Mine," he growled.

"Yes." My voice came out breathy, almost a beg.

"Tell me," he breathed into my ear as our bodies aligned.

"I'm yours."

He thrust into me, and I cried out in a soft pant. He thrust in again, harder than before. I was not going to be quiet. There was no way I was going to be able to keep this in.

"More."

He dropped me backward on the bed, burying himself even deeper inside of me. When my groans grew more insistent, he covered my mouth with his palm. My eyes widened as he drove into me again, holding me in place and claiming my screams for himself.

"All mine," he told me as my eyes rolled back in my head.

I was close. So close already.

I could barely hold on as he picked up the pace.

"Fuck," he ground out into my shoulder as I tightened around him.

Then, I couldn't hold on any longer. I released as wave after wave shattered against the rocks. I was incoherent, seeing stars, as he shuddered and finished inside of me.

"Oh my god," I whispered breathlessly.

He kissed my shoulder. "Good girl."

Every breath from my lungs, every beat of my heart, and every thread within my soul belonged to this man.

28

———

WHITLEY

After such a magical weekend, I wasn't ready to return to New York. I worried that the enchantment would burst when we went back to daily life. But things were just as wonderful in the city as they had been while visiting our families. We alternated sleeping at each other's apartment. He picked me up with coffee every morning for work. We lounged around with our friends every weekend.

And every day, the wedding drew nearer. A thing that I'd thought would terrify me but was now ... exciting me.

Are you sure I can't come with you?

I laughed at the text from Gavin.

I don't think the groom is invited to the wedding dress fitting.

But I want to see it.

You'll see it in a week.

He responded with a pouty face, and I sent him back a picture of me sticking out my tongue.

Yes please.

I rolled my eyes again. Ridiculous.

"For whom exactly are you all smiley for?" Katherine asked, appearing at my side outside of Cunningham Couture.

I put my hand to my heart. "Hey! I didn't know you were coming today."

"To see you in the dress I helped design?" Katherine arched a perfectly manicured eyebrow. "You should always expect me."

I laughed. "That's fair."

"So? Smiles?" She pulled the handle on the door. "Tell me everything."

"Just Gavin."

"Just? It seems someone is falling for their own trick."

I couldn't deny that even if I wanted to. When Gavin had shown up at my door a few short months earlier, begging me to be his fake girlfriend, I never would have thought we'd end up here. Where I'd be looking forward to my own wedding and not utterly dreading this thing we had ostensibly been forced into it.

Katherine laughed when I didn't respond to that and pulled me into the boutique. The Fifth Avenue shop was immaculate. Everything I would expect from a designer brand with a cult following. Brightly lit clothing racks lined the walls with only one or two sizes of everything on display. The woman in a smart skirt suit at the register brightened at the sight of Katherine Van Pelt in her store. Everyone knew who she was.

"Hello, Katherine," she said cheerfully. "Anything I can help you with today?"

"No, thank you. We're here for Harmony," Katherine said as she continued through the store as if she'd done this a million times. Maybe she had. She'd been a model for the company for years, and the second floor had long held the design team.

Katherine opened the back door, and we climbed another set of stairs into the madness of high fashion. My eyes roamed the space filled with scurrying designers and assistants holding bolts of fabric, rushing to a nearby sewing machines and gesturing emphatically to the drape of material on various mannequins.

An assistant saw us standing there and smiled. "Katherine, what a pleasure. Harmony is this way."

"Excellent," she said, following the girl down to Harmony's office.

Katherine seemed right at home, but I'd never been more out of my element. Even my short stint at a Fashion Week gala had resulted in a fistfight over me, and I'd sworn never to return. I would have been just as happy with a dress off the rack if Katherine hadn't been so adamant that I let her handle it. And I trusted Katherine with my life.

"Prompt as ever," Harmony said with a smile as she took in the sight of us. "I've been waiting for this."

She instructed her assistant to bring champagne to the suite, and then we were walking past the harried designers and into a private dressing room larger than most New York City bedrooms. The assistant returned a minute later, offering top-shelf champagne to the room as Harmony walked over to the only article of clothing in the room, covered by the purple garment bag that Cunningham Couture was known for.

My stomach tightened with anticipation. That was my wedding dress. Everything that had happened up to this moment had been going through the motions. Even the bridal shower wasn't all that different than a birthday party. I'd opened gifts and laughed with Gavin's family about the wedding. The closest I'd come to feeling like this was real was months ago when Gavin slid that ring on my finger. Now, it belonged there.

I glanced down at it now. It was crazy to think how much I'd gotten used to this ring. But once I had that dress on, the wedding was going to get twice as real.

"Ready?" Harmony asked.

I nodded because I couldn't get the words out. My emotions went haywire. I felt Katherine's eyes on me, as if she were assessing my every movement. She always saw straight to the heart of things, and I was sure she was seeing it right now.

"All right. Let's get this on."

I stripped out of my work clothes as Harmony unzipped the bag and let the layers of white material fall forward onto the floor. I couldn't get a good picture of what it looked like, but seeing the bright white color made my insides squirm. Harmony had me step into the dress, and as the bodice was fitted against me, the breath left my body.

It was perfect.

It was the most perfect dress I'd ever worn in my life.

Harmony was working on buttoning the dozen individual buttons up the back, but I was thunderstruck, staring at myself in the trifold mirror.

The balconette, corseted bodice had visible boning and tiny lace sleeves that widened slightly at the shoulders. My ample cleavage was visible, but not overwhelming. The corset held the girls in nicely, so I wasn't about to pop out even if I was dancing the night away. The boning made my waist look way smaller than it was in reality, and the layers of tulle skirt that fell past my feet somehow even made me look tall.

"You'll need heels," Harmony said. "I planned for you to be a few inches taller."

"I brought them last week," Katherine said.

The assistant eeped and rushed out of the room. A minute later, she returned with a box of Christian Louboutins. My eyes rounded in wonder at the sparkly diamond heels with classic red-lacquered bottoms. Harmony's assistant helped me into them, and they fit like a glove, lifting me off of the ground so that the dress barely grazed the floor.

Harmony finished with the buttons and pulled back to assess her work.

I was still too stunned to speak.

"Well," Harmony said, "do you like it?"

"It's ..." I swallowed hard, trying to find the word to describe the fluttering in my stomach when I wore it.

"She likes it," Katherine said, tilting her head to the side.

"Yes," I whispered.

Harmony buzzed around me, making notes about what would need to be taken in, pinned, and fixed before the wedding in a week's time. Her assistant hastened behind her, making notes and adding pins to the dress where Harmony dictated.

"Hey, Harm, can we have a minute?" Katherine asked.

Harmony glanced up at Katherine. You'd never know by seeing them now, but they used to have the biggest rivalry. But since Harmony's mom had married Camden's dad, they'd really worked on their relationship. I liked seeing them getting along. And when they looked at each other, I saw that Harmony understood.

"Yeah. Take as much time as you need. Lord knows I have more work to do. Just don't drink in the dress," Harmony said. She winked at me. "You look beautiful."

"Thanks."

Harmony and her assistant walked out of the room, closing the door behind them.

Katherine tilted her head as she came to her feet, setting her champagne flute on a nearby table. "What do you really think?"

"I love it. You couldn't have designed a better dress for me."

"That's who I am."

I laughed softly and met her eyes in the mirror. She was still looking at me as if I was a mystery.

"What?" I asked cautiously.

"I thought this would be the moment."

"The moment for what?"

"Where you ran."

I stiffened. "What do you mean?"

"Come on, Whit. You don't have to pretend with me. I know you for exactly who you are. I've been there through all your ridiculous stories. I figured at the end of this one, when it all came together, you'd do what you always do —run."

"I don't always run."

She arched an eyebrow. "Oh, no? Then, you didn't move to California instead of dealing with Robert and Gavin three years ago?"

"Well ..."

"Or disappear back to New York when your girlfriend of a year made one mistake in California?"

I bit my lip. "That was different."

"It's always different. You know you're like this. I don't even know why you're arguing."

"Fine." I brushed my hands down the skirt. "I'm a bad girlfriend. I know that. I don't want a relationship when it gets hard, and I won't deal with bullshit. Is that what you wanted to hear?"

Katherine smiled, slow and dangerous. "And yet"—she gestured to the wedding dress—"you haven't ripped the dress off of your body yet."

I turned back to the mirror to catch my reflection. I couldn't imagine stepping out of the dress and never wearing it again. It fit me as well as the diamond ring on my finger. As well as Gavin fit in my life.

"I like it," I finally said.

"No, you like Gavin King." She tilted her head. "Dare I say, you love him?"

I swallowed. "I ... I don't know. Do I? How do you know that sort of thing anyway?"

Katherine's smile grew. "Because you didn't deny it with every fiber of your being. You want to marry him in a week. Don't you?"

"Yes," I got out, my voice thick with emotion.

"This is your wildest story," she said with a laugh as she took my hand. For that second, both of us dropped the bravado that held us up. "I'm happy for you, Whit. I wanted this for you. I wanted Gavin for you. He's a good guy when he wants to be, and he wants that with you. I saw it before you ever did."

I flushed. "Thanks, Katherine. For the dress. For ... everything."

"Thank me by getting married in a week and being deliriously happy. That's all I want in return."

I nodded and pulled her unceremoniously into a hug. She laughed and hugged me back.

"Don't mess up the dress," Katherine said but with no real bite.

"I'm getting *married* in a week."

It felt surreal. I never thought the day would come. When I'd agreed to this fake marriage, I'd never once guessed it would turn completely real in the meantime. I couldn't wait to tell Gavin on our wedding night.

PART V

GENTLEMEN MARRY BRUNETTES

29

WHITLEY

"Y ou'll say your *I do*s," the officiant said from the front of the ballroom. "Then, you'll kiss."

I clutched the bridal shower bouquet that Cora had made for me tight in my hands until my knuckles turned white. Gavin stood across from me at the rehearsal for our wedding.

"Do we get to practice the kiss?" he asked with a mischievous smile on his lips.

Everyone laughed. Such a Gavin thing to ask.

He didn't wait for a response, just pulled my face toward him and kissed me in front of our friends and family. Everyone inside the Percy Tower ballroom cheered.

I pulled back breathlessly. He pressed another quick kiss to my lips.

He stared down at me in awe and whispered, "Tomorrow, we're doing this for real."

"Yes," I gasped.

"Then, you'll be my wife."

Wife.

In all the planning for the wedding, I hadn't considered that word. Wife. And he'd be my husband. Oh my god.

I dragged him forward and kissed him again to a chorus of laughter. But I didn't care. The thought had sent butterflies floating through my stomach. Tomorrow, at this time, he'd be my husband.

The officiant announced us, and then we followed the wedding planner's instructions to walk down the aisle and out of the room.

While she dealt with the rest of the bridal party, Gavin swept me off of my feet and swung me into a circle.

"I still can't believe you did this." He fingered the loose curl of my now-dark-brown hair. A color that I hadn't had in my hair since childhood.

"You don't like it?"

"I love it. I don't care what color your hair is. Pink or rainbow. Blonde or brown. Hell, let's get some red in there, so you match mine," he said, ruffling his own red-shot brown hair.

I chuckled. "You're ridiculous."

"I wanted to make sure this was what *you* wanted."

I touched the ends self-consciously. "To be honest, I wasn't sure. I sat down at the salon yesterday, prepared to touch up the vibrancy of my rainbow, and I decided I needed a change. That if I was going to marry you, I wanted it to be my natural color."

His eyes softened at those words. "Nothing to do with your parents, right? This is all you?"

"All me. Though my mom cried when she saw it, and my dad looked like he might cry."

"That sounds right." He drew me tight against him again. "Are you sure you won't reconsider about tonight too?"

I arched an eyebrow and weaseled my way out of his arms. "One night apart won't kill you, King. Think about what the wedding night will be like."

His eyes went molten. "Oh, I'm imagining it all right."

I pushed him playfully. "You're a scoundrel."

"I'm *your* scoundrel." He pressed a kiss to my fingers as the rest of our friends made their way toward us.

"Break it up. Break it up," English said. "We're stealing her for the night, King."

"By all means," he said, relinquishing me to my best friend. "Try not to have her still drunk tomorrow."

"No promises," Lark said.

"We make no promises either," Court said, slinging an arm over Gavin's shoulders.

Camden sighed and shook his head. "We will take care of him."

I laughed. "I bet you will."

Sam pressed a kiss to Lark's lips before helping the boys drag Gavin out of The Plaza. Gavin looked back at me once and winked.

What a ridiculous man I was marrying. And I *was* marrying him.

I hadn't yet told him all that I'd confessed to Katherine, but tomorrow night, I had plans of my own for our wedding night. He was going to lose his mind, and I was ready for it.

"Honey," my mom said before my friends could pull me out of the hotel as well.

"One minute," I promised my friends and then headed over to my parents.

"This looks like it's going to be magical," Mom said.

Dad pulled me into his arms unexpectedly. "Thank you for doing this, sweetheart."

"Of course, Dad."

"I know I rushed you into this, but I still love that it's happening. And seeing how much you and Gavin love each other ... well, I can't wait to walk you down the aisle."

I beamed at my father. The guilt that crept through was just a twinge after everything we'd gone through to get here. I did love Gavin, and this was all actually going to work.

"I love you, Dad."

"I love you too." He released me with a laugh. "Well, don't let us keep you from celebrating."

"Thanks. I'll see you here bright and early!"

"We'll be here," Mom said, waving as I headed back to my friends.

"Ready," I said, joining my friends out on Fifth Avenue. "Where exactly *are* we going?"

A limo waited outside. Lark slung a *bride-to-be* sash over my head while Katherine affixed a tiara into my dark hair.

English looked devilish. "Oh, you'll see."

I did indeed see.

A strip club.

Full of male and female strippers in tiny little string pieces. Laden with glitter. Dollar bills flying. Shots all around.

The night was wild and hilarious. All of my friends acting as if this were an everyday occurrence in their lives even though I wasn't sure that Lark or Katherine had ever been to a place like this. English and I used to go to strip clubs all the time in LA with our sorority friends. It brought back vivid college memories.

By the time we piled back into the limo, we were all wasted drunk and falling all over ourselves.

"Best bachelorette party ever," Lark declared, laying her head into Katherine's lap.

Katherine ran her fingers through Lark's hair. "Camden's going to kill me when I show up this drunk."

"You mean, fuck you," I quipped.

Katherine laughed. "Well, yeah, probably."

"I told Gavin we were going to be separate tonight."

"And now, you're having second thoughts," English slurred.

"Maybe I should text him."

"No!" all my girls called at the same time.

I nearly fell over laughing. They only agreed to drop me off after I promised I wouldn't see Gavin tonight, but, oh, I wanted to. Still, promises were promises.

I waved good-bye to my friends and lurched into an elevator in my building. I barely caught myself against the railing, saving myself from falling flat on my face, as it rose rapidly. The elevator doors dinged open on my floor. I stumbled out into the hallway and was almost to my apartment when I saw double of a figure sitting in front of my door.

I blinked twice, certain that I wasn't seeing what I was seeing.

"Safia?" I croaked.

All the alcohol drained out of my body as my ex-girlfriend came into full clarity. Her beautiful limbs stretched and straightened as she came to her feet, swiping at her tear-filled dark eyes. Her long black hair was pulled off of her face in a harsh ponytail. Her medium-brown skin was on full display in high-waisted shorts and a black crop top with Doc Martens.

"Hey, Whit," she said, wrapping her arms around her stomach.

"What are you *doing* here?"

"You know why I'm here." Her words were raspy and broken. The same voice I'd listened to as it breathed sweet nothings into my ear.

"How did you even find me?"

Safia shrugged. "It's not hard to search housing records, Whit."

I shook my head, reaching for my keys. "I can't do this tonight. I'm getting married tomorrow."

"You don't think that's why I'm here?"

"You're not going to change my mind," I growled.

"Just give me a few minutes." Her hand reached out and grazed my arm. I jerked back, and she retreated into herself. "Please. I flew all the way here."

I shook my head, but already, I was opening the door. "You shouldn't have come."

Safia followed me into the apartment. "I know, but I couldn't stay away."

"You should have."

I was the tiny pixie that barely grazed five feet, and yet I practically towered over my five-foot-nine ex. Our relationship hadn't been perfect. She'd taken advantage of my generosity and then ruined everything with her ex.

"You never let me explain."

I whirled on her. "And whose fault is that? You let your ex into *my* house. She was in *my* bed."

"Our bed."

"Don't," I hissed. "You even being here right now goes against everything I believe in. We don't work. I walked away. This is *done*."

Safia held solid and just waited for me to finish. "I know."

"Then, why are you here?"

"Because you can't marry him."

I stared at her, waiting for the punch line. Because my ex-girlfriend couldn't actually be here, trying to convince me not to get married the night before my wedding.

"What?" she whispered when I said nothing.

"Waiting for the end of the joke because this whole thing is ludicrous."

"This isn't a joke," she argued. "I still love you. You can't be with me for a year and then get married to *some guy* after knowing him a matter of months. That's not even who you are."

If anyone had told me a few months ago that I'd be marrying Gavin King, I would have laughed in their face. So, she wasn't wrong. But it didn't change what had happened between me and Gavin over those months. Something I never felt with Safia. Words I was never able to express. And that was because I hadn't felt it.

"You don't know who I am anymore, Safi. You should go."

"Please," Safia said, grasping my hand and tugging me closer to her. "Please, can we just talk?"

I closed my eyes and breathed out heavily. "Why are you doing this?"

"Because I love you."

Three words. So easy for someone else to say. Impossible ones for me to get past my teeth. Why couldn't I say them like everyone else? Why couldn't I tell Gavin even though I was sure that must be what I was feeling? Still, I couldn't say it.

I tugged my hand back. "Fine." I sighed. "*Fine.*"

"When Roni showed up, I wasn't home. She *broke into* the house, Whit."

I furrowed my brow. "She didn't say that. She said she was waiting for you in my bed."

"I know. I know she said that. I tried to tell you. But you'd already made up your mind. You'd already boxed all my stuff up and changed the locks. Without allowing me to even explain."

I pushed past her to pour myself a glass of water. I didn't want to be having this conversation. I'd avoided it long enough, and now, it was here, where I couldn't avoid it any longer.

"Don't talk to me like I'm stupid," I said after I had a long drink. "I had all the proof I needed right in front of me."

"Roni and I didn't get back together. I was furious with her for the shit she pulled."

"What? Like the shit you're pulling right now?"

Safi took a step back, her hand going to her heart. "It's not the same."

"No? You're not here to ruin my wedding?"

She bit her lip. "I wasn't going to come, but I heard the worst about him, Whit. He's a player. He's slept with half of New York. How do you know he's the one for you? A year with me and a few months with him? I don't understand what you're even doing."

"Gavin was a player," I said meeting her dark gaze. "I was actually his wingman for a few years before I ever met you. We were friends. When I came back, things changed. People can change, Saf."

"Is that what you think? That you've changed?" Safi took two long strides, boxing me against the counter.

I glared at her. "What are you doing?"

"You still love me. I know you do."

"I never told you that I loved you."

"And you've told him?" she demanded.

I turned my face away from her.

She snorted. "Of course not. You're doing this, and you

don't even love him." She put two fingers under my chin and tipped my face back up to hers. One I had adored for so long. The girl I'd thought I might have a future with. Only for it to shatter so effortlessly. "You don't *have* to do this."

I jerked my head out of her grasp and pushed myself away from her. "I will not become the thing that I hate," I snarled at her. "Of course I had feelings for you, Safi. But I don't go back to mistakes. No matter what I felt for you. You being here is not only cruel, but also insulting."

Safia nodded, swiping tears from her eyes as she looked away from me. "I see."

"You should go."

"I'll go," she agreed slowly. "If you tell me you love him."

"I don't have to tell you anything. I'm happy. Isn't that enough for you?"

"As I thought." She was silent for another few seconds. "It's not enough for me. It shouldn't be enough for you either."

"Then, I can't help you. If you came here, hoping for another outcome, then you're going to leave disappointed."

"Well, at least I tried," she muttered as she crossed to the door.

"Safi," I groaned.

She stopped with her hand on the handle. "Maybe you don't love me, but if you don't love him either, then you shouldn't go through with it tomorrow."

Then, she wrenched open the door and left.

I watched her go, feeling more melancholy than I had in months. And wondering if, in some way, she was right. I hadn't told Gavin that I loved him. I'd said the words in my head, but that wasn't the same. If I couldn't tell Gavin how I felt, was there any way I could get married tomorrow?

30

GAVIN

"I'm cashing out," I declared to the party.

Strangers at the poker table groaned in relief. My friends began to protest, but I held my hand up to stop them.

"I'm up fifty thousand for the night. I have never had a winning streak like this in my life. I know when to bow out." I pushed my chips toward the dealer. "Color me up."

Alcohol and good luck coursed through my veins. I'd won more hands than I'd lost at poker. Something that never happened with my friends. Either Sam was feeding me cards or luck had truly been on my side tonight. I wouldn't put it past them to have rigged the game so that I won at my bachelor party. But I wasn't stupid enough to let the game fall out of my hands. I could barely see straight. The cards weren't going to get any better when I was seeing double.

"Other than the wedding, this might be the smartest thing I've ever heard you say," Court joked. "Get out while you're still ahead."

"Worried I'll take all your money, Kensington?"

Court rolled his eyes. "Good luck with that, King."

Camden stood from the table and buttoned the top of his suit coat. "I was never worried."

Court and I exchanged a look. Nothing ever fazed Camden Percy. Well, nothing since everything with him and Katherine had worked out. And even then, he'd really never shown his displeasure with that arrangement.

"I could keep going," Sam said as he pushed his chips to the dealer next, "but I would like to get home to my wife."

"I can't believe you'll all be fucking married before me," Court grumbled. He punched me in the arm. "Especially you."

"Well, it wasn't exactly in the plan. Then, you had a two-year engagement," I reminded him.

"It hasn't been that long," Court said. "Though, some-times, it feels like it. I should have gone to the courthouse. The whole elaborate wedding is such a mistake. Penn tried to warn me."

"Since when have you ever listened to your brother?"

Camden laughed under his breath. Camden and Penn had long been rivals. He probably would have disagreed with him on principle.

"Never," Court agreed. "But in this, we're agreed. He was the smart bastard to elope. My mom would never forgive me if I did the same. So, here we are. At least you and Whit made it all happen quickly."

"I mean ... her dad is dying," I reminded them. "Hence the expediency."

"Hence the whole reason you decided to go through with it," Sam added.

"But not anymore," Camden said.

"No, not anymore," I said with a drunken smile on my face. "Tomorrow, she'll be my wife for real."

Once we had chips colored up, Camden set down several thousand-dollar pieces as a tip for the dealer and then gestured for us to leave. Only Camden could be that casual about tipping like that. We exchanged our chips for cash, exited the gambling hall, and fell into an awaiting limo. Court poured another glass of whiskey, which Camden took, but Sam and I declined. I couldn't drink another drop. I had to be semi-coherent tomorrow. I wanted to be fully coherent for Whitley.

Maybe I had plans to be lucid for tonight too. Because Whitley had said that we should spend the night apart, but I had no interest in that. I had every intention of sneaking up to her apartment and seducing her. Neither of us was a virgin or innocent by any means. I didn't want to spend another night away from her again.

"Man, you're a goner," Court said with a laugh.

I glanced over at him in confusion. "What?"

"I was talking to you, but you were off in your own world. Thinking about your wedding night?" Court winked at me.

"Thinking about tonight actually."

Sam grinned. "I thought you weren't seeing each other tonight."

I shrugged. "Plans change."

Camden clapped me on the back. "Go for it."

That was all the encouragement I needed. Camden was always right.

The limo dropped me off first. I said good-bye to my boys and then headed into the lobby of my building. I clutched the door as I entered. Everything was spinning. Fuck, I'd had more to drink than I thought. I could barely stand up. A laugh escaped my lips.

I just had to get to the elevator. The rest would work itself out.

I walked to the bank of elevators on the other side of the black-and-white tiled room. I jammed a finger onto the button. A second later, the elevator dinged open, revealing a woman who looked vaguely familiar.

"Excuse me," she said, trying to bypass me.

"Oh. Sorry." I stepped out of the way. My back hit the other wall, and my vision blurred again.

Why did she look familiar? It wasn't someone I'd hooked up with. Or at least, I didn't think it was. I didn't remember them all, but still, that wasn't why she looked familiar. I couldn't place her.

She was tall with brown skin and lush, long hair. Her clothes were edgier than the normal inhabitants of the Upper East Side apartment building. As if she belonged in Brooklyn and had wandered into the wrong part of town. She looked like she'd been crying.

"Do I know you?" I stammered out as she walked past me.

"That's not a very good pickup line," she snapped as she continued to walk away.

Then, it hit me.

I'd only ever seen her in pictures. Pictures that Whitley had shown me from when she lived in California. Pictures of her actress ex-girlfriend.

"Safia?"

She stopped walking and slowly turned around. "How do you know my name?"

"Fuck," I spat under my breath.

Because if this was Safia, then there was only one reason she was here. One person she had come to see. On the eve of our wedding at that.

Her hackles went up as I cursed.

She crossed her arms over her stomach and then finally took a look at me. She sighed heavily. "It's Gavin, right?"

I nodded once.

We stared at each other across the space of that lobby. Only a few paces between us. The last couple of years of Whitley's love life. Her past and present. I'd never known Whitley to ever go back to someone after they hurt her. But she'd come back to me, and we'd made it work. She had been with Safia a lot longer than our two-night stand in Puerto Rico.

"I guess you won," she finally said.

"What the fuck does that mean?"

She just shook her and walked out of the building.

Confusion clouded my features. I'd won? Had Safia come to try to change Whitley's mind? Had Whitley chosen me? What exactly had happened?

I pulled my phone out to see if Whit had tried to call or text. Surely, she would have let me know that her ex had shown up on the night before our wedding. But there was nothing there.

The alcohol in my system was clouding my mind, but it was draining away as I stared down at the blank screen. Not a word from her? That didn't seem right. Whitley was the *burn the world down* kind of person. If Safia had shown up at her place and she'd turned her away, she would have told me to clear the air.

I didn't want to make assumptions, but finding her ex walking out of the elevator was pretty damning. Especially with no fucking explanation. It wasn't Safia's job to tell me any of this. If I hadn't stumbled into her, I wouldn't have even known.

I jotted out a text.

You still up? I want to come up and see you.

I pocketed my phone as I stepped into the elevator and pressed the number for her floor. I expected a text by the time I got there. If Safia was just leaving now, she must still be awake.

But the text stayed on *Delivered*, not *Read*. Fuck.

I headed down the hall to her apartment. I fumbled the keys out of my pocket. I dropped them once, cursed under my breath, and picked them back up. I flipped through the keys until I found hers.

Then, my phone dinged.

haha why am I not surprised that you're trying to break our agreement? Go to bed. I'll see you in the morning!

I had the key to her place in my hand. I could walk right inside and talk to her about seeing Safia. I could figure this all out now. But ... she didn't want to see me.

I frowned. I wasn't accustomed to this feeling. Much like Whitley, whenever things got complicated, I left. And now, disappointment coursed through me. I could ask her about Safia. I could start an argument with her right before we tied the knot. Or I could trust her.

Safia was gone.

She said I won.

What was I trying to prove by barging into Whitley's apartment?

Maybe she'd tell me all about it tomorrow.

31

WHITLEY

Today was my wedding day.

And I looked like a drowned rat.

My eyes were red and puffy from the alcohol ... and crying. I hadn't wanted to cry, but when Safia left and the events of the evening came crashing down, I'd crawled into bed and cried into my pillow like it was my own version of therapy. Now I felt sluggish from the lingering effects of drinking.

I forced myself into a shower. The scalding hot water helped dispel my queasiness. I towel-dried, applied light make-up, and hoped I looked like a human.

After all, it was a new day.

A brand-new day that just happened to be my wedding day. Something I had all been but convinced would never happen. And here I was, marrying Gavin King of all people. Maybe by the time I got to the venue and through hair and makeup, I'd figure out what I was going to say to him.

A knock sounded on my door, and anxiety spiked through me. Maybe that was him now. Maybe I'd have to decide sooner rather than later. But when I pulled the door open, Anna English was waiting for me.

"Happy wedding day!" she cried, throwing her arms around me.

I laughed. "What are you doing here?"

"What? You thought I'd leave something up to chance? Of course not. I have a car waiting to take us to Percy Tower. Katherine and Lark are meeting us in our private suite for hair and makeup."

"Bless you, English."

She winked at me and then ushered me out of the apartment. Sometimes, it was to my benefit, having a full-time celebrity publicist as a best friend. Champagne waited for us in the car, and we toasted my wedding day as we drove the short distance to the venue.

I stepped out of the car and inside the glossy lobby. This was where Gavin and I had seen each other for the first time after I returned. It felt like a million years ago when I'd been in that outrageous outfit for English's meeting with her mother-in-law and I'd flirted with Gavin like we hadn't missed a day instead of three years.

I did a double take as we walked by that same spot because Gavin King happened to be right there. My gorgeous groom in slacks and a button-up, holding two cups of coffee and watching me like a hawk.

"Gavin, you're not supposed to be here yet!" English groaned. "Didn't you read the itinerary?"

"Of course I did. That's how I knew to be standing right here." He stepped up to me and pressed my favorite coffee into my hand. "Didn't think you'd survive without this."

My heart leaped at the gesture. Coffee was how we'd reconnected all those weeks before I was willing to let myself take a chance. Now, here we were, on our wedding day, and I was tongue-tied and uncertain. There were things we still needed to say. So many things. But I had no idea how to get them out.

"How was your night?" he asked, as if seeing straight through my makeup to my puffy eyes.

I shivered at the words. "It was ... interesting."

"So was mine." He tilted his head, as if expecting me to say more, but I didn't know what he wanted.

"Okay, lovebirds, I need to get Whit to her hair and makeup in exactly three minutes, or we'll be running behind," English said. Her eyes were on the Rolex on her wrist.

"Can you give us a minute?" I asked English.

She looked ready to argue with me, but there must have been something on my face that stopped her. Because she sighed and said, "Five minutes."

English stole Gavin's coffee, much to his displeasure, and then gave us the space we so needed.

"What did you do last night?"

"Poker," he said. "I won."

"That's good. Doesn't Sam normally win?"

"Yeah. Pretty sure he was feeding me cards. What about you?"

"Strip club," I said with a stilted laugh.

"Yeah? Bring anyone home?" He asked it so innocently that there was no way that he'd know that I'd found Safia sitting outside my door.

I should just tell him, but fuck, how did I even begin to explain? I didn't care about Safia anymore. Yet I couldn't get the words out that I needed to say to make this real. Because, without them, was this all as real as we claimed it was?

"Of course not," I forced out. "I thought we only brought someone home to share."

His face fell slightly, and he nodded. "Right. Yeah."

"Gavin ..."

"Whitley Jo Bowen," a voice cut across the lobby, silencing anything I'd been about to say.

I whipped around with wide eyes to see my father storming toward us. He looked furious. No, beyond that. He looked apoplectic, as if at any moment, he was going to burst from the anger coursing through him. I'd seem him look at me like that before when I was in high school, but normally, Mom yelled, and he was the calm one. What the hell had happened?

"Dad?"

He stopped in front of me with fire blazing in his eyes. "How could you do this?"

I blinked in surprise. "Do what?"

He ignored me, turning to face Gavin. My father pushed him full-on in the chest. Gavin took two steps backward, more in shock than because of the strength of the shove. Dad had always been a big man, but with his bout with cancer, he'd shrunk before my eyes. Losing weight until he was almost unrecognizable. It hadn't been a good sign, but Mom didn't want to talk about it until after the wedding.

"Dad!" I gasped.

"You!" he snarled in Gavin's face.

Gavin stared at him in disbelief. "What's going on?"

"You fucking liar."

I shuddered at the word. My parents didn't cuss. I'd heard words like that out of my parents' mouths only a handful of times. Usually when they were *really* mad at me.

"Dad, stop!" I shouted.

He rounded on me, as if remembering where his real

anger lay. He was shaking from head to toe. The exertion of the last few minutes catching up with him, but doing nothing to dispel his anger.

"You lied to me, Whitley Jo. You're a liar."

I shrank backward at the accusation. He wasn't wrong. But ... how did he know?

"I came to you with my entire life on the line and said I wanted to walk you down the aisle as my final wish. And you two lied and conspired to have this *fake* wedding," he snarled. His shaking progressed as his breathing became labored. "I don't care what reason you had for doing it, but you've made a *mockery* of my wish. A mockery of my illness. A mockery of *me*!"

He coughed violently for a few seconds.

"Dad, you need to calm down. You're too sick ..."

"Don't talk to me ... about my sickness," he raged. "You don't care about any of it. And this is ... this is over!" He took a step away from me, as if he couldn't stand to look at his only daughter another second.

My jaw was on the floor at the words, the horrible words filtering through my brain. The realization that he was right. That we should have come clean from the start. We'd done it all wrong, and now, there was no going back.

"I won't be made fun of," he spat. "This wedding is ... over!"

With his final pronouncement, he collapsed onto the floor in the lobby of Percy Tower.

"Dad!" I screamed as I fell to my knees at his side.

All of my training kicked in at once. I hadn't been in medical school in years, but that didn't make it go away. So, I got to work.

I looked up at Gavin. "Call 911."

My father was still breathing, but it was labored, and his

heart rate was through the roof. We were going to need an ambulance.

My mom came rushing toward us and dropped down next to me with tears in her eyes. "Oh my Lord, Whitley, what are we going to do?"

"Get through this moment," was all I said.

That was all we could do.

32

———

WHITLEY

When the ambulance finally showed up, I was shaking and exhausted. They put him on a stretcher with a breathing mask on his face and carted him onto the ambulance. Mom went with him, and I promised that I would be right behind them.

My father could be dying.

He could be dying from his cancer.

And it was my fault.

"Whitley," Gavin said carefully, reaching for me.

"Don't." I broke away and turned to English, who had stood by through all of it, keeping the lobby clear and working her magic. "Will you take me to the hospital?"

"Of course. Let me get the car back." She got on her phone and began demanding a quick response.

Gavin looked hurt, and I couldn't deal with any of this. I couldn't even think about it until I knew that my dad would be all right.

"Whitley," he said again.

"Don't," I repeated. "Please don't."

"We have to talk about this."

"About what?" I asked, suddenly just as angry as my dad had been. "He's right. He's right about all of it. We lied to him. We lied to basically everyone from the beginning. Your family. My family. It was all a lie."

"You don't believe that."

"Don't tell me what I fucking believe," I growled as those pesky tears came to line my lids again.

"I didn't mean it like that."

"Didn't you? I'm just supposed to feel exactly how you want me to feel at any given moment?"

"Whit," he groaned. "Come on. It's not about this."

"What is it about?"

"I don't know," he snapped and then sighed heavily. "Safia."

I froze at that word. My head swiveled to him in shock. "What about Safia?"

"You sure it's not about her being in your apartment last night?" he asked, his voice hard.

I shuddered. "How do you know that?"

He chuckled sardonically and took a step back, shaking his head all the while. "The question is ... why didn't *you* tell me?"

"It's complicated."

"And she didn't get in your head?"

She had. She had absolutely gotten in my head. But not the way he thought. And right now, I was so furious with everything happening that I couldn't even see straight.

"If you knew she was there, why didn't *you* say anything?"

"I thought you'd tell me yourself."

I scrubbed my face with my hands. The light makeup I'd put on earlier was now a hot mess. "We're so fucked up, Gavin. I sent Safia away, but none of that even matters. It started as a lie." I swallowed. "None of this was ever real anyway."

He stepped forward. "What if it was real to me?"

"It wasn't. We wouldn't be standing here right now if it was."

"That's not true." He reached for me again. "Whit …"

"My dad could be *dying* right now. He's in the hospital. And he's pissed that we lied to him. We did that. If he dies tonight, then it'll be my fault." The tears ran freely down my face. "So … nothing else matters. The wedding is off."

Then, I pushed past him and out of the lobby of the hotel. English hurried on my heels. She knew enough to stay silent after what just happened. I rubbed my eyes again, ignoring the flash of a camera before darting into our awaiting car.

I turned to face the entrance of the hotel through the blackened window and found Gavin rushing out after us. He kicked something on the sidewalk, bellowing his rage as the car pulled away.

"Whit," English whispered.

I didn't respond. I buried my head in her lap, curling up on the backseat in the fetal position and sobbing like I was a child. English ran her fingers through my brown hair. The muddy natural color I'd changed it to so that I could marry this man. And then we'd just fucked it all up. Royally fucked it up.

English didn't say anything until we got to the hospital. "We're here."

I sniffed and sat up. "Thank you."

"Anytime, sis." She ran her thumbs under my eyes to clean up my mascara. "I've got your back."

She didn't say that I'd made a huge mistake. She didn't

tell me that Gavin and I would work it out. She just smiled her brilliant smile and followed me inside.

In that moment, she was half publicist and half best friend. Maybe I'd hear all of that later, but for now, she wanted to take care of me. I appreciated it more than she'd ever know.

English announced who we were at the front desk, and we were ushered through the ER to a waiting area, where my mom was sitting in tears.

"Oh, Whitley!" she called, rushing to me.

We hugged tightly.

"What's going on? What did the doctor say?"

"No one has come to talk to me yet. They're still trying to get him stable."

"I'm going to go find someone to talk to."

"Don't leave me," she said with a pointed sniffle. "Your brother is on his way too. He feels terrible."

"Why? It's not his fault." The unspoken *it's mine* weighed between us.

"No, he's the one who told your father. I don't think he had any idea that your dad would confront you about it or ... any of this."

Well, that explained a lot. I'd told my brother about the relationship starting out fake in confidence. Or at least, I'd thought it was in confidence. He'd insisted even then that he didn't think it was a fake relationship. I hadn't asked him not to tell anyone. What had he been thinking?

"We all need some coffee," English said. "I'm going to see what I can do. Text me if you get an update."

"Thanks, English."

My mom reached out and touched English's hand. My mom, who had never liked English. She smiled wanly. "Thank you, sweetie."

English beamed. "Anything for Whit."

"She's lucky to have you."

"I'm lucky to have her." English hugged me again and then left for coffee.

"I was wrong about her. She cares about you."

"You were," I agreed easily. "She's the best."

"And that young man ..."

I sighed and looked to the ceiling. "Please, let's not do this right now. I know you're mad about Gavin. The wedding is off. Let's deal with Dad, okay?"

Mom bit her lip like she had so much she wanted to say. But what could she say that Dad hadn't already thrown in our faces? There were more important things to deal with right now than her anger.

So, we sat in the cold plastic hospital chairs for word about Dad. English returned with coffee and my brother.

Mom jumped up and threw her arms around him. "Where's Carrie?"

"She's with the kids. I came as soon as I could get them settled. How's he doing?" Wyatt asked.

"We haven't heard," I told him as I came to my feet.

Wyatt's gaze shifted to mine, and guilt was in every crease on his face. "Whitley, I'm so sorry. I didn't mean for all of this to happen."

"It's fine," I told him, accepting his hug.

"You told me everything, but I just laughed about it. I didn't realize that Dad would blow a gasket, and I tried to tell him that it was real now."

"It's not," I nearly choked out. "It's over."

Wyatt's face fell. "No. No, it can't be. I didn't mean for that to happen ..."

"I wreck everything I touch, big brother," I whispered,

sinking back into my seat. "This should come as no surprise to anyone."

Mom and Wyatt exchanged a look of despair, but at that moment, the doctor came out to speak to us.

"Is he all right?" Mom gasped.

I jumped to Wyatt's side, waiting for the worst.

The woman held her hands up. "He's going to make a full recovery. We're keeping him sedated, but he can have visitors in his room."

I nearly fell over with relief at the news. My mom was speaking animatedly to the doctor about his diagnosis and whether she thought this would set him back, if they needed to do another round of immune therapy, and on and on. Mom knew more about what was going on with him than I possibly could, and still, I felt like I should have been the one there, figuring it all out.

Instead, I could barely keep my feet underneath me as relief and guilt flooded through me in a mix of emotions.

"I'm going to go see him," Mom said. "Are you two coming?"

"Go ahead. We'll be right behind you, Mom."

It was a testament to how scared she must have been that my mom left us sitting there to check on her husband.

"Whit," Wyatt began.

Then, I couldn't hold any of it back any longer. I threw myself into my brother's arms and cried great, heaving sobs. He held me, patting my back.

"It's going to be okay. Dad is okay."

"I could have killed him," I blubbered.

"If you're responsible, then so am I," Wyatt said.

"You just ... told him the truth. He probably ... loves you ... for that."

He pulled me back and looked down into my eyes. "But,

Whit ... I only said it as a joke. I didn't even realize how it would seem to him. After all, I assured him that you and Gavin were very much real. And if anything, Dad's diagnosis brought you two together."

"But it's not. It was a lie. Dad was right."

"That's not true. I saw you two together over the Fourth with my own two eyes. No one is more perfect for you, Whit."

I shook my head and pulled away from my brother, wiping at my eyes. "God, I'm a mess. Bad girlfriend strikes again."

"Would you cut it out? There's nothing wrong with you! You're a great person. A good girlfriend. A good fiancée. And I bet you'll be a great wife. Okay? All that stuff in your head is bullshit."

"Wyatt, you don't understand. I ... never even told him I loved him."

"Well, do you?"

"What?" I choked out.

He took me by the shoulders. "Do you love him?"

I stared up into my brother's determined expression, and for some reason, this time, it was so easy to admit. "Yes."

"Do you think that whether or not you've told him those exact words that he hasn't *felt them* for the last months you've been together?"

"I ... I don't know."

"He has. He knows exactly how you feel. Everyone knows exactly how you feel about him, except you."

"I don't think ..."

"He loves you, Whit, and you love him."

I shook my head as I pulled away from Wyatt. "You don't understand. None of that is enough if we can't even be honest with each other."

Wyatt sighed, dropping his hands. "Then, maybe today shouldn't happen anyway. Maybe it's a good thing the wedding was called off."

"Yeah," I agreed.

But the words felt hollow.

And I felt even worse as we walked together to Dad's hospital room.

33

GAVIN

I was fucked.

The wedding was off.

Whitley was gone.

No amount of texts or calls got me the answer to which hospital her dad had been taken to. So, there wasn't even a way for me to storm in there and make this right. I was stuck in the middle of New York City, the city that never sleeps, with no answers.

"Fuck," I said for the hundredth time since I'd watched Whitley get into that car and drive away.

Someone else, likely English, had contacted the wedding planner and the rest of our friends about what had happened. Camden and Katherine came downstairs and took control like they owned the place. Which they did.

Katherine took one look at me and rushed everyone away from me. Camden took me by the arm and plopped me into a seat at the bar.

"Give him whatever he wants on me," he growled at the bartender.

The man looked terrified under Camden's growing irritation and nodded. "What'll you have?"

"Start him on top-shelf bourbon and work your way down."

I nodded and took the first glass offered to me and downed it. I barely tasted it. Everything tasted empty and hollow with her gone. Somehow, I'd fucked this up as royally as I'd always thought that I would. Why had I brought up Safia then? Why wasn't I there for her when her dad freaked out? I could have been on the way to the hospital with her right now. We could have been dealing with this together.

Camden clapped me on the back. "I'll be back. I'm sending in reinforcements."

I waved him off. It didn't matter. Nothing anyone said could make any of this better. My wedding was currently being called off.

Fuck, money. I was supposed to pay people today. Balances were coming due, and I'd promised I'd pay it all. The money didn't fucking matter to me, but now, it was the time, and there was no wedding.

"Camden, the money."

He seemed to realize what I was saying without more explanation. "I'll take care of it."

Then, he was gone. And I trusted him to do exactly as he had said. He had more money than a god. I could pay him back later if need be. Right now ... I was going to focus on the next drink. And the next after that.

I didn't know how much time had passed.

Court and Sam came by and had a drink with me. They tried to cajole me to move from my seat. To go home and sleep this off. Promising that it would all be better in the morning. But I didn't move. I wasn't sober any longer, and I had no intention of sitting around at home, *alone*.

When home was where I was supposed to be bringing Whitley back to. Every inch reminded me of her. The way she lay across my bed, her full breasts spilling out of the top of the comforter. The smell of her on my sheets.

No. There was no way I was going home anytime soon. Maybe not ever. Not without her. I was going to have to fucking move if I couldn't figure this out. Because I'd never be able to walk into our building and not think of her.

The guys must have been running interference on access to me. I kept expecting my parents to show up or my aunt and uncle. Fuck, even my cousins. Malcolm would be knocking some sense into me. Nate would be disappointed. Trey would cross his arms and look cranky. I could picture it all, but that didn't mean I wanted to deal with any of it.

And as day turned into night with no answer from Whitley, one person made it through their defenses.

"Hey, Gavin," Maggie said as she slid into the stool next to me. She waved at the bartender. "I'll have a gin martini, extra olives, extra dry. Thank you."

"Coming right up."

"Mags," I said with a head tilt toward her. I wasn't quite seeing double of her. I'd been force-fed food from the restaurant next door when I refused to move. So, I wasn't on a completely empty stomach, but I wasn't sober either. "What are you doing here?"

"Well, I was supposed to be at your wedding."

I winced. "Yeah. Did you not get the memo? It's not happening."

"I was informed." The bartender slid her a martini, and she made a satisfied sound after she took a sip. "Delicious."

"And you're here why?"

"Oh, because I'm the only one who can even remotely relate to what you're going through."

I arched an eyebrow at her. "You and Locke got married."

"Locke and I were an arranged marriage, as you well know."

"Yeah."

"And yours was fake."

I winced at that word. Hearing it from Whitley had been one time too many.

"It wasn't."

Maggie took another sip of her martini. "No?"

"Well, yes. It started that way. It started because I needed a date to your wedding."

"And so you brought a fake fiancée?"

I groaned. "I know how it sounds, but I liked her from the beginning. I thought I could make her see the same if we moved the roadblocks out of the way."

"How'd that work for you?"

"Peachy," I said with a pointed glare.

"We're both stupid. We should have only agreed to get married for love. Not for any other reason. Not for an arrangement between our families. Not so Whitley's dad could walk her down the aisle. Not for any of it."

"And you don't love Locke?" I inquired.

She scoffed. "Hardly. I mean ... I wanted to. I tried to." She looked far away, as if remembering a time when it had seemed possible. "We're just too different. I saw it, but he didn't. It's never going to work the way we wanted it to. But it still could for you."

"I don't think so," I grumbled as I finished off another glass.

I called for another round, but Maggie shook her head.

"No more alcohol, cousin. You need to go home and sleep this off. It'll look better in the morning."

"I can't sleep at my place. It ... it smells like her."

Margaret's expression cracked then. "You really love her, don't you?"

"Completely."

"And did you tell her?"

I frowned and looked into the bottom of my empty glass. "No."

"Idiot," she spat. "Why didn't you tell her?"

"I didn't want to scare her off!"

Margaret sighed in exasperation. "Come on. You can stay at my place tonight. I have a guest room at Locke's."

"Yeah?" I asked, hope finally breaking through.

"Yeah. It's not a problem. I know you don't want to deal with anyone else right now. People who won't understand."

I really, really didn't want to have to deal with anyone else. That was for sure.

Maggie finished her drink and then helped me out of the bar. A car was waiting at the entrance to Percy Tower. Camden must have planned this. That sounded like him.

I fell into the backseat, and Maggie slid in next to me. She was silent as we sped through the Upper East Side toward her place with Locke. I'd never been there before, and I wasn't entirely sure where it was located. But none of that really mattered. All of it was a distraction from the reality of my fucked up life.

I wasn't marrying Whitley. No matter what I wanted, we'd ruined this thing. And if I knew anything about Whit, it was that she blew up relationships on the way out. This wasn't going to be any different.

Maggie slung an arm around my back as she helped me up the elevator to the top floor of her building. The living room looked out onto Central Park, and the enormous size of the place was dwarfed only by the Olympic-sized indoor swimming pool. I'd never seen anything like it before.

She rolled her eyes at it. "Locke is always working."

"He's an Olympic swimmer. It's pretty badass."

Margaret shrugged. "This way."

She hustled me down the hall and deposited me into the guest bed. My head was swimming now as everything caught up with me.

"Thanks, Mags."

"Anytime. But, Gavin ... in the morning, we're going to have to figure out how to fix this."

I stared up at the ceiling. "I don't think there's any fixing this."

"You know that's not true. You're a King! We can fix anything."

"And what if I can't?" I asked softly.

"Then, I guess you were right. It was fake all along, and ... you earned this."

The door pulled shut quietly behind her as I rolled her words around and around in my mind. Maybe I'd earned this after all.

34

———

GAVIN

I woke with clarity. We'd gone about this all wrong. I'd gone about this all wrong. I should have come clean to Whitley from the start about how I felt about her. Instead, I was so worried that she'd back out at the first sign of my affection. After all, it wasn't unprecedented. I'd watched her do it to others over the years. I'd seen the relationships implode, and I'd crossed my fingers and hoped it wouldn't happen to me.

Well, it had.

Now, what was I going to do?

Yesterday, I'd wallowed. I'd had every right to do so. The wedding was off. But I couldn't stay in that feeling forever. At some point, I was going to have to act.

As much of this was my fault as Whitley's. I'd asked her to be my fake girlfriend. I cajoled her into going to the wedding. I introduced her to my friends and family. I even convinced her that this would be the right step for her dad. I never stopped to think about the potential consequences. I'd been too far gone.

Consequences had happened anyway.

I rolled out of Maggie's guest bed, still dressed in my wrinkled shirt from the day before. I didn't want to go back to my apartment. I couldn't face the space where my wife was supposed to be sprawled across my bed.

Instead, I crept out of the bedroom to an empty apartment. Maggie had left a thermos of coffee on the kitchen island with a note, telling me to help myself.

"Bless you, Mags," I groaned as I poured myself a mug.

Splashing interrupted my drink.

Locke was home.

I yawned and headed toward the enormous pool at the other end of the house. I opened the glass door to find him swimming laps at such an incredible speed that I could barely track him in the pool. After a few minutes, he lifted his head from the water and looked up at me in surprise.

"Hey, you're finally up," Locke said. He hoisted himself out of the water and threw a towel haphazardly across his body. He was fucking rock solid.

Maybe I should take up swimming.

"I'm up."

"Sorry to hear about what happened. Any way I can help?"

"Actually, I was wondering if I could borrow some clothes."

Locke nodded. "Sure. Help yourself. Room is at the end of the hall. Take whatever you need."

"Thanks, man." I started toward the door but stopped. "Sorry about ... your marriage too."

Locke's eyes hardened. "We don't all get what we want."

"No," I agreed slowly. "I guess not."

"But good luck."

Then, he dived back into the pool, continuing his morning workout.

I left the pool behind and wandered into Locke's bedroom. We weren't exactly the same shape. He had broad shoulders and a trimmer waist, but we were about the same height. So, I found a pair of slacks and a button-up that didn't smell like the inside of a bar, and after changing, I headed out of my cousin's apartment.

I called English on the way downstairs.

"I don't feel comfortable giving you that information, Gavin," she said diplomatically.

"English, I don't have time for this. Whit isn't your client. You're not breaching confidentiality. Take your publicist hat off for a goddamn minute and think about your best friend."

"I am thinking about my best friend. She doesn't want to see you."

"I'm not going there to see her, So, give me the goddamn name."

She sighed heavily. "Fine. But don't tell her I told you."

"Thank you. I owe you one."

"More than one," she grumbled.

With the hospital name in hand, I called a car and headed across town. I didn't know how to fix what was broken with me and Whitley, but I knew where to start.

Walking through the ER as I headed to Whitley's father's room made me wish that I'd gone for a suit. Even though Locke and I couldn't possibly share suit coats. I wanted the reassurance of a solid suit coat and tie. A button-up didn't feel like enough as I went to my grave.

I stopped in front of the room Whitley's dad was currently staying in. I took a deep breath and knocked softly.

A minute later, Whitley's mom answered the door with eyes widened in shock.

"Gavin?"

"Hi, Cynthia," I said with my sharpest smile.

"What ... what are you doing here? Whitley isn't here. She went home."

"That's okay. I'm not here to see Whit. I'm here to talk to Walter ... if he's awake."

She blinked at me in surprise. "He is, but ..."

"Who is it, Cynthia?" Walter's deep voice called from inside the room.

She closed her eyes once in panic. "Don't say anything to upset him."

"I don't intend to, ma'am."

A small smile came to her mouth. "Well, at least someone remembers manners. I'll let you talk to him for a few minutes, but please be careful. He's fragile right now."

"I will, and ... thank you."

She touched my arm as she passed. "I'm going to go find us some breakfast and give you some privacy."

"Cynthia?" Walter called again.

I took another fortifying breath and then walked inside. "Good morning, sir."

Walter's eyes bulged. He looked worse for wear. As if the last twenty-four hours had drained so much of the life out of him. He'd been fighting for this wedding, and now, without something to look forward to, combined with our argument, the fight had been taken out of him.

"Gavin, I didn't expect to see you."

"No, I suspect you didn't." I gestured to the chair that Cynthia had likely vacated. "Mind if I sit?"

"If you must. What are you doing here, son?"

I took my time settling into the chair before meeting his

eyes. "Honestly, sir, I came because we have some things to work out."

Walter's eyes widened. "Is that so?"

"Yes. See, I'm sorry about what happened yesterday. I regret how you found out about my relationship with Whitley. It did start out fake. Actually, at first, it was because I'd told *my* family that I had a girlfriend, and I brought Whitley with me. We didn't think anyone else would even know, and we planned to have a big breakup."

"Why would you even do that?"

"To be honest, sir, I still have no idea why your daughter agreed. But I did it because I was already head over heels for her. But I also knew she was as stubborn as a horse."

Walter laughed and then choked on his own laugh, which resulted in him coughing.

"Do you need anything?" I asked, suddenly in a panic.

The coughing subsided, and he waved me off. "I'm fine. I'm fine. The doctors said I'm fine. Tell me more about Whitley."

"She's been hurt a lot, and she doesn't trust easily. She has this in her head that she's a bad girlfriend, but she's not. I wanted to get her past the fear phase to see that we could actually work out. I didn't anticipate you and Cynthia showing up. But I was the one to convince her that we should go through with it anyway."

"She didn't want to?"

"She wanted to tell you the truth, but I felt like it was cruel to deny you this request. Plus, I was already so deep that I thought if she spent more time with me, I could get her to fall in love with me."

Walter's expression was unreadable. "And did it work?"

I shrugged. "I don't know, sir. I thought it had, but now …"

"Hmm," he murmured.

"So, that's the truth. We should have told you from the start. I take all the blame. Don't put any on Whitley. She wanted to make you proud."

He waved me off. "We were so proud that she was following what we thought was the right path that we didn't even think about it. But then when I found out the relationship was fake ... I just got so mad. I know that we've done wrong by Whitley. And I handled this all wrong."

"I don't blame you for being upset."

"No," he said slowly. "But I should have let you explain first. I shouldn't have done it publicly. Then, maybe I wouldn't even be in this hospital room."

"Are you going to be here long?"

He shook his head. "Not if I can help it. I want to get out of here before the end of the day."

I suppressed a smirk. That sounded a lot like Whitley. No wonder she was so stubborn.

"So, what do you want from me?" he finally asked. "You didn't come here just to apologize."

I took a deep breath. "No, I didn't. I'm sorry for how it all happened, but I love your daughter. I want your permission to marry her."

He scoffed. "It's not my permission you need. You'll still need to convince her."

"I'm up to that challenge, but it would be a lot easier if I could tell her that you're okay with it."

"You were man enough to show your face here after what happened." Walter held his hand out, and I stuck mine in his. "You have my blessing. And Lord knows, you're going to need it."

I laughed, letting my smile widen. "She is difficult."

"A little spitfire."

"And that's why I love her," I told him as I rose to my feet.

Walter chuckled. "Well, go get her."

"Yes, sir," I said as I headed out of the room.

Cynthia was just coming back with breakfast. I held the door for her, and she looked furtively up at me.

"Everything all right?"

"If you don't mind, I plan to marry your daughter."

The shock was so evident on her face that she nearly collided with the door. "Still?"

"Of course."

"But you called it off. You spent all that money."

I waved off her objections. "I love her."

Tears came to her eyes. "That's all we've wanted for her."

"Now, I just have to convince her."

She laughed softly. "Good luck."

"Yeah, I know. I'll need it."

35

———

WHITLEY

"I'm really not up for this," I grumbled as English directed me down the pathway toward Bethesda Fountain in Central Park.

Katherine and Lark were also on duty, walking on either side of us.

"I know, but you need this," English said.

Katherine nodded. "It's true. You slept for fifteen hours. You need fresh air."

"And sunshine," Lark added.

There was no point in arguing. I hadn't argued when they showed up at my apartment and escorted me into an awaiting car that dropped us off at the edge of Central Park. I'd barely had enough time to change. Katherine had applied makeup to my splotchy face in the car. I wasn't sure what I looked like, but if Katherine approved, then I guessed I was safe for a public appearance.

"Are the pictures from yesterday everywhere?" I asked, biting my lip.

I hadn't thought much about it at the time. But someone had definitely taken pictures of what had happened. Not to mention, my tear-stricken face. Gavin and I had been on *Page Six* for our official engagement announcement. Of course the vultures would be more than happy to see our downfall.

Katherine and English exchanged a look.

I groaned. "Is it that bad?"

"I suppressed them as much as I could," Lark said.

"Same. I did all I could," English said.

"But you're news," Katherine said with a shrug. "Hard to quash real news."

English flipped through her phone until she found the offending pictures and then let me see.

"That's the best of them," English told me.

If this was the best of them, then we were fucked. I hardly recognized myself in the horrible image as I'd rushed out of Percy Tower yesterday morning. I passed the phone back to English. No use in looking at any of the others. It was weird enough to be treated like a celebrity just because I was marrying a King. Well, that hadn't exactly happened, had it?

"Lovely," I mumbled.

"What did you expect?" Katherine asked me.

"I don't want to talk about it."

Katherine arched an eyebrow. "That's a first."

I scowled right back at her. "This isn't one of my stories."

"No?"

Lark nudged Katherine. "We're on her side."

"Yeah, Jesus," English grumbled.

"I'm on her side, but I'm not going to pretend like nothing happened. This is a hundred percent a classic Whitley story. Complete with a public argument and ending in a dramatic demolition of your relationship."

"That is not what happened," I snapped at her.

"No? What happened?"

I stumbled over my words. That *was* what had happened. I'd blown a gasket. All of my fears had escalated into the worst possible scenario, and I'd set the world on fire. Like I always did. Why did I have to do that?

"I don't know," I said, backing down from Katherine's intensity. "You're not wrong."

Katherine smiled triumphantly. "Well, don't tell us that. Tell him."

I blinked up at her rapidly. "What? Who?"

Then, my friends grinned devilishly and pushed me forward. That was when I saw him. Gavin King. He stood at the edge of the fountain in a shirt that was too big for him and pants that might have been a little too short. Despite the disheveled appearance, his gaze was steady. And it was fixed purposely on me.

"I hate you three," I told my friends.

"We know," English said.

"We love you too," Katherine said.

"Always and forever," Lark agreed.

I left my friends behind and strode over to Gavin. The man I'd thought would be my husband only a day earlier. Until everything had crumbled to ash.

"Hi," I said hesitantly as I met him.

"Hey, pixie."

I stifled a grin at the nickname. "What are you wearing?"

He fingered the too-big button-up with a shrug. "I haven't been home. I stayed with Locke and Maggie, and he let me borrow his clothes. It turns out, Olympic swimmers have broader shoulders than the rest of us mere mortals."

"Who has ever called you a mere mortal?"

He sighed. "Well, I fell from Olympus yesterday."

I glanced at my feet and kicked a loose rock. "Why didn't you just go home?"

Gavin took another step forward, putting two fingers under my chin and lifting it for me to look up into his endless emerald eyes. "As if I could go back to a place that held every memory of you. As if I could smell my sheets that still had your scent on them. As if I could lie there alone when I had every intention of bringing my wife home to that bed."

I swallowed at the intensity in his statement. "Gavin ..."

"Wait," he said quickly. "Let me go first."

I arched an eyebrow. "Okay."

"I was wrong."

"About what?" I couldn't help but ask.

"Asking you to be my fake girlfriend."

I stared at him in confusion. "Um ... okay?"

"I should have asked you to be my date to the wedding from the start. My *real* date to the wedding. And then seduced you into falling for me the old-fashioned way so that you'd be my *real* girlfriend all the time. I shouldn't have put any tricks on it, and that was my fault."

"I don't ..."

He barreled forward over my uncertainty. "Because I wanted you to go to that wedding with me. Just you. It's not that I didn't have any other options. I did. I could have taken anyone that I wanted, but the idea of that was abhorrent. I'd stopped dating the previous year because every person I'd met over the years bored me. Well, everyone but you."

I blushed at that assessment. "Why didn't you say that then?"

He laughed, as if the very thought was absurd. "Say that to *you*? Whitley, the very thought of being with me three years ago had sent you running for the hills. Literally. The Hollywood Hills, halfway across the country."

"That was about Robert."

"Was it?" he demanded. "Because I remember him laying me flat on my ass."

"You said that didn't happen."

He shot me a look that said he was putting aside his pride here. "We both know Robert punched me flat on my ass. And what happened when I came asking for more? You bolted."

"I mean ... yes, but I didn't want to come between friends and ..."

"I get you had your reasons, but from my point of view, it was like a sucker punch. I let you go. I never stopped thinking about you, but what could I do half a country away? But then you were back." He blew out a breath. "Can you imagine what I was thinking? How much I wanted to make it work this time and not scare you off? It was as delicate as threading a needle, and I was a fucking wrecking ball."

I bit my lip as I tried not to grin at his mixed metaphor. "It still doesn't explain you being here."

"Well, I came up with the insane idea that if you thought none of this was serious, then you'd go with it. We'd joked before. We'd played wingman so many times that I couldn't count. What would a new game be to you? And if, in the meantime, I could make you fall for me, then I'd win." He met my gaze with his sincere eyes. "But I was always a hundred percent in, Whit."

I could barely breathe at those words. All this time that I'd been wondering if it was real, he was telling me ... it had been real for him all along.

"The only one who needed convincing was ... *me*?"

He nodded. "You were the only one who didn't know. Katherine gave me a good, long talking-to about making sure I took care of you so you wouldn't bolt. And look ... I fucked that up too."

I was still reeling.

My mind was a map of memories. I plotted every step of our relationship that had ended up at this very moment in Central Park. I'd thought that I was calling the shots. All along, I'd been on Gavin's trajectory. He'd been leading me exactly where he wanted to be. He'd been the mastermind of our fate.

And I ... I liked it.

I liked that he knew me well enough to know that I needed leading. That I would have left at the first sign that he wanted me as bad as he said he did. I'd laughed at Robert for the sheer audacity. And here Gavin was, saying that it had all been exactly right.

"You really planned this all out?" I asked, still in disbelief.

"I'd say I regret it, but for ninety-nine percent of it, it was perfect. All up until I flubbed the ending."

"I think we both did."

"Well, you weren't planning any of this," he said solemnly, looking at his feet. "The real problem was how I reacted about Safia."

I winced and stepped back. Safia. His words from yesterday still cut deep. He wasn't wrong that I should have told him what had happened, but was the trust there if neither of us had been able to have that conversation?

Gavin pressed forward, following me in that step I'd taken. "It's not that Safia showed up. It's that I should have been there for you instead of confronting you about her in the worst possible moment." He ran a hand back through his hair. "I already knew that nothing happened with Safia when I confronted you about it. She told me that I won."

"She did what?" I gasped.

"Yeah. When she realized who I was, she told me that I won. But I kept expecting for you to tell me about it. To let me in on the secret, you know? If we were past the point of being fake, then you'd confide in me the hard things too. But you never did."

He clenched his hands into fists. I could see the anger still right on the surface of everything. The months of unspoken words left between us. And how, right now, they were coming to bear fruit.

"I should have told you," I whispered. "It was stupid."

He nodded. Satisfied that I'd admitted to being in the wrong as well. "I thought that you didn't trust me. And somehow, that became more important than anything else in the world."

"I didn't trust you." The admission pained me beyond belief. And I could see the grief on Gavin's face mirroring mine. "I should have, but I ... I was so worried."

"About what?" he demanded. "What could you possibly fear from me?"

"That you'd never forgive me for seeing her."

He laughed once, as if he couldn't believe it. "Why? Whitley, you know me!"

"I know." I shook my head. "But part of it wasn't even about you. It was ... this was why I'd *left* Safi. Her ex showed up at my apartment, and I assumed the worst and kicked Safia out. I'd ruined the whole thing over her ex showing up without even proof that anything had happened because I didn't trust her. Then, I assumed *you* wouldn't trust *me*."

"Your history didn't help that one."

"But there's more," I said, choking on the words. "You

were right all along. Safia got in my head. I told you I've never told anyone that I love them. Well, she made it seem like, if I couldn't say those words, then what we had was fake."

Gavin frowned. "You believed that?"

I met his gaze as tears came to my eyes again. "Should I have?"

He rushed forward, pushing his hands up in my hair. "Absolutely not."

"Why? Why not?"

"Because I love you, Whitley."

The entire world narrowed down to those words. The words Gavin had never said to anyone before. The words I'd never spoken to another living person either. It was almost too much.

"You do?" I gasped as tears ran down my cheeks. I'd never thought I'd hear that from Gavin. Not ever. Not after what happened yesterday.

"Of course I do. I've loved you since the moment you walked back into my life with that pretty lavender hair and threw my entire world off its axis. And I've loved you every day since."

"Oh, Gavin!" I slung my arms around his neck and buried my face in his shoulder. He laughed as he lifted me into the air, pressing a kiss into my hair. "Say it again."

He set me on my feet, swiping the tears from my eyes. "I love you, Whitley Bowen. And I always will."

I swallowed once hard and nodded as I said. "I love you too."

His eyes closed on instinct as euphoria lit his face. "Perfect words. Say it again."

I chuckled and pressed my lips to his, murmuring, "I love you," over and over against them.

When he set me back down on my feet, he fell to one knee. I stared down at him in shock as I realized what he was doing down there.

"Whitley Bowen, will you marry me?"

I gasped. "Gavin!"

He held my left hand that still had his grandmother's diamond ring on my finger. The diamond I still hadn't been able to take off. I had removed it only once since the day that he'd put it on my finger. Fake or not, it belonged there now. And here he was, offering for it to all be real—very real —from the start.

"But my dad," I said softly.

He grinned. "Your dad said I didn't need his permission to marry you. Just your acceptance."

I gaped at him. "You talked to my dad?"

He nodded once with that mischievous grin that I loved so much. "Cleared the air. Now, it's only you that I need an answer from. And maybe quickly because this stone is not comfortable on my knee."

I burst into laughter. Only Gavin could make something so ridiculous so romantic at the same time.

"Yes, yes, yes! I'll marry you. Of course I'll marry you!"

He rose up in one swift moment, catching me around the middle and swinging me in a tight circle.

When he set me back down, he was grinning from ear to ear. "Today."

"Today?" I asked, unsure what he meant.

"Your family is already here. My family is already here. We already have the rings and the marriage license. Marry me today."

"What?" I gasped. "But ... we don't have a venue or anyone to marry us or ..."

"We'll do it here, and we can get someone last minute.

Just marry me. Let me take you back to my place as my wife."

There was no way I could deny him.

Everything was set, and nothing was. We'd been planning several hundred people at an enormous wedding. But hadn't English always said that eloping was the way to go? Everyone was here. What else did I need?

"Okay. Let's do it!"

36

WHITLEY

"I can't believe this is happening," I said from the top of the Bethesda Terrace stairs with my three bridesmaids.

"It's happening," English said, barely containing her glee.

Somehow, all the months of planning our wedding had been condensed down to a matter of hours. Katherine got me into emergency hair and makeup. Harmony brought over my dress. Gavin and I had sent texts to our friends and family to meet us at the fountain, dropping the guest list from hundreds to thirty with the snap of a finger.

My dad had even been discharged from the hospital in record time and approved by his doctor to participate. Now, it was time to go, and I could hardly believe it.

I had whiplash from my utter despair over yesterday to delight that this was *actually happening*! It felt like a fairy tale. And I couldn't believe it was mine.

"Showtime," English said.

She'd taken complete control of all the finer details. I hadn't even had to worry about it, as she had assured me it would be better than I even expected. Knowing my groom was waiting for me at the bottom of the stairs was enough for me.

Wesley and Wynona headed out first. Wynona gleefully throwing flowers as Wesley walked stoically beside her. Lark went down the stairs next, followed shortly by Katherine, and then it was English's turn.

She pressed a kiss to my cheek. "I love you, sister. You deserve all of this and more."

I choked back tears. "Don't make me cry yet."

She laughed. "No. Not yet."

Then, she walked down the stairs in the matching red dress that Harmony had apparently designed for my bridesmaids. Leave it to Katherine to get the most from her *IOU*.

Finally, the music shifted, and it was my turn. I took a deep breath, letting it out slowly, and then walked down the middle of the stairs. Tourists still roamed Central Park, looking on at me in awe. Many of them took pictures as they walked past, but my eyes were only on the bottom of the stairs, where my dad waited, holding a cane. The concession from his doctor to let him leave the hospital. My dad hadn't been happy, but he'd relented.

"Daddy," I whispered.

He pulled me into a hug. "You look beautiful, honey."

"Thank you."

He offered me his arm and I slid mine through his. He fingered my mother's diamond bracelet. "It suits you."

"Thank you."

"Shall we?"

"Absolutely."

Together we turned and walked across the cobblestones and through the terrace. When we reached the stone entranceway, we both took a deep breath as we exited out into the sunlight again.

A small group of buskers had been paid to service our wedding. I didn't know who had arranged that, but three violinists, a female guitarist, a man playing an erhu, a saxophonist, and an actual *opera* singer were playing the music as I walked down the makeshift aisle toward where our friends and family were assembled.

On my side was my mom, brother, and Carrie as well as my boss, Dr. Varma, his wife, and three daughters. That was all I'd wanted there. On Gavin's side was his mom, dad, aunt, uncle, and five cousins, plus Locke. His three groomsmen were arranged on one side and my bridesmaids on the other.

And then there was Gavin.

My heart leaped into my throat at the sight of him in a tailored tux that must have been made for him. I was certain that was also Katherine and Camden's doing. Though he had enough style that it could have been all his. But the beauty of it all was the smile on his handsome face. And how everything lit up at the first glimpse of me.

I stopped with my dad before Gavin, my eyes only for him.

"Who presents Whitley to be wed today?"

My eyes broke for that one second as I realized exactly who was marrying us. And I found Mayor Leslie Kensington in a smart Chanel suit with a wide smile on her face. Of course the mayor had the authority to marry people in her city, but I'd *never* suspected that anyone would ask her to. That must have been what Lark had said when she said she'd handle it. Holy shit.

The mayor nodded at me once at my look of astonishment.

"I do," my dad responded to the question.

Gavin stepped forward and shook my dad's hand. They

shared a sincere smile, and then I was walking forward with Gavin, up to the mayor.

Before I could even hope to stop them, tears came to my eyes. I was holding my fiancé's hands in the most beautiful dress of my life, prepared to marry the man of my dreams. I'd been certain that this day was never going to come. Only yesterday, the entire thing had been up in the air.

Now, I was speaking my vows to him, declaring my heart, body, and soul to him, and hearing the words in return. But right before the moment of saying our *I dos*, I stopped the ceremony.

Gavin looked stricken. "Whitley?"

I laughed, squeezing his hands. "There's a tradition in Gavin's family," I announced to our friends and family. "To sing the song 'Love Me Tender.' I sang it at Margaret's wedding, and I wish to continue that tradition today."

I glanced at the buskers, who had no idea what I was about to do. "Any of you know the tune?"

After several seconds of chords being struck, a tune became clear in the middle of it. A song that I'd sung under duress months ago, I sang now with all the love in my heart now. A song that was about devotion and a promise of forever.

It might have been the song that his grandmother sang to all the grandchildren, but now, it was as much our song. Tears came to not just his family's eyes as I sang the song with so much meaning, but my friends' and family's too. This sealed us all together more than even the vows could.

At the end, Gavin brought my hands to his lips and kissed them tenderly. "I love you."

I nodded. "I love you too."

"After that amazing tribute," Mayor Kensington said, "I ask, are you both ready to declare yourself to one another?"

"I am," we said in unison.

We spoke our vows to one another, letting all the world know our desire to be wed. And then Court removed the rings from his pocket, handing them to Gavin with a smile. He slid mine on my hand, and then I gave him his. There was only one thing left.

"I now pronounce you husband and wife. You may kiss your bride."

Gavin tugged me toward him, dipping me dramatically and kissing me for all the world to see as everyone cheered —friends, family, and gawking tourists alike.

This was everything I'd ever wanted with Gavin.

Everything I'd never thought I'd be worthy of.

Maybe I wasn't actually a bad girlfriend. Maybe all of that had been in my head. Because for the right person at the right time, Gavin King had proven that we could be perfect for each other in every way.

And now, he was my husband.

For now and always.

EPILOGUE
ONE YEAR LATER

"So, I was thinking," I said as I watched Gavin's naked ass through the window of our villa in Puerto Rico.

He was currently in the shower, and this time, I didn't have to pretend not to be watching.

"I was thinking," he said, turning around to give me a full-frontal view, "you need to get your ass in here."

I laughed. "I already showered."

"And?" He grinned at me. "Do I need to jack off to get you invested?"

"I mean, it wouldn't hurt anything."

He stroked himself a few times as I stripped out of my bikini and jumped into the shower with him. He grabbed me around the middle and pinned me to the shower wall. Our lips crashed together, just as demanding and ravenous as we had been our first time in Puerto Rico when I fell for him.

Now, we were a year married. A year of living together in his Upper East Side apartment. A year of sharing our lives together. And things had only gotten better and better.

He lifted my legs around his waist, slamming me backward against the wall even harder this time. I raked my nails down his back as he thrust home inside of me. I cried out, tilting my head back and letting the spray of water run down between us.

"Fuck, Gavin."

"I love you," he said as he pumped faster and faster into me.

"I love you too," I gasped.

Then, stars burst across my vision, and I came with such force that I could barely contain myself from shouting. Luckily, our closest neighbors were yards away. And if they heard ... oh well.

Gavin grunted and finished with me, letting me back down onto my feet and pressing heady kisses to my swollen lips.

"Going to have to come back here on every anniversary."

"I think you've convinced me," I murmured.

"Now ... what were you thinking?"

I laughed and shoved him playfully. "Before your rude interruption ..."

He arched an eyebrow and grabbed me by the ass. "Oh?"

"I was thinking we should meet all of our friends sometime while the sun is still up. They're throwing us a party tonight, you know?"

"Hey, I know, but you weren't supposed to."

"Like anyone can keep a secret."

He laughed. "Well, be surprised. English has been working on it."

"Done."

English and Court had had the magical wedding of his mom's dreams. The mayor had won in a historic landslide. Good for all of them. Even better that they'd then spent the next month in Bora Bora without internet. I didn't blame them one bit.

Gavin and I cleaned up and then headed down to the clubhouse for our "surprise" party. I looked properly shocked as everyone jumped out at us. We'd invited all of them to our anniversary celebration. And they'd all come.

Not that I'd been expecting a party, but my friends couldn't help but celebrate at every opportunity. I hugged Lark, Katherine, and English. Before turning to the other friends that I didn't know as well, but was getting to know.

Katherine and Lark's old friends—the Crew. They were a knot of Upper East Siders that they'd known since they had been children. Natalie and Penn had their own private villa. Lewis and Addie, and Rowe and his husband had come in later and were on the other side of the island. I didn't know them as well as the rest of the New Yorkers who had grown up there, but I was glad that the animosity had dissolved. That Court could be around his brother, Penn. That Katherine and Natalie were no longer at each other's throat. That Camden didn't want to kill Penn at every opportunity. It sure helped that Katherine was pregnant with their third child in so many years.

"Congratulations again," Natalie said, pushing her signature silver hair off of her shoulders and grinning brightly.

"Thank you for coming."

Natalie looked around at the world we'd both somehow ended up in. Outsiders to our core, but somehow belonging all the same.

"It's who we are now, isn't it?"

I nodded. "It sure is."

Gavin grabbed my hand then, tugging me onto the

dance floor as "Love Me Tender" filtered through the speakers.

"It's our song," he breathed into my ear.

Our song.

I loved that. Even if I hadn't been able to listen to it since Halloween last year, when I'd sung it at my father's funeral. He'd made it another couple of months after our wedding, but the prognosis had always been low. Gavin and I had spent as many weekends as we could back in Dallas, trying to get as many memories in as we could. But none of it had been as much as we all deserved.

Dad had passed.

I still mourned him every minute of every day. Sometimes, I'd find myself going a whole day without thinking about his absence, and then it would hit me. He was gone. Really gone. I'd never hear him call me honey again. I'd never hear his voice. Or his laugh. And then I'd freeze up, and deep sobs would rack through me.

Everything would be terrible. Despite my entire life being more wonderful than ever.

Luckily, Gavin was there every time. We talked about my dad. The highs and lows and everything in between. I didn't want to forget him, and I was grateful that Gavin known my dad even briefly.

And maybe "Love Me Tender" had been taken from us at that funeral, but it'd also made it all the more special.

A tribute and a blessing.

Because my dad had loved me tenderly in his own way. He'd given his blessing to Gavin to love me forever after he was gone. Which was as good as I could have asked for.

"I love you," I told Gavin, swiping at the lone tear that tracked down my face.

"I love you too, pixie."

We kissed on the dance floor as our joy and sorrow mingled in an inexplicable way. The way only Gavin could ever know me, which was why we were perfect together. And I'd never choose otherwise.

312

THE END

ABOUT THE AUTHOR

K.A. Linde is the *USA Today* bestselling author of more than thirty novels. She has a Masters degree in political science from the University of Georgia, was the head campaign worker for the 2012 presidential campaign at the University of North Carolina at Chapel Hill, and served as the head coach of the Duke University dance team.

She loves reading fantasy novels, binge-watching Supernatural, traveling to far off destinations, baking insane desserts, and dancing in her spare time.

She currently lives in Lubbock, Texas, with her husband and super adorable puppy!

Visit her online:
www.kalinde.com

Or Facebook, Instagram & Tiktok:
@authorkalinde

For exclusive content, free books,
and giveaways every month.
www.kalinde.com/subscribe